"I know it sounds weird, Matt, but it's a vast conspiracy *aimed* at making me look crazy.

"They were trying to make it look like Jenna Moon never existed," she finished in a rush of excitement.

"It sounds too incredible to be true," he said slowly, taking her hands in his. "And that might have been just what they were counting on—whoever 'they' are."

He had a nice voice, she thought inconsequentially. It was such a sexy contrast to his tough exterior that it ignited a string of wildly imaginative paradoxes in her mind, like a chain of Chinese firecrackers exploding—controlled but unleashed....

His thumb began idly stroking the inside of her palm. This time she was quite willing to accept that she was going a little crazy as the world around them seemed to recede into nothingness.

And Jenna was suddenly certain she would never be the same person she'd been half an hour ago.

Happy New Year, Harlequin Intrigue Reader!

Harlequin Intrigue's New Year's Resolution is to bring you another twelve months of thrilling romantic suspense. Check out this month's selections.

Debra Webb continues her ongoing COLBY AGENCY series with *The Bodyguard's Baby* (#597). Nick Foster finally finds missing Laura Proctor alive and well—and a mother! Now with her child in the hands of a kidnapper and the baby's paternity still in question, could Nick protect Laura and save the baby that might very well be his?

We're happy to have author Laura Gordon back in the saddle again with *Royal Protector* (#598). When incognito princess Lexie Dale comes to a small Colorado ranch, danger and international intrigue follow her. As sheriff, Lucas Garrett has a duty to protect the princess from all harm for her country. But as a man, he wants Lexie for himself....

Our new ON THE EDGE program explores situations where fear and passion collide. In *Woman Most Wanted* (#599) by Harper Allen, FBI Agent Matt D'Angelo has a hard time believing Jenna Moon's story. But under his twenty-four-hour-a-day protection, Matt can't deny the attraction between them—or the fact that she is truly in danger. But now that he knows the truth, would anyone believe *him*?

In order to find Brooke Snowden's identical twin's attacker, she would have to become her. Living with her false identity gave Brooke new insights into her estranged sister's life—and the man in it. Officer Jack Chessman vowed to protect Brooke while they sought a potential killer. But was Brooke merely playing a role with him, or was she falling in love with him—as he was with her? Don't miss *Alyssa Again* (#600) by Sylvie Kurtz.

Wishing you a prosperous 2001 from all of us at Harle~ Intrigue!

Sincerely,

Denise O'Sullivan
Associate Senior Editor
Harlequin Intrigue

WOMAN MOST WANTED

HARPER ALLEN

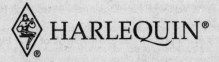

HARLEQUIN®

TORONTO • NEW YORK • LONDON
AMSTERDAM • PARIS • SYDNEY • HAMBURG
STOCKHOLM • ATHENS • TOKYO • MILAN • MADRID
PRAGUE • WARSAW • BUDAPEST • AUCKLAND

ISBN 0-373-22599-7

WOMAN MOST WANTED

Copyright © 2001 by Sandra Hill.

Visit us at www.eHarlequin.com

Printed in U.S.A.

ABOUT THE AUTHOR

Harper Allen lives in the country in the middle of a hundred acres of maple trees with her husband, Wayne, six cats, four dogs—and a very nervous cockatiel at the bottom of the food chain. For excitement, she and Wayne drive to the nearest village and buy jumbo bags of pet food. She believes in love at first sight because it happened to her.

Books by Harper Allen

HARLEQUIN INTRIGUE
468—THE MAN THAT GOT AWAY
547—TWICE TEMPTED
599—WOMAN MOST WANTED

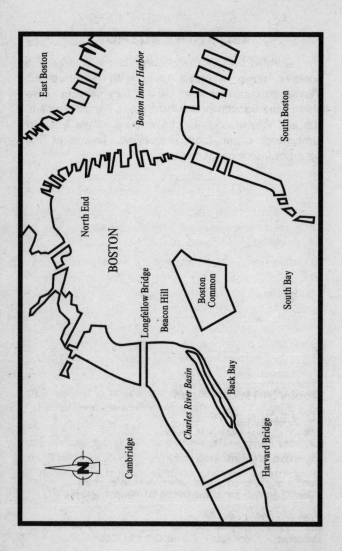

CAST OF CHARACTERS

Jenna Moon—Gorgeous but flaky, she's convinced that her identity has been stolen from her.

Matt D'Angelo—Gorgeous but stuffy, he's convinced he can kiss his career as an FBI agent goodbye once he starts believing Jenna's zany story.

Zappa—Cross-eyed and a little overweight, he's the Siamese cat that Jenna insists was stolen from her.

Franklin Moon—Jenna's late father, he spent his whole life running from the imaginary enemies he thought were out to get him. Like father, like daughter?

Sara Moon—Jenna's mother, she died when Jenna was just a child—but somehow she's never really left the daughter she loved so much.

Carmela Tucci—Matt's sister, she's a world-renowned physics lecturer. She sees her brother as a hopelessly immovable object who may have met his match in the irresistible force of Jenna.

Mrs. Janeway—The sweet, elderly lady whom Jenna nearly brains with a can of cat food. She uses a walker to get around—but Jenna's pretty sure she's a lot sprier than she lets on.

Edna Terwilliger—The vinegary dragon of the law firm where Jenna worked, she says she's never seen Jenna before in her life.

Charles Parks—The senior partner at the law firm, he may have been involved in some shady deals. Then again, Jenna may be completely offbase about the poor man.

Rupert Carling—The missing tycoon whom Jenna insists she saw skulking around the law firm's basement—which has got to be another one of her delusions.

With all my love to Joan Mary Foley Hill—
the original adventurous redhead.
You have no idea how much you mean to me.
And a Special Mention To: The real Zappa,
aka Walker Percy Cat, Siamese *extraordinaire*.

Chapter One

The lady was late. *Real* late.

Somehow Matt D'Angelo wasn't surprised. On the phone she hadn't sounded like the type who would wear anything as practical as a watch, he thought in resignation, glancing at his own. He leaned back against the headrest, his gaze flicking warily to the rearview mirror of the Taurus. Then again, he admitted, she hadn't sounded like the type who would choose a borderline neighborhood of graffiti-sprayed businesses and grim little apartments like this one to live in either. Her voice had evoked completely different images in his mind.

He'd give her another half an hour. Another hour, tops.

He was acutely aware of the fact that he could still just make Fenway Park for the start of the first inning, but even as he tapped the ticket on the rim of the steering wheel, he knew he wasn't really considering skipping out. Like any red-blooded Boston male, he took his baseball seriously, but he took his job even more seriously. If she showed, he'd be waiting for her.

Sighing, he tossed the ticket on the dash and opened the car door. As he stepped from the government-issue sedan to stretch his legs, his attention was caught by the slim figure heading in his direction, still half a block away.

He'd never seen her before in his life, but as crazy as it seemed, that didn't matter. Without even thinking about it, he was certain it was her.

So what the hell did she want with him?

Unconsciously raking a renegade strand of thick black hair off his forehead, Matt leaned against the side of the car and narrowed his eyes against the June sun to watch her approach.

On the phone this afternoon her voice had been soft, as if she was afraid of being overheard, but there'd been an incongruous trace of huskiness around the edges that prevented it from sounding too sweet. He definitely wasn't a fanciful man, but that voice breathing through the receiver into his ear had sounded like…he groped for the right comparison…like *honey,* he thought lamely. Honey with a dash of cinnamon. Listening to her, he'd felt an uncharacteristic desire to lean back, prop his feet up on his desk and just let that voice wash over him.

He'd resisted the impulse with an effort. Straightening in his chair and conscious of the fact that all calls coming into the Bureau field office were monitored, his own tone had been strictly business as he'd asked her why she needed to meet with an agent.

The softly conspiratorial whisper had taken on a surprising stubbornness. She was calling from a pay phone on her break, she'd said, the huskiness more pronounced. There wasn't time to go into detail and risk getting fired her second day at a new job for returning late from lunch. Irritatingly unswayable, she'd rattled off the address of her apartment, insisted that he meet her there after five and had been just about to hang up when he'd cut into her monologue.

It would help, he'd said, keeping his words even with an effort, if he knew *who* he was supposed to be meeting. With a contrite gasp that had instantly made him feel like a heel,

Jenna—all she would divulge was her first name—had lowered her voice even further and told him he'd be able to
recognize her from her dress. It was green, she'd said with
absolute seriousness—the *exact* color of a leaf against sunlight. He couldn't miss it. Before he could get in another
question, she'd hung up.

Most likely a kook, he'd told himself. The Agency got
its fair share of conspiracy nuts, alien abductees and plain
old garden-variety paranoids. No one would fault him for
writing her off as one of the above and forgetting about
her, but he'd check her out just to satisfy his own sense of
duty.

The Sox had been on a losing streak lately, anyway.

Actually, her offbeat description had been right, he
thought unwillingly as he saw her walking toward the di-
lapidated sixplex where he was parked. The tie-dyed dress
she was wearing *was* the exact color of a leaf against sunlight. But what she hadn't thought to mention was the molten red-gold hair that rippled halfway down her back, the
luscious legs that went on forever and the tinkling noise
like little silver bells that seemed to fill the air as she came
closer.

She was carrying a badly dented can of cat food. She
looked like a sexy angel.

Matt grabbed his suit jacket out of the car and shrugged
into it, tightened the knot in his tie too vigorously and wondered what had gotten into him. Silver bells? He had to
stop skipping lunch, he told himself repressively as he approached her, the leather case containing his badge and ID
already in his hand. He could still hear that damn tinkling,
like glass wind chimes being stirred by a summer breeze.
But although he darted a furtive look at the apartment
building, he already knew this wasn't the type of neighborhood where anyone hung out wind chimes.

Just then Jenna looked up and saw him. She stopped, and the sound stopped with her. As he got closer she took a tentative step forward, and a single silver note rang out.

Around one slim ankle she was wearing a fine chain with tiny bells on it. Relief swept through him.

"Agent D'Angelo?"

The voice was the same as he remembered, but combined with wide eyes the color of cornflowers, and spoken through those lush lips, the effect was even more sensual than it had been over the phone. For a moment he just looked at her, his brain refusing to shift into gear. Then he snapped out of it. She was *way* too much, he thought with sudden illogic. Too much hair, too much leg, too much satiny skin. Generous curves that even the short straight shift she wore—the famous leaf-green dress—couldn't conceal. The ankle bracelet was like an unnecessary cherry on top of warm caramel sauce and whipped cream.

He realized that he'd been holding his open ID in front of him for the last few seconds, and those amazingly blue eyes were beginning to hold a hint of uncertainty. Snapping the leather case shut and stuffing it back into his jacket pocket, he nodded curtly and held out his hand to shake hers, but even as he did he saw what he should have noticed from the first.

She'd been crying. And as she switched the can of cat food to her other hand and automatically met his grasp, he could see a raw scrape on the side of her arm by her elbow, as if she'd fallen on pavement.

"Matt D'Angelo," he acknowledged, the formality he'd intended to project falling away as his glance took in the pinpoints of dried blood on that smooth skin. "What happened to your arm?"

"I—I got mugged on my way home, just as I was coming out of the grocery store." The honeyed tones shook slightly as her hand rested briefly in his and then withdrew. "I had eggs and a jar of low-fat mayonnaise, too, but they broke on the sidewalk."

The last few words came out in an unsteady rush. When she closed her eyes, for a second Matt thought she was about to faint, but before he could make a move toward her she took a deep, controlled breath. Holding it for a long moment, she let it out slowly, her lashes fanning her cheekbones. She exhaled as softly as if she were blowing a kiss.

For some reason, he couldn't tear his gaze from that mouth. He was beginning to get annoyed with himself.

For God's sake, she wasn't even his type. He liked cool-looking blondes. He liked short hair grazing a woman's jawline in a blunt cut. He liked women who wore tailored clothes in neutral colors and women whose idea of appropriate jewelry was a pair of classic gold earrings. All of his past girlfriends had more or less fit that pattern.

Unfortunately, for the past five months he hadn't been seeing anybody on a steady basis. That had to be why this woman's overwhelming lushness was getting to him.

"This is the first time anything like that's ever happened to me. Before I knew what was happening, my shoulder bag was gone and I was lying on the ground." Again she breathed, her breasts rising against the thin cotton of the dress. "Pranayama," she said, opening her eyes and meeting his carefully blank gaze. "Tantric breathing. It's a yoga exercise to restore serenity."

Her serenity, maybe. Matt cleared his throat.

"What was taken?"

Resuming normal breathing and starting up the walkway to the shabby apartment building, for a moment she didn't answer him. Following her, he saw her shoulders slump a little, and at that he felt a familiar emotion—one that he could deal with—override the inappropriate flicker of attraction he'd just been feeling. It was anger. It was directed at the unknown scumbag who'd done this to her.

He was willing to bet that losing even the ten bucks or so she'd probably been carrying in her purse had been a major financial blow. What the hell was the matter with the world, when a woman couldn't even walk home safely in the daytime anymore?

"Nothing that really mattered." They'd reached the front door of the building, and as he held the door open for her, Jenna fished inside the front of her dress, finally pulling out a couple of keys hanging around her neck on a piece of string. She looked up at him and flashed a weak smile. "A hundred and fifty dollars. It was all the money I had till I get my first paycheck Friday, but Franklin always used to say that money's the least valuable commodity in the world. Anyway, maybe the mugger needed it more than I did."

Slipping the string over her head, she tried to insert the key in the peeling foyer door but she seemed to be having trouble. Silently Matt reached over to take the awkward can of cat food from her and she bent to her task again, her face hidden by that fabulous cloud of red-gold hair, her voice slightly muffled. "Franklin was my dad. He never trusted banks, but then again, he never really had much need for them." She dropped the keys and he was sure he heard her muttering a singularly unangelic phrase.

"It's not working." She pushed the mass of hair back from her face and turned to him. "Why isn't the stupid thing working? Can't *anything* go right today?"

Those honey-and-cinnamon tones sounded decidedly peevish. Two seconds ago she'd written off her life savings with the calm saintliness of a Mother Superior, he thought, bemused. Now she was getting cranky because her key wouldn't fit smoothly. He handed her back the can, picked the keys up off the cracked linoleum floor and tried the first one in the lock.

"This one's obviously the key to your own apartment," he said. "That's why it wouldn't fit."

Behind him, he heard her taking a deep breath.

His sisters always had problems with keys. Privately he was convinced it was built in with the XX chromosome, although the one time he'd run that theory by his older sister, Carmela, she'd hit him over the head with her physics textbook.

He straightened up in abrupt annoyance. "The stupid thing's not working. Which apartment does your super live in?"

Jenna took her keys back and pressed a button on the intercom board. "I don't understand," she said. "I didn't have a problem this morning. I forgot my bus pass, and I had to let myself back in to get it."

She gave the buzzer another halfhearted little tap and turned back to him without waiting for a response. "He's not home. Let me try the keys again. Men always have trouble with keys."

"Trust me—they don't work." Biting off the words with unnecessary emphasis, Matt jammed his thumb on the buzzer and kept it there. Whatever information she had for the Bureau, he thought wearily, it had better be good. By the time they got into her apartment and she spilled her big secret it would be midnight, at the rate this meeting was going.

He felt a twinge of guilt. It wasn't her fault she hadn't shown up on time, he told himself. And if his evening wasn't turning out exactly the way he'd planned, hers had been a disaster. She'd been mugged, for God's sake. She'd been left penniless by some creep who'd knocked her down and taken her purse, and she was right—the money was going to be the least of her problems. Replacing credit cards and identification would be a major headache.

No wonder her serenity was beginning to crack a little.

"What do you want, mister?" The man who opened the door was about fifty. He was shorter than Matt's own six-two by about a foot, but he had the bad-tempered pugnaciousness of a bantam rooster. Under the dirty white T-shirt he was wearing strained the hard potbelly of a serious drinker, and his tattooed biceps, stringy as they were, looked as if they'd served him well in decades of barroom brawls.

He didn't even glance at Jenna, but instead kept his glare pinned on Matt. "If you're a goddamn salesman for something, buddy, you've got about five seconds to get your butt off—"

"Mr. West, my key's not working." Jenna didn't seem intimidated by his stream of invective. "When I moved in last week you said you'd get a spare set cut for me. Can I use them tonight and have some copies made tomorrow?"

He swung round to her, the scowl on his face deepening. "And who are *you,* lady? What is this, some kind of freakin' scam?"

Matt had been watching the super, ready to step in if the man's hostility crossed the line into action, but this newest tactic caught him by surprise. Flashing a quick look at Jenna's dumbfounded expression, he realized that she was as taken aback as he was. Her polite smile had faded into confusion, and her cornflower-blue eyes widened.

"I'm *Jenna,* Mr. West—Jenna Moon, from 2B. Remember, you helped me move in my futon and I dropped it on your foot? And last night I gave you an aloe plant and told you how it could heal burns and cuts?" She gave an uncertain little laugh. "You were going to fix my faucet this weekend."

"You're crazy, sweetcheeks." West looked from her to Matt and grunted. "Get your flaky girlfriend out of here before I call the cops."

He started to close the foyer door, but Matt had had enough. Swiftly he stepped forward and shoved his shoulder and right arm through the narrowing space between the door and its frame, his ID and badge already open and dangling from his fingers.

"I *am* the cops," he said in a flat voice. "And the lady's a tenant of yours. How about you start showing some co-operation here, *buddy?*"

He could have sworn he saw a flash of something like fear behind West's hard stare, but that was a common re-action. Men like him always had something to hide, Matt thought with disgust. Usually their dirty little secrets had nothing to do with the case on hand, but as soon as they realized they were dealing with the authorities they started lying automatically, unwilling to give a straight answer to any question.

West was probably just a mean drunk who'd drawn a temporary blank on his newest tenant. But Jenna—what had she said her last name was?—Jenna Moon didn't need any more problems tonight. She was doing that deep-breathing thing again, he noted resignedly.

"Just let her into her apartment. I'll even sign for the key if you want some kind of official receipt." He forced a civility into his voice that he didn't feel, at the same time exerting enough pressure on the half-open door to make the surly superintendent step back. Giving Jenna a slight nod, he kept his body between her and West as she nervously slipped past him to the short flight of stairs leading to the second floor.

"Look, mister." West dropped his voice and darted a look at her, now climbing the stairs. "I'm being straight with you—that little sweetheart don't live in 2B or any other freakin' apartment here. If I have to, I'll prove it to you.''

His attitude had changed from abrasiveness to an unpleasant kind of man-to-man confidentiality. For a second, Matt wondered if there was any way the man was telling the truth. His earlier impression of Jenna resurfaced.

West had called her flaky. During her brief phone call to the Bureau, he'd figured himself that she'd sounded like a kook—secretive, refusing to give him any hint of what her vital information was and hanging up after that unconventional description of the dress she was wearing. Her reaction to losing her life savings hadn't been normal, and even her appearance was a little offbeat. He frowned. On the other hand, this lowlife superintendent was just the type to run some kind of scam himself, and, with her obvious openness and artlessness, he would have pegged his new tenant as an easy mark. The last thing he would have expected was for her to show up with an FBI agent in tow.

"There's someone in my apartment!" Jenna's voice was outraged, and glancing up to the first-floor landing he saw her bent over and peering at the crack under the door. "There's a *light* on. I didn't leave any lights on when I left this morning!"

"Okay, that's it." Matt jerked his head grimly at the man in front of him. "You're going to let the lady into her apartment, and if we find anything missing you better be ready with some real fast explaining. What is this, some sweet little deal you've got going with a few light-fingered friends?"

West gave a short bark of humorless laughter, shedding the false bonhomie he'd displayed a few seconds ago as if it had never been. He rubbed his unshaven jaw thoughtfully, a thin smile on his lips. "You're as crazy as she is.

But I don't want no trouble with the feds.'' He shrugged and started for the stairs, reaching around the back of his belt for the collection of keys that hung on a steel ring there. "Come on, let's see how Miss Looney Tunes explains this.''

They were close enough now to Jenna that she overheard this last remark, and the expression in those wide, guileless eyes made Matt think of a deer, shot without warning. She'd obviously trusted this jerk. He felt a sudden spurt of irritation at her naiveté. Where the hell had she been all her life, that she seemed so ill equipped to deal with the real world? She had to be twenty-three or twenty-four—not a susceptible teenager anymore. It was as if she'd been living in some peaceful utopia up until now, where everyone could be taken at their face value, and the sordid side of life—money, violence, dishonesty—never intruded.

"Use your damn key, West,'' he snapped. The man had raised a meaty fist and was knocking on the door. "Let's get this over with.''

Even as he finished speaking, he heard footsteps coming from inside the apartment and all his senses went on full alert. Jenna had heard them, too, and she turned to him, shocked.

"What's going on, Matt? Does he have the right to let someone in when I'm not at home?''

"Move away from the door, Jenna.'' He ignored her question and gave the command in a low, urgent voice. Standing to one side of the door himself, he reached inside his jacket for the shoulder-holstered Sig Sauer he wore during working hours and narrowed his eyes at West, who hadn't moved.

"If your pals are armed, you stand a good chance of being the first casualty. And if you're not the first, you can bet I'll make damn sure you're the second.'' He gripped the gun in both hands, the barrel pointing at the floor. His words were barely above a whisper, but the threat was unmistakable. "Tell them to open the door slowly, and no sudden moves."

The man's shrug of reply was almost insolently unconcerned. One side of his mouth hitched up in a mocking half smile. "This is a real career-breaking move you're making here, D'Angelo. Maybe you should go home tonight and start packing for Anchorage. The Bureau's probably going to send you as far out of town as they can after this foul-up." He tapped with almost ludicrous courtesy on the door as the footsteps shuffled to a halt. "Mrs. Janeway? It's Pete West. Can I talk to you for a minute?"

Matt's finger was tight on the trigger, and for one fleeting second he could see himself—Matt D'Angelo, who never rushed into things without carefully considering every angle, standing armed and ready to kick down a door if necessary, all on the word of a woman he'd met only minutes ago. *What's wrong with this picture, D'Angelo?* he thought in momentary confusion. *This isn't you, man—step back and think this out, for God's sake!*

Then he stopped trying to reason, and let instinct take over completely as he saw the door swing slowly open.

"FBI—*freeze!*" Out of the corner of his eye he could see Jenna edging nervously but resolutely up to the other side of the door, the dented can held high above her head like a weapon, and he felt his heart skip a couple of beats. "Step out into the hall with your hands up!"

For a second there was no reply, but then a voice answered him in a hesitant quaver. "I can't, young man. If I let go of my walker, I'll fall. If you'll give me a minute, though, I think I can spread 'em, as you policemen say."

Even as Matt pivoted swiftly from the side of the door frame to confront the intruder, his brain was scrambling into overdrive, desperately trying to pull in every scrap of information it was receiving and process it into something that made some kind of sense.

Except when he realized that he was holding a gun on a little old lady in an aluminum walker, a little old lady with white hair, orthopedic shoes, and bifocals that glinted in front of curious faded blue eyes, he suddenly got the feeling that there was going to be no way this was ever going to make sense.

God, D'Angelo, you could have blown away Grandma Walton, he thought with numb horror. Well, it hadn't been *that* close a call. But he'd be willing to bet that West, standing behind him, would embellish the encounter to the first reporter he could get on the phone.

"Who are you and what are you doing here?" Jenna asked the woman.

For a second he'd forgotten about Jenna, but that had been another mistake, he thought, his heart sinking. Hair flying around her shoulders in a burnished copper cloud, breasts heaving in indignation under the thin Indian cotton of her dress, and shaking the can of cat food at Mrs. Janeway, she looked like an angel, all right. Only this time she looked like an avenging angel, ready to drive the old lady out of the Garden of Eden.

Or at least out of the apartment that Jenna obviously still felt she had a claim on. A sudden thought struck Matt, and he turned with renewed hope to the superintendent behind him, ignoring West's triumphant grin. "What are you trying to pull? It's the wrong damn apartment!"

"What do you mean, the wrong apartment?" Jenna whirled on him angrily. "I *know* where I live, Matt! This woman might look like a sweet little old lady to you, but she's got no right to be here! Look, I'll show you!"

Before he could stop her, she'd sidestepped past the aluminum walker with a dancer's agility, but even as he edged cautiously past the old lady with a muttered apology and reached out to grab Jenna's arm, she froze.

"What have you done to my apartment?"

Her gaze swung wildly around the comfortably cozy living room as if she was looking upon some terrible desecration. With a trembling finger, she pointed at a row of potted African violets on the radiator by the window.

"They—they're *artificial!* Where's my fern and my spider plant?" She gestured at the colonial-style recliner sitting in front of a small television set. On a low table beside the chair was a half-knitted child's garment, in an insipid color combination of peach-pink and cream. Her voice rose. "And what's all this? This isn't my furniture! I had my rattan set here, and I don't even *own* a television! *What's going on?*"

It was time to step in, he told himself. She'd made some kind of colossal mistake, and she just wasn't admitting it to herself. Again, the first impression he'd had of her flashed through his mind, but he shoved it aside. She'd only lived here a week, and tonight she'd gone through a traumatic experience. She wasn't necessarily crazy—maybe she'd hit her head when she'd fallen and received some kind of mild concussion. That had to be it, he thought compassionately. She was suffering from some kind of short-term memory loss.

It was a convenient theory, but it was full of holes, and he knew it. She'd given him this address over the phone this afternoon—*before* she'd been accosted by the mugger.

If there had been a mugger.

"You don't believe me." She was staring at him, her face pale, her white-knuckled grip still hanging on for dear life to the cat-food can, and Matt found it impossible to say anything. The smart way out would be to lie, to play along with her until he could get her out of here quietly, but suddenly he knew he couldn't do it. As the silence between them lengthened, she seemed to be searching his expression intently.

"You think I'm *crazy*." Her voice was a thready, incredulous whisper. She stared numbly at the fussy flower-sprigged wallpaper, the embroidered pictures of pastoral scenes on the walls and the stack of Agatha Christie mysteries piled on an ornately ugly coffee table in front of the plaid sofa. "You've *got* to believe me, Matt! When I left here this morning that ceiling was painted sky-blue with white clouds I'd sponged on this weekend. The walls were a lighter blue. I was making canvas cushions for my furniture, I had photographs of my parents on the wall, and my plants were growing on the windowsill. Somebody's made it all *different!* You *have* to believe me!"

Her last few words were an urgent entreaty, and though he tried to soften his response, he knew it was the last thing she wanted to hear. "That doesn't make any sense, Jenna." He kept his voice quiet, hoping to soothe the raw anguish in her eyes. "What reason would anyone have for doing that?"

Instead of answering him, she held his gaze unwaveringly for a moment as if giving him one last chance to change his mind. Then whatever hope she still had ebbed visibly out of her and she turned slowly away. Walking to a half-open door, she flicked on a light switch. Matt remained where he was, his hands clenched at his sides, watching her as she looked in, switched off the light and turned back to him, her voice toneless. "Everything's changed. My futon's gone, the quilt my mother made for me when I was a little girl—it's all disappeared. And you don't believe me, do you?"

"Would anybody like a nice cup of tea?" Mrs. Janeway

had hobbled back into the room. At the doorway, West surveyed the scene with a tight grin and Matt suddenly felt a violent urge to knock the smile from his face. But Jenna didn't even spare the man a second glance. Her attention was directed at the old lady, and her head was tipped to one side, quizzically.

"It's all an act, isn't it?" She gave Mrs. Janeway a coldly appraising look, and the older woman halted in her slow progress across the room, her faded eyes sharpening as she met Jenna's glance. "You must be useful for something like this—who's going to suspect a sweet little old lady of being a crook?"

"I don't know what you're talking about, dear." Mrs. Janeway smiled sympathetically. "Mr. West says you had some idea that this might have been your apartment once, but that's just not possible. I've been here for over fifteen years now, and as you can see, I have all my little treasures and comforts around me. This has been my home since my husband passed away, God rest his soul."

The old voice held a wistful tremor, but instead of rousing Jenna to pity, what little composure she had left finally cracked. "You're lying! This is *my* home! You've stolen the first home I ever really had, you—you *criminal!*" She shook the can of cat food at West, standing in the doorway. "And you're in on this with her! You *rented* me this apartment a week ago, and you know it!"

Suddenly her gaze went blank and she stared frantically around. "Where's Zappa?" Her voice rose. "What did you do with him?"

"What's she talking about?" the old lady said in a loudly whispered aside to Matt, as if Jenna was incapable of understanding her. "Who's this Zeppo person she's looking for now?"

The wrinkled face held an expression of saccharine pity,

but behind the bifocals her eyes twinkled with avid interest, and suddenly Matt realized that he didn't like Mrs. Janeway either. But whether he liked the woman or not, they'd intruded on her long enough. He turned to Jenna.

"We have to go. I know you're upset right now, but—"

"Zappa! Not Zeppo—*Zappa!* My cat! Or do you think this is a delusion, too?" Now the tears that she'd been holding back spilled over, and those thick dark lashes were spiky and wet as she held out the dented can as if it was some kind of clinching proof. "He's Siamese; he's a little chunky around the middle, and his tail's covered with sky-blue paint from when I was sponging the ceiling." Her voice shook. "And you've made *him* disappear, too!"

From the doorway West's glance caught Matt's and he winked. "Like I told you," he said in a stage whisper. "Miss Looney Tunes."

Matt's heart sank.

Chapter Two

"He called me crazy. Miss Looney Tunes." Jenna sat across from Matt in the nearby coffee shop where he'd hustled her after the fiasco at her apartment. Her gaze looked as if it could start a flash fire on the cracked Formica of the tabletop between them. "And you're thinking the same thing."

She never should have let him persuade her to walk away from West and that deceitful old woman who called herself Mrs. Janeway, she thought in angry self-recrimination. She should have refused to leave, at least until she'd found out what they'd done with Zappa. Except that in the middle of her near-hysterical outburst she'd caught a glimpse of the expression, quickly veiled, on Matt's face and for a moment she'd felt as if she'd actually taken a physical blow.

His expression had frightened her. Suddenly she'd realized that she'd lost her only ally, and that the man she'd thought was on her side wasn't even able to meet her eyes.

He wasn't meeting them now.

"I don't think you're crazy," he said a shade too heartily. There was a container of paper-wrapped toothpicks on the table, and he'd already mangled two of them. Now he stripped the wrapping off a third and snapped it in half. "It's obvious that you're a little confused, but that could be the result of a lot of things—stress, for example. It could be an aftereffect of the mugging.'' The third toothpick lay in pieces by his coffee cup as he fell silent.

Right from the start he hadn't known what to make of her, she thought despondently. She'd seen him glancing dubiously at her ankle bracelet and tie-dyed dress, and even on the phone this afternoon she had the sinking feeling she'd come off as a flake. When she'd met him, she'd realized that Agent D'Angelo was just as alien to her as she appeared to him.

It was no wonder he'd felt uneasy with her. It had been almost inevitable that he'd jumped to the conclusion that she was suffering from some kind of delusion.

The phrase ''just the facts, ma'am,'' could have been coined for him. He was the perfect FBI agent, from his unobtrusive but well-cut suit right down to his gleaming shoes. Maybe he was just a little too good-looking to pass unnoticed in a crowd, but even there he'd done his best to conform. Not a strand of that thick black hair was out of place, and that sensuously full lower lip that seemed so at variance with the rest of the hard angles of his face was usually thinned in a tightly controlled line. It must have taken him years to submerge his own personality so completely, Jenna mused. Now he probably didn't even have to think about it.

But he'd slipped up once, and for a startling moment she'd seen past the conservative facade to the original Matt D'Angelo. The man she'd glimpsed had looked at her with a sudden flare of heat in those cool golden-brown eyes, and for a heartbeat his gaze had lingered searingly on her, as if he couldn't stop himself. Then he'd pulled back with a visible effort, and she'd almost been able to see him convincing himself that what he'd experienced hadn't been real.

Just like he was trying to persuade her now.

"Refill?" The waitress, a tired-looking woman in her late forties with a name tag that said Marg pinned to her uniform, was standing beside them with a full coffeepot in her hand and a mechanical smile on her face, but as she looked at Jenna her expression changed to one of interest.

"Beautiful dress, honey." Almost reverently she reached out and her fingertips brushed the thin multihued cotton. "I used to know a girl in the '60s who designed and dyed her own—Tamara, her name was. She used to give them away."

"Tamara Seagull?" Jenna looked up eagerly. "She still does—this is one of hers. She lives on a commune in Vermont and barters them for produce and firewood. I traded a couple of bushels of tomatoes and a wheelbarrow-full of zucchini for this." She laughed for the first time that evening, feeling suddenly as if she'd run into a friend.

Matt was looking at them as if he didn't know what they were talking about. She ignored him.

"When I knew Tamara we were both still in our teens," Marg the waitress said reminiscently. She set the coffeepot down on the table, forgotten, and her expression was faraway, as if her dingy surroundings had faded into the background. She smiled dreamily, and it was possible to see that she'd once been vibrantly pretty. "Everything seemed so simple then—she'd make her dresses, and I was going to set up a pottery studio. But then I met Dwayne and fell madly in love, and the next thing I knew, I was married and expecting a baby. Dwayne took a job for a few months at a factory, but he hated it, and two weeks after Debbie was born he took off. I never heard from him again." She stared unseeingly through the steam-fogged window of the coffee shop to the darkness outside, and then blinked. Slowly she picked up the pot and one of the thick, chipped mugs. "I'll never forget that summer. I still have one of the plates I made back then. But you wouldn't even have been born in the '60s—how do you know Tamara?"

"My father and I lived on the Sunflower Commune for a while about three years ago," Jenna said. Out of the corner of her eye she saw Matt frown uncomprehendingly. He probably thought the lifestyle she'd lived up until recently had died out with sit-ins and peace medallions, she thought impatiently. "It's a well-respected artists' colony now, with a self-supporting organic farm attached—their stone-ground bread is famous all over the state. They didn't have a resident potter when I was there, though," she added. Beside her, Marg bit her lip thoughtfully.

"It'd take a while before I could turn out anything good again," she said slowly. "But I'm a hard worker, and a bakery can always use an extra pair of hands. Since Debbie got married and moved away, there's been nothing to keep me here."

She poured Matt another cup of coffee almost briskly, and her smile at Jenna as she left their table was nothing like the mechanical one she'd worn earlier. As soon as she was out of earshot, Matt spoke.

"How'd you do that?" His voice was almost accusatory. He looked baffled. "I've seen agents with years of experience who can't draw that much out of someone in hours of interrogation, but she spilled her most secret hopes to you after two seconds. Where'd you learn that?"

Jenna shook her head, momentarily taken aback. "I didn't *learn* that. It's not a technique, Matt—I just thought she looked kind of lonely. And when she noticed my dress, she reminded me of the people I grew up with."

"Ex-hippies." He couldn't keep the skepticism out of his voice. "You really were brought up on communes? I didn't know they still existed."

"It's not *that* unusual," she said with a spurt of defensiveness. "A lot of people still choose to opt out of mainstream society and live an alternative lifestyle closer to nature. It's not as if we painted our bodies blue and sat around contemplating blades of grass all day."

"Well, it explains the ankle bracelet, anyway," he muttered, and at that her temper flared.

"And it explains what happened back at my apartment, right? I'm just an off-the-wall flake that lives in a fantasy world half the time, is that it?" She took a deep breath. "I *know* it must have seemed weird, Matt, but you've got to believe me—somebody went into my home today and completely changed everything!"

Put like that, it did sound outrageous, she thought in sudden uncertainty. Why *would* anyone in the world want to discredit her? What threat was she to anybody?

All of a sudden the answer was right in front of her. Her breath caught painfully in her throat as she considered her theory, examining it for flaws and finding none. Of course, she thought with growing certainty—that had to be it! And once she explained everything to Matt, he'd *have* to believe her, because with this missing piece in place, the whole thing made sinister sense. Jenna looked around the coffee shop, leaned across the table and lowered her voice to an urgent whisper.

"It's a vast conspiracy *aimed* at making me look crazy," she said in a rush of excitement. "That's why it's working so well—because it was *planned* that way! They wanted you to discount everything I said, so they created the whole setup—changed the locks so my keys wouldn't work, repainted and papered my apartment and got rid of all my furniture, and installed that terrible old woman in there with her phony walker. I was watching her, Matt." She gave an unladylike little snort of derision. "She wasn't even putting her weight on that thing! Heck, she probably teaches swing dancing when she's not busy with her criminal career—'' She stopped in mid-sentence, taking in the expression in the dark gold eyes across from her.

It was pity. But that was only because he still didn't know the reason she'd called him today in the first place, Jenna thought, exasperated at herself. She *did* sound like a kook, spilling it out like that. She took a deep, calming breath to center her thoughts, but Matt's voice broke into them.

''A vast conspiracy.'' His tone was placatingly noncommittal, as if he was taking care not to set her off on another tirade. ''Sure, Jenna, that's probably what's going on. But right now let's try and find you a place to stay for the night—since Mrs. Janeway and her cohorts have stolen your apartment.''

He paused, and invested his next words with a casual carelessness, shredding another toothpick to sawdust as he spoke. ''And it might be a good idea to take you to the hospital and have that graze on your arm attended to in case it gets infected. In fact, we should do that first. My car's still outside the apartment, so we'll walk back. I'll drive you over to Mass. General straight away.''

He couldn't have telegraphed his meaning more clearly if he'd been wearing a white coat and chasing after her with a net, she thought in annoyance. She discarded her plan of leading up to the subject logically and dispassionately.

''I saw Rupert Carling today, Matt. *That's* what this is all about.''

Across the table from her he let the last remnants of the toothpick fall from his fingers. His features smoothed into a bland mask, revealing nothing of what he was thinking, but the gold glints in his eyes intensified and he flicked a glance around the half-empty room before he spoke. When he did, he sounded as perfunctory as if she'd made a comment about the weather. "Run that one by me again. You saw who?"

"Rupert Carling. You know—the missing tycoon who disappeared two days ago," she elaborated impatiently. "His photo's been on the front page of all the papers with the story about how the police think he might have been murdered. You must have seen it!"

"I've seen the articles. I know who Rupert Carling is." He held her gaze with his own. "I still don't get the connection between his disappearance and what happened tonight at your apartment."

"It's obvious! For some reason, no one's supposed to know where he is or even that he's still alive, and when they found out I'd seen him at Parks, Parks, and Boyleston today in the basement, they had to totally discredit me before I told the authorities." Jenna tapped her thumbnail nervously on her bottom lip. "They couldn't simply kill me. I wonder why?"

"And Parks, Parks, and Boyleston is...?" he inquired politely.

"The law firm where I started work yesterday." Her hair had fallen forward in her excitement and she pushed it back with a quick gesture. "Don't you see? This whole thing makes sense now— I'm simply a crazy lady with one crazy story after another." A thought struck her and her eyes darkened. "The mugger! He wasn't after my money, he was after my identity! Everything that could help me prove I'm who I say I am was in my wallet...."

Her voice trailed off as the enormity of the plan became clearer. "They couldn't kill me for some reason, so they did the next best thing. They were trying to make it look as if Jenna Moon never existed, Matt. As if everything about me was a lie or a fantasy.''

Outside it had begun to rain heavily, but she hardly noticed the downpour through the plate-glass window beside them. All her attention was focused on him, and when he finally spoke she realized she'd been holding her breath.

''It sounds too incredible to be true,'' he said. At her stricken expression, he continued, voicing his thoughts aloud. ''And that might have been just what they were counting on—whoever 'they' are.''

He was silent for a moment. Then he sat up straighter and took a pen and a small notepad from the breast pocket of his suit jacket. ''Okay, take it from the top and don't leave anything out, no matter how insignificant it seems. How did you run into this man you thought was Rupert Carling?''

He wasn't convinced—not yet. But at least he was giving her the benefit of the doubt, instead of writing her off as a flake, Jenna thought shakily. A wave of relief rushed over her and she felt the sharp prickle of tears behind her eyelids, but she blinked them away and tried to keep her voice steady as she answered him.

''Miss Terwilliger is training me as a records clerk, and like I said, today was only my second day on the job,'' she began. He interrupted her.

''Miss Terwilliger? What's her position at Parks, Parks, and Boyleston?''

''We call it Parks, Parks for short,'' she said helpfully. ''Miss Terwilliger is the head of the office staff, and she's been there forever. Parks, Parks is her life— I don't know what she'll do when she's forced to retire.'' Matt rubbed his temples in an unconscious gesture and she went on hurriedly. ''Anyway, she's a dragon, but today she said she thought I might have the makings of a first-rate records clerk in me, so I think she likes me. She even gave me some files to put away in the archives but the building's old, and I got lost going down the wrong passageway."

"And you ran into Rupert Carling in the basement of this law firm?" The note of disbelief was back, not as strong as before but still distinctly audible. "What was he doing, catching rats?"

Her thoughts skidded to an abrupt halt and she stared blankly at him. "If you *knew* already, why the big pretense with the notebook? Why didn't you tell me somebody'd already reported it?" She drew away from him in annoyed disappointment, and the bells on her ankle bracelet tinkled sharply.

"I don't know anything about Rupert Carling being seen except for what you're telling me now," Matt said. He lifted a skeptical eyebrow. "Call the rat-catcher thing a lucky guess."

"Oh." She looked dubiously at him. "Well, he wasn't catching rats when I saw him, but he *was* wearing coveralls with the name of an extermination firm on them."

"You're serious? Rupert Carling really was posing as a rat-catcher?" He looked incredulous, but at her nod he scribbled something in his notebook. "Did you notice the name of the firm?"

"It was something unimaginative like Pestex. Oh—and he had one of those weird gas-mask things on."

"A respirator?" He started to make a notation in his book but then paused and looked up. "Wait a minute. Wouldn't that have covered his face?"

"If he'd been wearing it, yes, but he had it hanging by the straps around his neck." She frowned slightly. "I hope you're getting this down right. I probably should read it over when we're finished in case you miss something vital."

"Someday you'll have to teach me that deep-breathing technique you use." Matt laid his pen carefully on the table and smiled thinly at her. "The serenity one."

He sounded touchy. "Sorry. It's just that this is the first time I've ever given a statement, and I want to make sure I remember everything."

"That's understandable." Sighing, he raked his hand through his hair and picked up his pen again. "If you did see Rupert Carling and someone's trying to cover it up then you've obviously stumbled onto something big. Any little detail could be important. What happened next?"

"Nothing." She shrugged helplessly. "I turned a corner, barreled into the man, apologized and kept going. The next corridor was the right one, and I was almost back at the file room when I realized who he was. All I could think of was to phone the FBI, so when Miss Terwilliger said I could take my lunch break I ran out to a pay phone, got the number from the operator and called you."

"Hold on a minute." Tossing his pen down, he narrowed his eyes. "Why waste precious time waiting for your lunch break? In fact, why didn't you just phone from the office and tell me all this right away?"

Jenna shook her head. "No personal calls at work. Miss Terwilliger says that's like stealing from the company. I knew you'd want to ask questions and go over my story a few times, but I only had half an hour for lunch and it was obvious Carling had no idea I'd recognized him." Color rose to her cheeks. "Look, Matt—I wouldn't have traded my life for anything up until now. But I'm twenty-four years old, and I've never had a regular job or stayed in the same place for more than a few months at a time. Franklin wasn't the type to settle down and since it was just the two of us, I guess I felt I should stay with him until—until he died earlier this year. It was hard enough to find a firm that was willing to hire someone like me in the first place, and I'm not about to do anything to lose this job. I *need* it. I've got rent to pay. For the first time in my life I've finally got a place I can call my own—''

She broke off, suddenly remembering. To her chagrin, this time the tears wouldn't be contained and she felt one sliding down her cheek. She looked up through flooded blue eyes and attempted to pull herself together, but to her surprise, instead of looking uncomfortable and grabbing for another toothpick to destroy, Matt reached over and took one of her hands in both of his. He'd forgotten to thin his mouth into his usual straight line and he looked more approachable than she'd yet seen him.

''Here's what we're going to do.''

He had a nice voice, she thought inconsequentially. When it lost its businesslike edge, it was as warm and silky as melted chocolate, and it was low enough so that the person he was speaking to felt compelled to keep quiet, just to catch what he was saying. Big family, she decided promptly. That had to be something he'd learned growing up in a noisy household. She felt ridiculously pleased at having guessed a little of his background.

''I'm going to make a quick call to the Agency before we leave and alert them to what you've told me.'' He glanced at the public phone on the wall by the exit. ''Not the most secure place to give a report, but I want to get this information to the office right away. Then we're going to head back to the apartment and start searching for your cat. The most likely way they got rid of him was simply by opening the window and letting him out, and if he's not familiar with the neighborhood, he's probably still somewhere close by. Siamese, kind of chunky around the middle, right?'' He gave her a one-sided and quizzical smile.

She could feel the stupid tears coursing down her cheeks,

but this time she didn't care. "Don't forget the blue paint on his tail," she laughed shakily. "Oh, Matt—I *knew* your aura couldn't lie! I can't see them very often but when I can they're always right, and today when I met you I was pretty sure I saw yours. It was pale pink, like a cloud."

He looked nonplussed. "Aura? I have an aura around me?" She saw his eyes flick involuntarily to the air above his head.

"Don't worry, everyone has one." She laughed again, and then somewhere deep inside her it suddenly felt like a bird had started fluttering around, trying out its wings for the first time. It was an oddly exhilarating sensation. "They're—they're a reflection of your inner being. Pale pink is good," she finished breathily, her gaze locked onto his.

"Even for a man?" He had that melted-chocolate voice thing going again, she thought hazily. It was such a sexy contrast to the tough pragmatism the rest of him projected that it ignited a string of wildly imaginative paradoxes in her mind, like a chain of Chinese firecrackers exploding one after another—controlled but unleashed, lazily casual and then intense, slow and sweet and strong and hot...

His thumb was idly stroking the inside of her palm. This time she was quite willing to accept that she was going a little crazy.

"*Especially* for a man," she managed to say. Whatever was going through her mind had to be going through his right now, too, she thought. That lower lip was pure sensuality and his eyes were half-veiled by those thick dark lashes. His breathing had deepened and slowed.

For a long moment the world around them seemed to recede into nothingness. Far in the background of her consciousness Jenna could hear the clink of china as tables were cleared, the faint sound of a radio playing behind the counter and the rushing hiss of a bus coming to a stop outside in the rain. But nothing registered. She felt as if the whole universe had lasered down to a single pinpoint of reality that only included the touch of their hands, the electric awareness flowing between them.

"I—I should make that call."

Matt's reluctant words finally broke the silence, but instead of regretting that the moment had come to an end, she almost welcomed it. She felt shaky and disoriented, and as he abruptly pushed back his chair and walked over to the phone in the corner of the coffee shop, it was almost impossible to force herself to stop staring at the way he moved, from letting her gaze linger on the smoothly powerful shift of muscles under that suit jacket...

What had just happened between them? A silvery shiver ran down her spine. One moment they'd been slightly antagonistic near strangers, and the next minute they'd both been indulging in converging fantasies that had almost accelerated into reality. Only the fact that they'd been in a public place had kept them apart, Jenna thought tremulously.

It had been so *intense*. It was as if those wings she'd felt fluttering inside her had flown straight up to the sun, heedless of the fire that awaited them there and craving only the ever-increasing heat. A minute longer in that dangerously seductive flight and she would have never been able to return to the safety of the mundane world.

Even now she wasn't sure that she would ever be the same person she'd been half an hour ago.

He wasn't her *type*, for heaven's sakes! She saw him lift the receiver and casually turn his back to the room, but with heightened awareness she noticed that he was facing the broad, black expanse of plate-glass window. He was using it as a mirror, she realized. He knew everything that was going on behind him, and if anyone came close he'd probably start talking about something totally innocuous. Suspicion, caution, deception—they were all part of his job.

He was nothing like the men she'd known in the past. The two serious relationships she'd engaged in had been gentle and loving, and both Colin and Ted had been committed to the same lifestyle that she was used to—neither one of them could be called aggressive, and each relationship had ended with quiet affection when she'd moved on. She smiled faintly. Certainly neither man had come chasing after her, trying to persuade her to stay.

Matt D'Angelo might have a veneer of civilization and conformity about him, but if he ever wanted anything badly enough, he'd fight to get it—and keep it. Those gold-flecked eyes that could change so swiftly from bland opacity to raw desire gave him away every time he looked at her.

Those eyes were looking down at her now. With a slight start, she saw that he'd finished his call and was standing beside her silently…and as she met his shuttered gaze, she suddenly knew that her world was about to be shattered for the second time that day.

Chapter Three

She'd known it was going to be bad. What she hadn't been able to imagine was just how bad it could be.

Numb with disbelief, Jenna shivered involuntarily. Despite the steamy heat in the coffee shop, she felt as if a cold wind was cutting through her, numbing her to her very bones.

"They had to have made some mistake in identification." Even to herself, her protest sounded foolishly stubborn, as if she was insisting that the world was flat. "How do they know for sure it was Carling's body?"

Matt rubbed his forehead with the heel of his hand, not meeting her pleading glance. Under the harsh fluorescent lights the lines of weariness around his mouth were thrown into stark relief, and his eyes, when he opened them, were unreadable. He sighed like a man trying to hide his frustration.

"Forensics didn't make a mistake, Jenna. That's why they haven't released the news of his death to the media yet—because they wanted to make damn sure their suspicions were right."

"But even experts can—"

He cut in on her abruptly, as if he couldn't allow her to keep hoping any longer. His voice was low and emphatic.

"It's very important that you understand this. Rupert Carling is dead. He's been dead for over forty-eight hours—ever since someone turned his Mercedes into a ball of fire with a car bomb the night before last." His words were vehemently distinct and his gaze held hers with what seemed like desperation. "The man was a financial titan, so when word of his death gets out later tonight, Wall Street's going to tremble, Jenna—and with that much at stake, nobody could afford to make any creative guesses on what was left of his body. They located a Dr. Borg, Carling's dentist, and had him working alongside the forensics team to make absolutely certain that the dental records matched up with—" He saw the convulsive swallow that she tried to hide, and changed what he'd been about to say. "With what was found at the crime scene," he ended quietly.

"So I didn't see him today at Parks, Parks." Her voice was barely audible.

"There's no way you could have."

"And if I didn't see Rupert Carling, then there's no reason for anyone to try to make me look crazy," she went on. It was as easy as connecting the dots, she thought. One fact led to another, and although she knew she wouldn't like where this was leading, she had no choice but to follow the logic. "And if no one's trying to make me look crazy, the only explanation for what's been happening to me is that I really *am* crazy. Even Zappa was only part of my fantasy."

Her face was pale and the strands of hair feathering onto her forehead seemed to have lost their vibrancy and fire. Her eyes were dull. "Paranoid delusions. When I started using phrases like 'vast conspiracy,' it should have tipped me off right then. But of course, refusing to believe that they're delusions is part of the problem, isn't it?"

"You saw somebody in that corridor at work. It just wasn't who you thought it was," Matt said uncomfortably. The coffee shop was nearly empty now, but he lowered his voice. "There's got to be some other explanation for what happened tonight besides immediately jumping to the conclusion that you're suffering from paranoia."

"Another explanation for anyone else, maybe. Not for me!"

The unequivocal reply escaped from her like a cry of pain and her eyes squeezed shut, as if she couldn't bear to face his carefully phrased questions. Alarmed by her reaction, Matt reached across the table for her hand, but she drew away from his touch. A shudder ran through her and for a moment he tensed, ready to catch her if she fainted; but even as he watched, he saw her quell the trembling with a visible effort.

A few hours ago she'd made him think of caramel sauce and whipped cream, he thought slowly—lush and desirable and frivolously disconcerting. Who would have guessed that that almost confectionery-like exterior hid a will as tough and unyielding as stainless steel? Whatever other problems Jenna Moon had, the woman had an inner strength that was imposing a rigid control on her.

When she spoke again, her words were delivered in a flat, dead whisper that sounded as if it was being wrenched out of her. "Let me tell you about my father. Then you'll understand."

She folded her hands carefully in her lap, pressed her lips together tightly for a moment, and then continued, the normally husky edge to her voice harsh with pain. "Franklin Moon was a student radical in the '60s—passionately committed to making the world a better place through peaceful protests and demonstrations. He was typical of the best of that era, and he should have become one of the most influential people of his generation. But no one's ever heard of my father—and no one ever will now.''

A car sped by on the rain-slick pavement outside, throwing up a sheet of muddy water against the coffee shop, and she flinched as it slapped loudly against the window beside them. Her shoulders hunched forward. ''Sometime during his last year at Berkeley, Franklin Moon became convinced that 'they' were out to get him—a sinister enemy or enemies who would stop at nothing to destroy him. He left without completing his degree. My mother, Sara, was his girlfriend back then. She loved him enough to throw away her life and her future—she cut all ties with her family and disappeared with him. They lived like nomads, never staying in one place for more than a few months, sometimes packing up their Volkswagen van and moving on after only a day or two. Franklin would have seen or heard something that convinced him that 'they' were on his trail again.''

She couldn't completely disguise the rawness in her voice, and this time when Matt reached forward he was too fast for her. His hand, strong and warm, encircled her wrist. ''You don't have to go on.''

For a moment she hesitated. Her fingers curled reflexively, resting on the pulse point at the base of his palm as if she needed to reassure herself that he was real. Then she firmly disengaged herself from his clasp.

''For a long time I thought everybody lived that way— starting a new school just as soon as you made a friend at your old one, never owning anything that couldn't fit in a suitcase, waking up sometimes and forgetting exactly where you were. And then when I was seven, my mother died suddenly and the bottom fell out of my world. A few days later Franklin started loading up the van again and I began screaming and hitting at him, telling him that this time I wasn't going with him, asking him how he could just leave the place where she was buried when he knew that he'd never come back.''

Her eyes filled with tears. She made no attempt to wipe them away and they fell unheeded from her bowed head to her lap. She continued as if it was vitally important to relate every last painful detail.

''That's when he told me. He pulled me into his lap and stroked my hair while I cried myself into exhaustion, and he explained that there were people looking for him—people who would *never* stop looking for him...people who wanted to kill him. The next morning I got in the van and we drove away from the town where my mother had died.''

''How the hell could he have put a child through that?'' Matt exploded angrily. ''No roots, no stability—what was he thinking?''

''He was trying to *protect* me,'' Jenna interjected. ''He really believed that he was in danger, and that whoever was tracking him wouldn't hesitate to kill his daughter too. In every other aspect Franklin is—'' She stopped and her lashes dipped briefly as she closed her eyes and sighed. She corrected herself softly. ''*Was* the gentlest, kindest man I'll ever know. Most people never guessed there was anything the matter with him, and he tried his best to make my childhood as full of love as possible. That's one of the reasons we lived on the communes—he hoped that being part of caring communities like that would make up for me not having any family but him.''

She fell silent, and beside her Matt stared unseeingly through the plate-glass window into the wet night. When he spoke, his words were hesitant. ''Was there ever anything that made you think he wasn't fantasizing this mysterious enemy? Anything, however far-fetched, that might have indicated that there really *was* someone trying to find him and kill him?''

"Forget it, Matt." She smiled tightly and shook her head, just barely holding on to her composure. "After a lifetime of living with Franklin Moon, maybe I sometimes persuaded myself that I'd seen the same car following us in two different states, or that the casual curiosity of a complete stranger was reason for alarm. But there was never any solid proof. How could there have been? It was all in his mind—all part of the same outlandish delusion."

His gaze searched her face intently. "And you're afraid that whatever compulsion drove Franklin to think he had to run for his life has been passed on to you." It wasn't a question. One look at her haunted eyes was answer enough.

The smart money at the Agency was on Agent D'Angelo becoming the next area director. The man was tough, pragmatic, and nothing ever threw him. That was the image he seemed to have acquired, Matt thought wryly. But all bets would have been off if any of his co-workers had been around to see the indecision on his features as he searched for something—*anything*—to soothe away the fear that had taken control of the woman across from him. Dammit, he was supposed to be good at handling people, he told himself in sudden anger. Why was he just sitting here, letting the silence between them lengthen?

He said the first thing that came into his mind, and as soon as he had, he wished he could recall his words. "Even one shred of proof that you'd ever lived there would have given me grounds to investigate further, Jenna. The Carling thing could have been a simple case of misidentification. But coupled with what happened at the apartment and the fact that none of the other tenants in the building would cooperate when I tried to question them before we left—" He broke off, cursing himself for his clumsiness. Jenna had been pale before but now the only color in her face was her eyes, bluer and wider than ever.

"Coupled with the apartment that I insisted was mine, the apartment that obviously belonged to someone else— the apartment where no one *knew* me—there really isn't any doubt, is there?" She met his gaze and held it almost challengingly. "Crazy Jenna Moon who sees auras, dead tycoons walking around in exterminator coveralls and whose whole existence is turning out to be a fantasy. And what's really scary is that I almost had *you* believing it all, didn't I?"

"For God's sake, I'm not the bad guy here." He shifted uncomfortably in his chair, acutely aware that Marg the waitress was looking narrowly over in his direction. "I know what you must be going through. I just wish there was some way we could back up part of your story, but there isn't."

"You have no idea what I'm going through." The brief flash of emotion that she'd displayed had subsided, to be replaced once more with a hopeless acceptance of the situation.

The cornflower-blue of her eyes was blinded with a sheen of tears. Even stainless steel snapped under enough pressure, Matt thought worriedly. And although he still thought it was more likely that whatever mental aberration she was suffering from was temporary, she seemed to believe that her condition was permanent—a legacy from a father who'd lived his whole life running from a fantasy enemy. She needed professional help, he thought reluctantly.

A psychiatrist, D'Angelo, he told himself roughly. *Face it—it's possible she needs a shrink.* This gorgeous, sexy, warm woman who didn't look as if there was anything the matter with her at all was going to have to be checked into a hospital. And he had the sinking feeling that she wasn't going to go along with that plan willingly. He'd been wrong, Matt thought with a twinge of self-condemnation. He *was* going to have to be the bad guy here.

"We've got to find you a place to stay for tonight." He attempted a reassuring smile, feeling like a Judas. His voice sounded a shade too hearty even to his own ears. "There's a hotel downtown that the Agency uses sometimes. We'll put you up there for the night, okay?"

For a moment she didn't answer him. She stared at him assessingly, the unshed tears glittering at the edge of her lashes, and Matt had the feeling that she knew exactly what he was planning. If she ran, he'd have to go after her. It wasn't something he wanted to do, but she couldn't wander around the streets in her condition. Then, with a sense of deep relief, he saw her nod in agreement. Jenna Moon trusted him—which made it a whole lot easier to lie to her. He felt like a heel.

"I guess that's the best solution. I'll start looking for another place tomorrow, but if you're sure it's okay for me to stay at the hotel tonight, that would solve one problem at least." She managed a smile. "I owe you, Matt. Just give me a couple of minutes and then we can leave. I'd feel better if I splashed some cold water on my face."

She got up from the table with that long-legged grace that had caught his eye the first time he'd seen her—had it only been a few hours ago? A gallant spirit, Matt reflected somberly as he watched her approach the waitress standing by the counter. Marg gestured toward the back of the coffee shop. If what Jenna feared was true, she'd need all the courage she had to battle the demons that had beset Franklin Moon throughout his life, and that at his death had seemingly transferred themselves to his daughter. She was going to hate him for deceiving her, but with time maybe she'd realize that he hadn't really had a choice. The hospital was the only place for her right now. He was doing the right thing, he told himself weakly.

So how come words like *betrayal* and *abandonment* kept running through his mind?

Probably because she'd come to him in good faith, asking for his help. She certainly hadn't expected that he'd end up taking her freedom away, no matter how much he felt his actions were justified. He rubbed the side of his jaw tiredly, hardly noticing the pinprick of stubble against his hand, and as he did he caught the sidelong glance the waitress threw him. Their eyes met, and she switched her attention quickly to her order pad, but not before he saw the guilty flush of color on her cheeks.

For crying out loud, D'Angelo—she's taken off on you. And that pottery-making waitress helped her escape!

He pushed his chair back swiftly and crossed the distance between them in three strides. Flustered, Marg looked up with an expression of innocence that wouldn't have fooled a Cub Scout—which was no guarantee that it couldn't fool him, Matt thought disgustedly. He'd screwed up royally.

"She left by the back exit, didn't she? Where is it?"

"It's past the kitchen, mister." Marg snapped her order book closed defiantly and crammed it into her apron pocket. The only other customer left in the place, a bleary-eyed old man in a security-guard uniform, looked up with interest as the waitress's voice took on a sharp edge. "And she's had a good five minutes' start on you, so you might as well just kiss her goodbye. She's gone. What the heck did you say to her, anyway?"

Matt didn't answer. He pushed past her and down the short hall at the back of the room. A slightly overweight boy in a white apron over a stained T-shirt was filling jelly doughnuts with an enormous pastry bag. His boredom was replaced by dull interest as first Matt, then Marg, then the geriatric security guard went by at a fast trot, and he stared hopefully at the hallway as if he was expecting more to the parade. The doughnut he'd forgotten he was filling exploded, sending raspberry jelly and powdered sugar all over the counter.

"You a fed?" The security guard pushed importantly past Marg and wheezed out his question at Matt, watching with avid interest as he unlocked the heavy metal door at the end of the hall with some difficulty. "I switched my hearing aid up full blast when you were on the phone and I heard you talking about that big shot that's gone missing. That redhead with the great gams was a witness—and you let her get away."

Ignoring the excited old man's running commentary, Matt slid the lock back on the door.

Behind the coffee shop was an alleyway that seemed to run parallel with the street in front of the building, but it was hard to see more than a few feet. The rain was a silvery curtain blocking out everything but the basic shapes of the buildings backing onto the alley.

"Calm down, Jimmy," Marg snorted. "It's just a lovers' argument."

"It wasn't a lovers' quarrel." Even though he was standing in the doorway, already the front of Matt's suit jacket was beaded with moisture. The rain-haloed glow of a streetlight shone fuzzily on the three of them as they huddled there. "And she wasn't a witness, old-timer. She was just a lady with a problem."

"It looked to me like the only problem she had was you," Marg said with a scowl. "One minute the two of you are practically melting the frosting off my Boston cream doughnuts, and two seconds later she looked like she'd just lost the only friend she ever had. She was a basket case when she ran out of here—no sane girl would take off into this downpour.''

"Yeah, well..." Matt turned his suit collar up and looked out into the night. It wasn't going to stop anytime soon, he thought, and somewhere out there Jenna was getting soaked to the skin. "The question of her sanity was what I was worried about. I was about to take her to a hospital.''

"The redhead was crazy? She looked all there to me.'' The guard pushed his cap to the back of his head and whistled in disbelief. "Didn't seem like there was *anything* wrong with her, if you catch my drift.''

"There wasn't anything wrong with her.'' Marg's fists went pugnaciously to her hips and her voice rose in scorn. "*You're* the one who's crazy if you were planning on having her locked up in a padded room somewhere. You were sitting right across from her, mister—didn't you take a good look at her? She was upset, sure. I guess to you she looked a little offbeat, what with her clothes and all. But that sweet girl was as sane as you and me, and if you'd even thought twice about it instead of jumping to conclusions, you'd have realized that.''

"Hold on, Marg,'' the old man said uncomfortably. "He's a federal agent. He must know what he's doing.''

"He works for the Establishment, Jimmy.'' Anger sparked in her eyes, making her look suddenly younger. "He's the *Man*—what does he care about ordinary people like you and me and that beautiful, gentle girl, people who think peace and love and doing your own thing are more important than wearing a suit and tie and toeing the corporate line? He probably thinks we all should be carted off to a padded room!''

Jimmy tugged nervously at his jacket, partially hiding the holstered gun and the handcuffs that hung from his belt.

Matt didn't blame him. He felt as though he'd been dropped into the middle of an early Peter Fonda film. Jenna Moon might be Miss Looney Tunes, as the apartment superintendent had so sensitively phrased it, or she might be the saint that this fiery holdout from the '60s, with her faded apron and work-roughened hands seemed to think she was, but one thing was definite. She certainly had an effect on anyone she came in contact with—and if proof was needed, all he had to do was examine his own emotions.

He felt a sudden affinity for Marg. She'd only known Jenna for a few minutes, but in that short time the course of her life had taken a drastic turn. She'd been given back her hopes and dreams, all because Jenna had taken the time to care about her. Of course she was going to defend her and blame him for the situation she thought he'd created.

"Okay, I was a jerk," he said. "I lied to her and she knew I was lying and she ran. But I feel the same way about her as you do, Marg, and whether you agree or not, I feel I've got a responsibility to find her and get her some help. Did she say anything about where she was heading?"

"No." The waitress surveyed him stonily for a second, and then sighed. "Sorry for the outburst. I guess I was having a flashback or something." She glanced over at the kitchen and shrugged. "You could ask Tom if he saw which way she went—he probably had to open the door for her."

Jimmy, now that the crisis was over, had regained his swagger. "Nice kid, but no rocket scientist, if you catch my drift," he confided to Matt. He raised his voice. "Tom, get your butt out here! Man's got a question for you!"

"He's a little slow, but he's not deaf." Marg shot the security guard a black look. As the younger man lumbered out of the kitchen toward them, she fixed a smile on her face. "Tom, you know the red-haired lady who went out of here a little while ago?"

"The pretty one? Sure." Tom nodded judiciously. "I had to open the door for her. She couldn't do it all by herself, so she asked me. Her hair smelled good."

Marg reached out and touched the boy on the arm. "It's pretty important, Tom. Did she go to where the alley comes out on the street, or did she turn right and head for the back of those apartments?"

With a start, Matt realized that the apartment building she was talking about was the one where he and Jenna had had that ill-fated encounter with West and Mrs. Janeway earlier—the building where she'd insisted she'd lived. It made sense that she'd head back to what she imagined was familiar territory, and he grabbed Tom's arm, his voice urgent. "Did she go toward the apartments? Is that the way she went?"

With slow deliberation the pudgy teenager looked down at Matt's hand. Then, as if he'd come to a momentous decision, he shook his head and pursed his lips. "*Not* toward the apartments, mister. She ran toward the street and a bus was coming and it stopped for her. She got on it and then she told the driver she wanted to go downtown, and he said okay. Then the bus drove away with her on it." His voice rose. "But she *didn't* go toward the apartments. She never even *looked* that way! She went toward the street, okay?"

He was lying as best as he knew how, Matt thought with rueful admiration. Jenna had done it again—passed a few moments with a stranger and gained another friend for life.

"He couldn't have heard a conversation on the bus at this distance," Jimmy said in a low tone. "Not with this downpour making such a racket. The kid's lying—she musta headed for the back of those apartments like you figured.''

"She got on the bus and it drove away with her," Tom said. He folded his arms across his chest, adding a new smear of raspberry jelly to the stains already on his apron. There was a smudge of powdered sugar on his cheek. "She didn't go anywhere *near* those apartments, mister."

"Poor kid, he's trying to protect her," Marg murmured to Matt. She patted Tom's arm. "Thanks, Tom. You'd make a pretty good detective."

"Okay, Marg. I'm going to start making more lemon doughnuts now." Pointedly ignoring Matt, he turned away from the open door.

If anything, the rain was heavier now. Down the cracked pavement of the alleyway small streams ran and merged together, sweeping bits of paper and cigarette butts and other flotsam along with them. Jenna was out there, Matt thought. He'd been responsible for making her run. Anything could happen to her, and it would be his fault.

"Thanks, Marg. Jimmy, forget anything you thought you heard me talking about on the phone." Hunching his shoulders, he sprinted out into the downpour, heading toward the apartment building.

THE KID HAD suckered him in. For the third time in as many minutes, Matt wiped the rain from his eyes in frustration and wondered briefly if it was too late to switch careers. A few feet beyond him was the dead end to the alleyway, beside him was an industrial garbage bin with the refuse from the apartment building spilling out of it, and behind him was the building itself—the building where this doomed nightmare of an evening had begun. Jenna hadn't come this way at all. He'd been finessed by a donut-making teenager who, if he definitely wasn't a rocket scientist, as

Jimmy the security guard had said, certainly had managed to pull a fast one on one Matt D'Angelo, future area director of the Agency.

Jenna could be anywhere by now. He'd lost her.

He was halfway back down the alley when he heard the sound—an unearthly scream that floated eerily through the night. The hair on the back of his neck lifted in an atavistic reaction and he whirled around, his hand going automatically to his gun before he checked himself.

It had sounded like a baby's cry—but not like any *human* baby he'd ever known. A chill that had nothing to do with the rain spread through him. From out of his childhood came, full-blown and as spine-tingling as when he'd first heard it, the memory of a story his great-grandmother had told him and his sister Carmela; the story of the goblin's child who sobbed and wailed in the forests of her native Calabria to draw soft-hearted maidens to their deaths.

The cry came again, an unearthly, soulless entreaty that turned his blood to ice.

Matt blinked the rain from his eyes, and his mouth thinned to an angry line. He didn't believe in ghosts or fairy tales or fantasy. He believed in hard facts. He started running, heading blindly toward where the sound had last come from and he felt his foot connect with something.

With a raucous clatter, the lid of a trash can fell to the pavement and rolled a few feet before its noisy progress ended. The next minute he saw a small figure leap from the edge of a nearby garbage bin and felt a searing pain rip its way across his left bicep. Immediately the cold clamminess of his shirt was overlaid with the warmth of blood.

His blood. Dammit, he was bleeding. And he was holding a damn *cat!*

For the second time that evening he found himself gazing into impossibly blue eyes, but this pair was cross-eyed.

They glared myopically out of the triangular, brown-masked face peering from his arms, and even as Matt met that disconcerting gaze, the cat opened its mouth and let out a sobbing wail that gurgled off into an irregular purr.

He'd insisted on proof. He'd refused to believe anything she'd told him, he'd let her run out into the night believing she was what that lying bastard West had called her—Miss Looney Tunes—and now she was on the run, alone and frightened, just because he had to have everything by the book. How could he have been so damn *stupid?*

The cat in his arms yowled miserably and lashed a rain-drenched tail—which was covered, Matt saw, with a streak of sky-blue paint.

Chapter Four

Jenna was stiff from spending the night on a hard bus terminal bench, her hair looked like the proverbial burning bush, and her dress had wrinkled as only a natural fiber could. Jenna smoothed ineffectually at it with the palms of her hands and realized, for the first time in her life, that there was something to be said for polyester.

The bus station washroom was empty, so when her stomach gurgled the sound echoed hollowly around the tiled room. A skimpy lunch yesterday, no dinner, and she didn't have any money to buy breakfast.

She shifted slightly, and the muted silvery chime of her ankle bracelet tinkled off into a delicate echo. At the sound, Jenna's chin lifted and her slumped shoulders straightened.

She hadn't been able to sleep much last night, and her insomnia hadn't been because she'd kept slipping off the plastic bench. She'd run a whole gamut of emotions before she'd finally dropped into a fitful doze; from fear and anguish to a sense of betrayal to bewildered confusion. And just as dawn had begun to filter through the grimy terminal windows she'd come to a conclusion that had brought her a faint ray of hope—enough so that she knew she could go on.

Maybe Franklin had passed on the instability that had

robbed them both of a normal, settled life. It seemed as if he had, judging from everything that had happened in the last twenty-four hours. But she was Sara Moon's daughter, too—Franklin had always said that Jenna took after her mother more than she did him—and Sara Moon had been the sanest person Jenna had ever known.

She didn't remember much about her mother, but she could recall a voice that was never raised in anger, a calm acceptance of Franklin's spur-of-the-moment upheavals and a reassuring presence that had managed to turn each new and bewildering town into a comforting home for a lonely little girl. Sara Moon was as much a part of her as her father was, Jenna thought. Her mother's strength would keep her from veering over the edge as Franklin had.

From now on she would live a dull, uneventful, *normal* life, Jenna decided. If she saw Elvis walking down the main street wearing blue suede shoes and eating a peanut-butter-and-banana sandwich this afternoon, she'd smile politely and walk on. She wouldn't tell anyone, she wouldn't phone anyone and she wouldn't try to convince anyone of her crazy story.

Least of all that snake in the grass Matt D'Angelo.

She walked casually through the bus terminal, drifting by the vending machines and surreptitiously pulling on their handles to see if anything dropped out. Nothing did. There was a line of pay phones flanking the far wall that she'd tried earlier, but just in case, she glided like a hungry shark by them again, flipping open the coin return on each one hopefully. She was walking dispiritedly away from the last one, the bells on her ankle bracelet jingling sadly, when she heard a cascade of coins dropping to the ground behind her.

Jackpot! Jenna stuffed the money into the pocket of her dress and dodged out the nearest exit door as guiltily as if she'd just pulled off a major heist. Half a block away she stopped to count her winnings—four and a half…no, five dollars in quarters. If she was careful, she could get breakfast *and* lunch out of that.

The tiny corner diner was packed with truck drivers and, for some reason, six or seven young women dressed as if they were going out for an evening's club-hopping, instead of sitting hunched over cups of coffee and half-eaten pieces of toast at six-thirty in the morning. Just looking at them while she placed her order at the counter, Jenna felt like a wreck, but when a seat at one of the tables became vacant, she slid in with a murmured apology.

At one of the communes she'd lived on a few years ago there'd been a woman who made all-natural herbal cosmetics, but her beeswax lip balm had felt sticky and the buttermilk and orrisroot eyeshadow she'd given Jenna had smelled like—well, like sour buttermilk. She'd never really gotten the knack of makeup after that, Jenna thought.

Out of the corner of her eye she cast an envious glance at the woman sitting beside her. Her lipstick was an iridescent mauve, and her eyelashes were thick and black and the longest Jenna had ever seen. She wore a white denim bomber-type jacket that was so short it showed her navel, and under it was a black lacy bra top. Her skirt was some kind of stretchy fabric that clung to her curves, and under the table five-inch-high stiletto heels lay toppled over on their sides. One of her feet was wrapped around the rungs of her chair. She was massaging the other one when she met Jenna's interested gaze.

"You a working girl, Ginger?"

It took a moment to realize who she was speaking to, but then Jenna flushed, embarrassed to be caught staring. She tucked a fiery strand of hair behind her ear. "Oh. Yes,

I guess I am. I just started a couple of days ago. Sorry I was staring, but I love your lipstick. What's it called?"

The other woman fished in a tiny purse with a chain-link strap that lay on the table, finally pulling out a black plastic tube. She squinted at it. "Mauve," she said in a disappointed tone. "What a rip-off name. So who do you work for, Ginger?"

"The Skipper. And the Professor's her best customer," another girl said. She flipped open a compact and checked her teeth in its mirror, then snapped it shut and started humming a tune. The other two girls at the table started giggling and humming along with her, and even the woman with the mauve lipstick grinned and joined in. The only words they seemed to know were the last few, and the whole table finished on cue.

"Here on Gilligan's Isle!"

It had to be a television thing again, Jenna thought in frustration. She smiled weakly. There was so much she'd missed through Franklin's vow never to own one. People were always using catchphrases that meant nothing to her— "Book 'em, Dano," or "I'll buy a vowel, Pat," or "Lu-u-ucy, I'm home!" For a while it had seemed that every second person was hitting his head and saying, "Doh!" and she'd never figured out what *that* had been all about. This song had to be something along those lines.

"I work for Parks, Parks," she said as the laughter subsided. "At the corner of Barton and South Streets." Just then her breakfast came; scrambled eggs and toast with a side order of home fries and a cup of tea with the tea bag still in it. Jenna stopped talking and started eating.

Nothing had ever tasted so good in her whole life. The eggs were a little greasy and the home fries were a lot greasy and the toast was soggy, but she was so hungry it wasn't until she was scraping the last blob of grape jam out of the tiny plastic container onto her last triangle of toast that she realized that the table of women had fallen silent.

She looked up in midchew.

"You sure can pack it away." The woman with the mauve lipstick was staring at her in awe. "You better hope that the johns on the corner of Barton and South like 'em a little chunky, Ginger, 'cause at that rate you're not going to fit into a size eight much longer."

Jenna swallowed the last bite of toast and started jiggling the tea bag up and down in her cup. "I don't usually—"

Johns? She took another look at the table of women, but this time her perceptions weren't dulled by hunger. Short clingy skirts, full makeup, high heels...not exactly a.m. attire. Not unless a girl had been working all night....

"You're not one of us, are you?" The question came from the woman who'd started humming the song, and there was an edge of suspicion in her tone. "What are you doing here, slumming?"

"Cool it, Crystal." The woman with the mauve lipstick stared curiously at Jenna, taking in her wrinkled dress and the faint smudges under her eyes. "She's right, though— you're no working girl. You running from some man, honey?"

The rough kindness in her voice was almost Jenna's undoing. She'd been up half the night, her thoughts chasing each other in ever-tightening circles, and although she'd finally come to a decision about her unanticipated legacy from Franklin, she still hadn't been able to bring herself to examine the hollow sense of betrayal and loss she'd experienced when she'd realized that Matt was trying to trick her into giving up her freedom.

How could he have done that to her? After that moment of electricity that had passed between them, how could he have reverted so swiftly to being the perfect Agency operative—to that stiffly correct, by-the-book persona that she'd thought was just a mask for the real Matt D'Angelo? He'd been willing to dump her at the nearest hospital and wash his hands of her, just because she'd come off as a little flaky.

Okay, a *lot* flaky, Jenna admitted to herself. But the man couldn't have it both ways. Either he should have treated her from the first with an arm's-length formality or he should have acknowledged that there was some kind of inexplicable bond between them and tried to help her, not have her locked up. He wasn't allowed to go touching her hand one minute and selling her out the next. That was just confusing, and irritating and…and *painful*.

"I guess you could say I'm running from a man," she said slowly. "On top of that, it seems like since I first met him yesterday my whole life's disappeared—my money's gone, I don't have an apartment anymore and even the cat I thought I had doesn't exist. Not that any of that was Matt's fault, of course," she added hastily.

"Honey, you might as well have Welcome written down the middle of your back." Crystal leaned forward, her earlier antagonism gone. "Don't be a doormat! Of *course* it's his fault. It sounds like he really did a number on you—just like when Tiffany's man trashed her place and cleaned out her bank account, right, Tiff?"

Mauve-lipsticked lips pursed together disapprovingly. "Stevie was no good, but he *never* would have had a cat whacked. That's just plain twisted. Listen, Ginger—if you ever need help or money or anything, here's the number of this place."

She rooted around in her purse again and came up with an eyebrow-pencil stub and a pack of matches. Scrawling something on the inside flap of the matchbook, she handed

it to Jenna and nodded her head at the unshaven man behind the counter. "Joe takes messages for me, and I'm in
here a couple of times a day. You need any money now?"

"No." Jenna felt a lump rise in her throat, and she gave
a hasty cough. "I really *am* a working girl—just not in the
way you meant, I guess."

"Don't apologize, Ginger." Behind the thickly
mascaraed lashes Tiffany's eyes held a hint of wistfulness.
"Somehow you didn't seem the type, anyway. But remember what I said—call if things don't work out or if this
Matt jerk tracks you down and starts hassling you again."

Jenna nodded, too touched to speak, and rose from the
table. She fished out a heavy handful of quarters from her
pocket, but before she could start counting out enough for
her bill, Crystal's sardonic voice stopped her.

"We'll cover the tab, Ginger. Just say hello to the Skipper for us, okay?"

All the way to Parks, Parks the catchy little tune they'd
been humming as she left the diner kept running through
Jenna's head. People were pretty nice, once you got to
know them, she thought. She'd never need to take Tiffany
up on her offer, but the generosity of spirit behind it just
bore out what she'd learned growing up on the communes—it didn't take much to turn a stranger into a friend.

And sometimes people you thought of as your friends
turned around and acted like complete strangers. Like cold
and *uncaring* strangers whose auras were as deceitful as the
rest of them. Jenna felt a tight hot squeezing feeling somewhere in the vicinity of her lower ribs, and she slowed her
stride a little, wondering if she had indigestion. The diner
breakfast hadn't exactly been the granola and fresh fruit
she was used to, she thought dubiously. She put her hand
to her ribcage experimentally.

Was it possible that she was experiencing...*rage?*

"Deep breaths, deep breaths," she muttered nervously to herself. "In...and out...and in—"

It wasn't working. *Darn* Matt D'Angelo anyway! In one evening the man had managed to get under her skin enough to undo a whole lifetime's worth of peace, love and understanding. He'd given her a couple of hot glances from those dark gold eyes and he'd tied her into as many knots as a macramé plant holder, and then he'd totally switched personalities and she'd come completely unraveled. She'd been born under the sign of Aquarius, for heaven's sakes! She wasn't *supposed* to feel this violently about anything!

"The next time I meet him I'm going to play it cool," she muttered, hastening her pace as the hewn-granite edifice of the offices of Parks, Parks, and Boyleston came into sight.

She stopped dead in the middle of the sidewalk, forcing the stream of other office-bound pedestrians to part and flow around her, but she didn't notice the impatient looks she was getting. She'd forgotten for a minute, she thought bleakly. He'd been so much a part of her thoughts that she'd allowed herself to daydream about meeting him again, but that wasn't going to happen. Matt D'Angelo, sexy and luscious and tempting as he might be, was the enemy. Maybe Franklin had run from an imaginary pursuer all his life, Jenna told herself, but his daughter knew only too well the face of her adversary. Straight thick eyebrows, a sensuously full lower lip and a hard, shadowed jawline— every detail was etched in her mind.

Now she'd have to forget him.

On legs that felt strangely shaky, she entered the heavy brass and plate-glass revolving door of Parks, Parks, and Boyleston behind a group of conservatively dressed secretaries and law clerks. Even if he'd changed his mind about getting her into a hospital, she thought, she'd never have any future with him. She'd never have a future with any man—not the future that she'd always envisaged having someday. She'd wanted children. That just wasn't an option anymore. How could she take the chance of passing on the frightening legacy that her father had bequeathed her?

And Matt D'Angelo was the type of man who should bring children into the world—lots of them, two or three at least. She smiled wistfully. They'd be gorgeous: tough little hellions of boys and dark-haired little charmers of girls. But there wouldn't be a blue-eyed redhead in the bunch.

"This stairway's for staff only."

Startled out of her bittersweet reverie, Jenna found her path blocked by an unsmiling young man in a blazer with a discreet badge on the lapel identifying him as security for the law firm. She'd seen him before, but this was the first time he'd spoken to her.

He didn't have to be so officious, she thought with a touch of impatience. By the enormous regulator clock above the reception desk she only had a minute or so to get to the file room before Miss Terwilliger marked her in as late.

"I *am* staff. I'm a records clerk." She started to go around him but he sidestepped, and once again his blue blazer was inches from her face.

"I'll have to ask to see your ID card, please."

"I'm a new employee—I just started this week. I had my ID photo taken yesterday, but they haven't given me my card yet." She bit her lip. "Can't you just let me through? I really do work in the file room."

Of course, this would have to happen the day she looked like she'd slept in her dress—which she had, and like she hadn't even bothered to drag a comb through her hair— which she hadn't, Jenna admitted honestly. Maybe it was partly her fault she'd caught the attention of security today, slopping into work looking like a bag lady. She wondered briefly if the receptionist would recognize her, but then she dismissed that hope. The blonde, efficient beauty behind the front desk never even glanced at the other employees as they rushed by her. Like a good bird-dog, she only came to quivering attention when she scented a monied and influential client approaching.

"I can't just take your word that you work here when you're not carrying any ID." The officious young man frowned as if she'd tried to bribe him. *With what?* she thought glumly. *My quarters?* "We're going to have to have your supervisor come and vouch for you," he said implacably.

"Oh, no! Miss Terwilliger isn't going to appreciate being called away from her work just for me." Jenna was aghast. She'd hoped she'd been making a good impression on the woman who'd been training her, but there was no denying that Miss Terwilliger was a stickler for appearances. To have one of her junior clerks detained in the lobby as a suspicious interloper would be seen by her as a black mark against her beloved filing department. It would be months before she'd ever look at Jenna without blaming her.

"Judy, can you page a Miss Terwilliger in the—" The young man turned away from the receptionist and back to Jenna. "You said the records center, right?"

She scuffed her foot miserably against the polished marble floor and the bells on her ankle bracelet chimed softly.

The receptionist stabbed a couple of buttons on her phone with the eraser end of a sharpened pencil, and then held the receiver slightly away from her glossy lips. "Miss Terwilliger from records, please come to reception. Miss Terwilliger, you're needed in reception immediately by security."

At one of the communes she'd lived on there'd been an Irish woman who'd hand-loomed mohair shawls and taught Celtic dancing as a sideline. For five months, until one night when Franklin had shook her awake and told her they had to leave immediately, Jenna had learned jigs and tap and Irish reels. She'd actually become quite proficient at it. Right now, she told herself, she might as well get in a few minutes of practice on this beautifully polished marble floor. She could do an intricate jig, rope a couple of by-standers in for a reel and finish off with a snappy display of her tap virtuosity.

Because even that wouldn't draw any more attention to her than the booming message over the building's loud-speaker system had just done. As half a dozen pairs of avidly interested eyes swiveled her way and then pretended not to be looking at her, she felt like hiding behind the curved oak barrier of the reception desk. And when she saw the bony, angular figure of Miss Terwilliger marching up the stairs that led from the filing section and the archives to the lobby, the notion of hiding became even more at-tractive.

"Hi, Miss Terwilliger." Her voice came out in a feeble croak and she nervously cleared her throat. "I don't have my ID card yet, and they won't let me in unless you vouch for me. Sorry to take you away from your work."

Miss Terwilliger was wearing a cable-knit navy vest over a brown wool dress. Over it all she had a beige sweater with the sleeves trailing over her shoulders like a cape— almost jaunty for Miss Terwilliger, Jenna noted. A bright gold chain clasped the two edges of the sweater together at her neckline. She flicked a blank glance at Jenna and then turned her attention to the security officer.

Jenna tugged at one of Miss Terwilliger's dangling beige

sleeves. "I told him not to bother you, but he insisted. Can you just tell him that I work here?"

Pale gray eyes under a corrugated gray perm slowly turned and focused on Jenna's hand, still plucking agitatedly at the beige sweater. Then that expressionless gray gaze scanned her from the top of her wildly tousled hair to the tarnished silver bells encircling one slightly grubby ankle. The thin lips pressed together tightly.

"Kindly remove your fingers from my person, young lady. I am not an exhibit in a petting zoo."

Jenna removed her hand in hasty consternation. "Miss Terwilliger, tell him who I am—Jenna Moon, junior records clerk trainee!"

"Young lady, if I'd ever met you before I'm absolutely sure I would have had a hard time getting your image out of my mind." The pale gray eyes closed briefly, as if she hoped that the wild-haired figure in front of her was a mirage that might disappear. When she opened them again she looked pained and turned to the guard. "I've never seen this woman before in my life."

"YOU STAY THERE, loudmouth."

Matt D'Angelo grimaced at the pelting rain bouncing off the Taurus's hood and got out of the car. This seemed to be his lot in life lately, he thought—dashing around in downpours. He swiftly slammed the door shut behind him just as a triangular, brown-masked face popped up at the window. Crossed blue eyes stared unbelievingly at him and then Zappa let loose with one of his patented yowls. Locking the door, Matt glanced nervously around him, but luckily there was no one within earshot. Twice already in the last two days some soft-hearted soul had threatened to report him to the humane society, but leaving the damn cat at home wasn't an option. The first time he'd done that, irate neighbors had told him Zappa hadn't shut up all day.

He'd been searching for her for three days now after hastily taking off some long overdue vacation days. He'd barely slept, half the time he forgot to shave, and this morning he'd put on the same sweatshirt he'd worn yesterday, because he'd come home too late last night to do a load of laundry. He was beginning to look like the bums he was paying to keep their eyes peeled for any sign of a long-legged woman with red-gold hair wearing a silver ankle bracelet, Matt thought grimly. And if this lead didn't pan out, he might just be tempted to take the similarity a little further. Jenna Moon could drive any man to drink.

That wasn't fair. On the other side of the street about half a block down he saw the diner Old Harry had told him about, and he found himself walking faster. He had no one to blame but himself for this situation—she'd come to him asking for his help and he'd taken the word of a couple of con artists over hers. West and the Janeway woman were playing some kind of angle, he thought, frowning—his discovery of Zappa had proven that—and though for the life of him he couldn't figure out what they'd gained by their elaborate deception, when he found Jenna he intended to investigate the matter thoroughly.

But finding her was priority number one.

Of course, she'd been completely mistaken about seeing Carling that day at work, and from what he'd found out she didn't even work at Parks, Parks, and Boyleston anymore. He'd phoned the law firm himself and talked to a woman in personnel who'd told him that Jenna wasn't listed as an employee. That had seemed slightly odd to him at first, but then he'd realized that she'd known he'd be looking for her there. She hadn't dared to return to her job. She might have turned his life upside down, but he'd forced her to abandon everything familiar out of fear that he'd find her and hustle her off to a hospital ward. Matt's mouth tightened. With her background of rootlessness with her father, it must have seemed to her that history was repeating itself. *He'd* done that to her.

He had a lot to apologize for. He pushed open the door of the diner with more force than was necessary and walked over to the counter.

The place was a dump, he thought as he sat down on an empty stool and shoved a used coffee cup away from him. He raked wet hair back from his eyes. Old Harry must have gotten it wrong, or perhaps he'd just told Matt that he'd seen a redhead here for the five bucks his information had garnered him, but there was no way Jenna would be working in a place like this, no matter how desperate she was. The counterman looked like a thug, and the table behind him was occupied by four or five hookers, obviously waiting until the rain let up. One of them, a brunette with iridescent purple lipstick, was eyeing him with more than casual interest.

"Coffee?" Without waiting for an answer, the man behind the counter poured a pitch-black stream of some noxious-smelling liquid into a chipped mug and pushed it toward Matt. The cigarette in the corner of his mouth barely moved as he spoke.

"Yeah, coffee's fine." Matt slid a ten-dollar bill across the countertop, detouring it around a splash of bacon grease and a stained serviette. He narrowed his eyes against the cigarette smoke. "Coffee and information, if you have it. I'm looking for a redhead."

"Natural?" The counterman took the cigarette out of his mouth and slanted a dubious look at the table behind Matt. "Because that might be a problem."

"What?" Matt followed the other man's glance. At the

table by the window a girl with brightly hennaed hair and a butterfly tattoo was filing her nails. Across from her the brunette with the purple lipstick was slowly licking the back of her coffee spoon. Her amazingly mascaraed eyes met his, and she slipped the spoon into her mouth before taking it out again and languidly stirring her coffee.

"No—you've got it wrong." Matt wrenched his appalled gaze from the brunette. "I'm looking for a *specific* redhead. Actually, her hair's more a kind of red-gold color, and she wears an ankle bracelet with bells on it. Her name's Jenna Moon." Without much hope he shoved the ten-spot closer to the counterman. "Seen anyone around like that?"

The room fell silent. Then he heard a hiss coming from the table behind him.

"You have some *nerve,* mister." The brunette had gotten up and was stalking toward him on lethal-looking stiletto heels. Her come-hither look had vanished, and her tone was barbed. "Look who dropped in, girls—it's that Matt jerk who did the number on Jenna! The one who had her cat whacked!"

Nothing she was saying made sense, but after thirty-six hours of being practically joined at the hip with an extremely vocal Siamese, that last accusation stung. "I didn't have her cat whacked! And I didn't do a number on her—" He stopped in midsentence. Four pairs of garishly shadowed eyes stared coldly at him. He cleared his throat uncomfortably. "Okay, maybe I did do a number on her. But that's why I'm looking for her—to put things right."

"You can't put things right for me. Nobody can."

The thready voice came from behind the counterman, and for a minute Matt couldn't figure out where she was. Then he saw her. There was a windowlike opening between the kitchen and the serving area, and Jenna had just placed two plates of sausages and eggs down on it.

"Two—two Babes and a couple of sunny-sides, Joe."
She kept her eyes from the sausages as she pushed the
plates forward. Her glorious hair was scraped back into an
elasticized white paper cap and she was wearing a grease-
spattered chef's apron that had to be at least four sizes too
big for her.

"You were right about me, Matt." Coming out of the
kitchen, Jenna reached around to the back of her waist and
started untying the apron. "I told myself that when you
finally showed up I wasn't going to run anymore."

"Ginger, you can't go back to him!" A bleached blonde
wearing thigh-high boots looked at Matt accusingly. "I
don't know exactly what you did to her, buddy, but the
girl's in rough shape. Jerks like you should—"

"None of this is his fault, Crystal. I kept trying to tell
you—it was all in my head."

Her voice shook. She'd forgotten to take the paper hat
off, and as Matt looked at her standing there, her shoulders
slumped dejectedly and all the fire that was so much a part
of her quenched, he felt his heart contract painfully.

Hey—come off it, D'Angelo! he told himself sharply. His
heart wasn't involved here at all. Why should it be? Now
that he'd found her he could tell her what he'd discovered,
and either he or some other agent would look into the apartment scam that West had pulled on her. Case closed. On
to the next one.

Those fabulous eyes were red and dry-looking, as if
she'd been crying on and off for so long that she'd run out
of tears. There was a cooking burn on her arm. And there
was something else wrong too, Matt thought worriedly, but
he just couldn't put his finger on it. There was something
missing...

She took the apron off and came quietly out from behind
the counter, and all of a sudden he realized what he wasn't

hearing. He looked down at her ankle. The silver bracelet was twisted around so that those tiny irritating bells had finally fallen silent.

Dammit, he couldn't stand to see her like this one more second.

"Don't move," he said shortly. "I'll be right back."

The half block to where he'd left his car was covered in a soggy sprint, and if anything, he beat his time on the way back to the diner, spurred on by the needlelike claws in his shoulder and the feline siren in his ear that must have been audible three streets over. But before he was halfway there, a white-hatted figure tore out of the diner and stood stock-still, peering through the rain at them. Then Jenna started running toward him, her arms outstretched, her hat falling off, and a mass of red-gold hair rippling down her back. Behind her a collection of spandex skirts, fishnet stockings and false lashes tumbled out of the diner to stand under the awning and watch.

"*Zaaappaaa!*" The scream tore from her throat. At the sound of her voice, the Siamese twisted in Matt's arms. With a vigorous rake of his back claws, he leaped through the air, landing in her grasp.

"You found him, Matt!" Tears mingled with the rain on her face as she hugged the small body to her tightly. "Zappa—you *found* him!"

She was doing it again, Matt thought in frustration. She was getting under his skin, and that wasn't the way it was supposed to be at all. Jenna Moon was supposed to be a job—nothing more—and the only reason he'd searched the city for her like a madman these last few days was because he'd felt responsible for her running. The *only* reason. Period. Anything else he might be feeling didn't make any sense—he hadn't really known the woman for more than a few hours, and despite the reaction that had flared in him, white-hot and uncontrollable, when he'd met her gaze in the coffee shop that night, there was no way he should be grinning like a fool right now just because he'd made her smile again.

He felt like a hero for bringing her damn cat back.

The silver bells on her ankle bracelet sounded like a small crystalline echo of her laugh as their eyes met. The rain kept coming down and they both kept getting wetter and their spandex-skirted audience under the awning fell silent and Matt didn't notice any of it.

Then Zappa's wail gurgled into a purr, breaking the spell. Jenna let her breath out in a ragged, shuddering sigh, lowered her gaze and looked down at the remnants of blue paint still dotting the cream-colored tail. One corner of that lush mouth curved up lopsidedly.

"Does this mean I'm not Miss Looney Tunes anymore?" she said.

Chapter Five

"So after the security guard threw me out all I could think of was to phone Tiffany at the diner. Joe's short-order cook had just quit that morning, and I started work right away." Jenna lifted a strand of her wet hair and sniffed it. "Thank goodness. I thought that fried-grease smell was permanent."

They were at Matt's house—the two-story home that he'd grown up in and that his mother had moved from a couple of years ago. After raising a son and three daughters by herself, her husband having died in a construction-site accident when Matt was ten, Maria D'Angelo was now enjoying the lively company of other active seniors in a modern condo-style apartment. But she hadn't wanted to give up the home she and her young husband had bought so long ago, with their dreams for a future together that hadn't come true. It hadn't been until Matt had told her he was buying it himself that she'd left willingly.

Carmela had told him he was crazy, but after moving back into the comfortable old house, Matt had known he'd made the right decision. It needed some work, sure, but he'd grown up around uncles and cousins who worked with their hands, and he'd never been a stranger to manual labor. Renovating the place had been satisfying on some elemental level, and he'd ended up with a home that had exactly suited his tastes and lifestyle.

But that was before he'd brought Jenna Moon into it.

She'd only been there for an hour, but already the cleanly masculine lines of his living room were blurring ominously. She was curled up in his favorite recliner, blissfully shaking herself to pieces, having discovered the vibrating feature and turned it on as high as it would go without actual liftoff.

After she'd showered, he'd loaned her a pair of fleecy sweats that Stacey, his oldest niece, kept at his place for overnight visits to her uncle Matt. Over those she was wrapped in a paisley silk dressing gown that Carmela had given him for Christmas one year. A too-large pair of his socks kept falling off her feet, but at least they muffled the jingling noise that was coming from her ankle.

"I just don't see that there could be any connection between those crooks at your apartment and a respectable employee of one of the city's oldest law firms." He looked over at her quizzically. "This Miss Terwilliger sounds pretty eccentric. She probably really didn't remember you. Maybe she's losing it."

"I don't know." Jenna sighed. "It's a possibility—she's spent most of her life in the basement of Parks, Parks and I guess that would make anybody a little strange. But none of that matters now. Like I said, I just want to forget any of this ever happened. It's been a nightmare, but it's over."

"You've got to report what happened. West and the old lady are running some kind of scam, although what's behind it is beyond me." He frowned. "It must have been an all-day job to refurnish and redecorate your apartment. The labor alone would have cost more than anything they made from the theft of your belongings."

He looked over at her. Her eyes were closed. She gave

no sign of having heard anything he'd just said and he reached over and snapped off the vibrator.

"I was listening," she said guiltily, her eyes flying open. "But I've made up my mind, Matt. I'll start looking for another apartment and a decent job tomorrow. Joe was only letting me stay overnight at the diner as a temporary measure, anyway." She picked up the mug sitting on the low table beside her and sipped delicately at the lemon tea he'd made her. He'd added a shot of rum to ward off the effects of her soaking, and she wrinkled her nose at the taste. "I'm grateful for you taking us in like this, but I want you to know that I certainly don't intend to impose on you. I should be able to find a place that allows pets by the weekend."

"That's not the point." He saw her hand creep unobtrusively toward the vibrator switch and glared at her. Slowly her hand withdrew, tucking itself into the opposite sleeve of the silk dressing gown. "Don't you want to know what this is all about? Don't you want to expose those two frauds and whoever they're working with? They had you convinced you were *crazy,* dammit."

"I'm trying to start a new life, Matt." The soft lips set in a mulish line and that usually open blue gaze slid away from the growing suspicion in his glance. "The story's just weird enough to get into the papers, and I don't want that kind of attention, especially when I'm looking for a job."

She fingered the cord of his dressing gown, plaiting the two ends together and not meeting his eyes. The silence between them lengthened.

She'd never been able to lie convincingly, Jenna thought miserably, and even if she'd been good at it, she didn't *want* to have to lie to him. Well...technically it wasn't a lie, she told herself with weak reassurance. She just wasn't able to tell him the whole truth. That wasn't really a lie, was it?

They had nothing in common, but these *moments* kept happening every time they met. Outside the diner when he'd brought Zappa back to her, their eyes had locked and time had stood still, just the way it had that night in the coffee shop. For a moment she'd felt as if she'd found something she'd been looking for all her life; something she hadn't even realized was missing until then. She knew her heightened reaction to his embrace had to be the result of the emotional roller coaster she'd been on for the previous nightmarish days, but even so, there was *something* between them that couldn't be ignored.

Lust, probably. He was an impossibly good-looking man, and that T-shirt he was wearing right now did nothing to obscure an extremely interesting torso. She liked men with muscles, Jenna realized suddenly. She liked men with linebacker shoulders and defined biceps—even if one of those biceps was sporting a nasty-looking scratch. She hadn't really thought about it before, but there definitely was a sexiness about a man who looked as if he would be able to hold his own in a fight.

After exhausting every avenue of nonviolent mediation, of course, she thought hastily.

Anyway, that was what she had to be feeling toward him—plain and simple lust, mixed in with gratitude that he'd offered her and Zappa a place to stay for the next few days. So why did she feel so guilty about the fact that she couldn't be completely honest with him? Why did she feel as if she was making some irreparable mistake that she would end up regretting?

Especially when she didn't have a choice anyway, Jenna reminded herself. All she could hope for was that he'd accepted her spur-of-the-moment explanation, and there was no reason why he shouldn't. It had sounded plausible enough. Maybe she *was* getting the knack of this lying business after all.

She darted a shifty glance at him from under her lashes.

"Give it up, Jenna." He sounded disgusted. "You can't lie worth a damn. What the hell are you trying to hide?"

Despite the jeans and T-shirt, he'd reverted to his suit-and-tie persona—stiffly remote and skeptically disbelieving. She glared at him.

"I'm not lying. I told you—I just want to forget this whole crazy episode ever happened and get on with my life like any other normal person, without seeing my face on the front page of a tabloid next to an alien autopsy."

She took a healthy slug of tea and coughed, swinging her mug around for emphasis. "Think about it. It's *exactly* the kind of oddball story that those papers like to print— Sweet Old Lady Stole My Life Woman Insists! I'd look like some kind of nut, no one would want to hire me and the best I could hope for would be that I'd get my apartment back. I wouldn't live there now if you paid me to!"

"It's the publicity, isn't it?" He spoke slowly, ignoring her histrionics. "You don't want to draw any attention to yourself if you can help it, even though for some reason you were willing to come forward earlier and testify about seeing Rupert Carling."

He was getting too close, she thought, panicking. "I *had* to come forward about Rupert Carling," she retorted. "Whatever your infallible experts say about him being dead, they're *wrong*—hours after that car bombing he was alive and wandering around the basement of Parks, Parks, and Boyleston, dressed up in an exterminator's outfit. I thought that was something the authorities might want to know."

She gulped down the rest of the tea, feeling a rush of

warmth spread through her like fire. "Of course, that was before I realized that anything that doesn't fit your neat little theories gets written off as *fantasy,* Agent D'Angelo. That was before you made it clear that you weren't interested in investigating the matter any further—since even if you *did* find out there was a possibility I'd really seen Carling, it would conflict with the official Bureau verdict."

"What the hell are you talking about?" Matt's detachment had vanished, along with any attempt at quiet reasonableness. "When I told you they'd identified Carling's body, you accepted it yourself!"

"That's when I thought I was *crazy!*" Eyes blazing, she matched his tone decibel for decibel. "I couldn't be sure *anything* I'd seen was real. But now I'm telling you I didn't make a mistake! Rupert Carling isn't dead, no matter how many forensics experts swear he is, and Miss Terwilliger deliberately lied about not knowing me. This isn't just some oddball little scam directed at me—it's a whole lot bigger than that, and it's all tied up somehow with Parks, Parks, and Boyleston!"

Matt stood up abruptly. "Fine. Let's go."

She stared up at him, suddenly uncertain. "Go where?"

"To pay a visit to your Miss Terwilliger." He narrowed his eyes at her. "It's the only way you're going to get over this Rupert Carling obsession."

She'd painted herself into a corner, Jenna thought—there was no way she could back out now without arousing his suspicions. Besides, if she was careful, she should be able to keep a low profile no matter what this investigation turned up.

She'd have to, she told herself uneasily. She owed it to Franklin.

She swung her feet off the recliner, the bells on her ankle almost inaudible under the borrowed sock. "It's not an obsession. The man's alive, and I'm going to prove it.'' She brushed haughtily by him. "And then I'm going to listen to you apologize to me a *second* time, D'Angelo.''

IT HADN'T BEEN HARD to track down Miss Terwilliger's address. She was listed in the phone book under "E. Terwilliger,'' and Jenna vividly remembered her displeasure when one of the junior lawyers in the firm had called her Edna.

"Mr. Barkin, for me to allow you to use such a familiar form of address would mean that we're either engaged to be married—a prospect, I'm sure, that fills both of us with equal horror—or that you are actually my sister Elspeth, who lives in Dayton and whom I have not seen in twenty years, masquerading as a young man with an odd taste in ties. That seems unlikely, but less inconceivable than the former. If neither is the case, I would thank you to call me Miss Terwilliger. Now, which file did you wish my staff to locate for you?''

The young lawyer had stammered out some reply and fled from Miss Terwilliger's domain, his boldly flowered tie streaming behind him in his haste. Jenna had been sure she'd seen a triumphantly satisfied gleam in Miss Terwilliger's pale eyes.

"There it is—turn here!'' She spied the sign for Tanner Street and barked instructions at Matt, who had already swung the Taurus onto the small dead-end crescent.

"Sorry.'' She sat back in her seat. The borrowed sweats she was wearing were powder blue, and in the fading daylight they seemed suddenly the same shade as her face. "I'm nervous, Matt.''

Her voice quavered slightly and she darted a doubtful look over at him. Now that they were almost there, all of a sudden she wanted to turn tail and run. "What if she

refuses to talk to us? This isn't an official investigation. We can't *make* her answer our questions.''

''I'd already thought of that.'' He didn't sound worried. ''But if you're right and she's mixed up in something shady, then it's my guess your Miss Terwilliger wants to talk to someone. All she needs is the right opportunity.''

He pulled the car up to the curb outside a small, neatly painted bungalow. The small lawn in front was flanked with a stiff border of red salvia, and the flagstones leading up to the front door looked as if they'd been measured off with a T square. The curtains at the bay window were drawn but as he shut off the ignition, Jenna thought she saw them twitch slightly.

''You called her a dragon,'' he said. ''You said that she rules the filing section with an iron hand, that she doesn't tolerate sloppiness and that she insists on keeping her relationships with the other employees of the firm on a businesslike footing.''

''That's right. But what's that got to do with—''

He continued as if she hadn't spoken, his glance flicking once again to the almost painfully neat facade of the bungalow. ''And she told you that making phone calls on company time was a form of stealing, right?''

Jenna nodded. ''Some people might call her old-fashioned, but there was something about her I admired. She had a code of conduct that she adhered to, and she was scrupulously honest.'' She stopped, and her gaze met his in dawning comprehension. ''If she deliberately lied about my working at Parks, Parks, then she must be finding it awfully hard to live with herself right now, Matt.''

''And she's lived with that guilt for three days,'' he said shortly. ''Maybe she's ready to confess so she can start sleeping at night again. One more thing—I'm used to this kind of situation. Let me ask the questions, Jenna.''

"But *I'm* the one she lied about. I've got questions for her too—like how could she have humiliated me like that in front of all those people!" Her voice cracked. "I thought she *liked* me, Matt. I'm not going to just stand there silently when I'm the one whose life got ripped apart."

"That's exactly why I want you to stay out of this."

There were two tiny lines between her eyebrows. He reached over and gently smoothed them away with his thumb, his hand resting lightly against her temple, his voice serious.

"Like I said before, you can't lie worth a damn. Everything that you're thinking and feeling shows in your eyes." As his hand slipped farther around the back of her head, she could feel her hair weaving itself around his fingers like tiny snares. "Miss Terwilliger might be honest enough, but you're transparent. Watching your face is like reading a book."

"That makes me sound dull and predictable." Jenna felt like purring the way Zappa did when she stroked him. It seemed as if minute electrical sensations were sparking from Matt's touch to her hair and spreading down along her spine. She let her lashes drift onto her cheeks. "Is that how you see me—predictably dull?" she asked huskily.

"God, yes." She couldn't see his face but there wasn't a trace of laughter in his voice. "It's been one yawn after another since I first met you."

Her eyes flew open in indignation and found themselves mirrored in a hazel-gold pair that held a glint of wry amusement. "No, never dull. Never predictable. I have no idea what I did for excitement before you blew into my life. Now get your butt out of the car."

She was startled into laughter, and it wasn't until they were standing in front of the immaculately painted front door and Matt was raising the brightly polished brass

knocker that she wondered if that had been his purpose—
to lessen, if only for a few minutes, the tension she'd been
feeling.

Maybe that had been part of it, she thought. But there'd
been something else going on between them—something a
lot more elemental and a lot less altruistic. She cast a sideways glance at him out of the corner of her eyes. Matt
D'Angelo liked touching her. She liked having him touch
her. And pretty soon just touching wasn't going to be
enough for either of them.

"Yes?"

The familiar vinegary voice was like a dash of ice water
on Jenna's imagination. Matt had positioned her to one side
so that Miss Terwilliger wouldn't immediately see her, but
she felt as if that gimlet gaze was boring right through her.
Matt didn't sound fazed, though.

"Agent D'Angelo, Miss Terwilliger. I'd like to ask you
some questions about a woman called Moon—Jenna
Moon."

"Presumably that was an identification badge you
flashed at me, Agent. I'd like to see it again—a little slower
than the speed of light if you don't mind."

Despite her nervousness, Jenna wished she could see
Matt's expression. It must have been the first time he'd
been admonished to be a little more by-the-book, she
thought, stifling her amusement. Right now he must be
thanking his lucky stars that he'd taken the time to change
into a correctly appropriate suit and tie. Miss Terwilliger's
next words took the smile from her face.

"Thank you. Now then—what was the name? Jenna
Moon?"

The day of that disastrous and humiliating encounter in
the lobby, she'd been too surprised and off balance to feel
anything more than stunned disbelief at Miss Terwilliger's

behavior. But now Jenna realized she was feeling something else—disappointment. She'd respected the woman. She'd admired her, acidic authority and all. But Edna Terwilliger's rigidly honorable image was a sham. For whatever reason, the woman was a liar.

"Of course. Now I recall why it sounds familiar." Miss Terwilliger sniffed dismissively. "A young lady calling herself by that name tried to sneak into Parks, Parks, and Boyleston a few days ago and security had her escorted out of the building. I'm afraid that's all I know about her."

The older woman's tone was final, and from her vantage point Jenna realized that she had started to close the door.

"I'd still like to come in and get a formal statement from—"

Matt's firmly polite request was never finished. Even as he was edging forward to block the door open, a wailing, desperate scream came from somewhere inside the house. Abandoning all pretense of concealment, Jenna moved to Matt's side just in time to see Edna Terwilliger's hand fly to her throat and her face blanch.

"My Lord! Ziggy!" She whirled around, her habitual self-possession shattered, and the cry shrieked out again, sounding even more desperate than before. Miss Terwilliger swayed, and for a moment Jenna thought she was going to fall, but then she took off down the hallway in a stumbling, frantic run.

About to follow her, Jenna was unceremoniously hauled back by Matt. His mouth was grim. "Get in the car and lock the doors. If I'm not out in a couple of minutes, drive to the nearest phone booth and call the police." He pressed his car keys into her palm, his eyes darting toward the darkened hallway down which Miss Terwilliger had disappeared. The scream split the air again, and he gave her a gentle shove. "Go! This could be dangerous!"

"But—"

"Just for once don't argue with me, Jenna." His voice was shot with anger and his grip on her upper arms tightened. She tried again, her own temper starting to fray a little.

"But it's a—"

"Don't you *get* it?" There was no trace left of the professionally detached facade that Matt D'Angelo usually showed to the world, she noted. Standing in front of her was the man she'd caught glimpses of before—involved, committed and almost archaically determined to shield the woman he felt he needed to protect from harm. His tone was impatiently urgent. "I don't want anything to happen to you. Get out of here—*now!*"

This old-fashioned manly-man attitude was endearing up to a point, she thought in exasperation. But she couldn't let him take it too far. As he turned away and started down the hallway, she sprinted past him.

"For God's sake, Jenna!"

His hand was on the collar of the powder-blue sweat suit, preparing to yank her back, just as they both came to the end of the hall and burst into the room beyond. The scream came again, this time from only feet away.

In the middle of the kitchen floor Miss Terwilliger was hunched over something. Around her were, incongruously, spools of thread and a spilled box of pins. A pair of scissors sat on the edge of the table. Her glasses were askew on the bridge of her bony nose and her skin was even more pallid than usual. Her mouth was trembling as she darted a beseeching glance up at Jenna.

"I don't know what's the matter with her! She won't even let me touch her!"

"What the—" Matt's grip loosened and his hands fell down at his sides. He sounded aggrieved.

This time the yowl was weaker. Miss Terwilliger gasped and drew back swiftly as a cream-colored tail lashed by her sensibly shod feet. "She scratched me! Ziggy *never* scratches."

"It's a cat." Matt shot Jenna a disgusted look. "It's a damn cat."

"Of course it's a cat." She pushed him aside and went to the counter briskly. Without looking at him, she quickly started to pull open drawers. "That's what I was trying to tell you, only you wouldn't listen. After taking care of Zappa this week I thought you'd recognize the sound of a Siamese by now. Oh—good."

In her hand she held a tea towel. Advancing on Miss Terwilliger, Jenna held it out to her. "Wrap this around Ziggy like a straitjacket and let me take a look at her. I think I know what her problem is."

With unexpected meekness, the older woman complied, her hands shaking clumsily. In a few seconds she held an explosive bundle of agitated Siamese cat, looking like a half-wrapped mummy with only its head sticking out of the towel. Jenna frowned and drew closer as Ziggy hissed at her.

"I'm pretty sure...yes, there it is." She held out her hand like a surgeon, her attention still on the cross-eyed, spitting cat in Miss Terwilliger's arms. "Oven mitts," she snapped impatiently.

"They're hanging at the side of that cupboard, young man," Miss Terwilliger gasped. "I don't think I can keep her still for much longer," she added to Jenna.

"Come *on,* Matt. We're running out of time here!" Even as she spoke, she felt the thick padded gloves slapping into her outstretched hand. She looked up with a flash of compunction. Matt hunkered down beside her, one eyebrow lifted.

"What's your diagnosis, Doctor?" he asked dryly.

"She's got a sewing needle stuck at the back of her throat." Jenna peered dubiously at the struggling cat. "I'm going to try to keep her mouth open with one hand while I get the needle out with the other."

"I'll hold her mouth open." He pulled on the oven mitts as if he was girding himself for battle and tentatively moved toward Ziggy. Crazed blue eyes bulged at him and the tea towel heaved convulsively. Matt flinched.

"You won't feel anything through those gloves. Jam your thumbs in between her back teeth and keep her head still."

Miss Terwilliger's grip was weakening, Jenna saw. As Matt grabbed the distressed cat and forced open its mouth, she reached in as far as she could. Ziggy started gagging and the yowl that came out of the wide-open mouth sounded tortured, but just as the tea towel started to unwrap and an angry paw shot out, Jenna's fingers closed around the sliver of steel at the back of the cat's throat and she plucked it out.

"Hell!" Matt jerked backward and looked at the fresh scratch on his arm.

"You can let her go, Miss Terwilliger. I've got the needle." Holding it up to the light, Jenna squinted and shook her head chastisingly. "Never, *never* leave sewing supplies out if you've got a cat. I'm surprised you didn't know that."

As the now-shredded towel flew into the air, a small cream and brown bomb streaked across the kitchen, almost knocking Matt off balance. Ziggy hunched under a chair, glaring balefully at her rescuers.

"Of course I know that, Jenna." Miss Terwilliger said stiffly. "But I'd just finished sewing up a small—a small rip in the seam of her collar." She sat down heavily in one of the chairs and passed a shaky hand across her forehead. "Sorry," she mumbled. "So foolish of me—but I thought—I thought—"

The pursed lips worked soundlessly and under the ubiquitous beige sweater the thin shoulders shook. Jenna gave Matt an anguished look.

If it was anyone else, she thought, she wouldn't hesitate to put her arms around those shaking shoulders in comfort. But Edna Terwilliger seemed to have a horror of human contact. In fact, before today Jenna would have said that the woman shrank from any affection at all, human or otherwise, but after seeing her with her obviously beloved Ziggy, she realized that Miss Terwilliger had one soft spot in an otherwise flinty personality. Still, the dragon of Parks, Parks, and Boyleston wouldn't thank her for drawing attention to it.

Jenna cleared her throat, but before she could venture a suitably impersonal comment the bony shoulders straightened. From the cuff of one of her sleeves Miss Terwilliger pulled a spotless white handkerchief. She blotted her eyes, dabbed at the beaky nose and gave a businesslike sniff, and skewered Matt with a still-reddened gaze.

"You're staring at me, young man. Mr. D'Angelo, I think you said your name was?"

Matt nodded, unperturbed. "You actually have a pretty good memory for names when you want, Miss Terwilliger." His voice softened, whether in sympathy or persuasion Jenna couldn't tell. "You remembered Jenna's a moment ago with no problem."

The pale gray eyes wavered and Jenna saw slightly arthritic fingers clutching tightly around the handkerchief. Just then, Ziggy came out of hiding and leaped lightly onto her owner's lap, bunting the top of her head under Miss Terwilliger's sharp chin in affectionate forgiveness. The older woman gathered the cat to her, stroking the creamy fur with an unsteady hand. She spoke finally, but her words were directed at Jenna, not at Matt.

"I'm a silly fool who lives with her cat—practically a cliché. But Ziggy's all I have and the thought of something happening to her…"

The trembling voice trailed off and the blue-veined eyelids squeezed shut for a moment. Ziggy mewed in protest as the arms around her tightened and Miss Terwilliger opened her eyes. "Sorry," she said to the cat. She spoke as matter-of-factly as if she was apologizing to another person, and all of a sudden Jenna understood. She looked around her in belated comprehension.

The plastic casing of the electric clock on the wall was cracked and the small radio on the counter had to be at least twenty years old. The floor was covered with linoleum, which, though gleamingly clean, had started to lift away at the baseboard. The chrome-and-vinyl chairs had seen better days, and the refrigerator and stove were straight out of the fifties.

In the corner of the room on an embroidered doily was a pair of matching blue ceramic bowls with gold stars around the rims. One bowl was filled with water. The other held scraps of chicken in what looked like a deliciously thick gravy. Beside the bowls sat a small pink foam-rubber ball and a toy mouse with a bell on its tail lay a few feet away.

Parks, Parks wasn't Edna Terwilliger's life. Edna Terwilliger's life was here, in this house that was starting to be too much for her, with these possessions that she couldn't afford to replace and centered around this adored little cat that was given all the love no one else had ever asked of her. And Edna Terwilliger, as ramrod-straight and conscientiously honest as she was, hadn't hesitated to toss

a lifetime's worth of scruples aside to protect the only crea-
ture who loved her back.

"Why did you lie about not knowing her?"

There was no accusation in Matt's question, but at his
softly spoken words Jenna saw a flash of fear dart across
Miss Terwilliger's pinched features. It wasn't worth it, she
told herself suddenly. Nothing—not even finding out who
was behind this whole scam—was worth terrifying this
lonely woman like this.

"No, Matt." She put her hand on his arm, feeling the
silky sprinkling of hair there and the strength of the muscle
underneath. He felt warm and alive and vital, and she kept
her fingers on his skin, for some reason not wanting to
break the contact between them. All Miss Terwilliger had
was her Ziggy, she thought with a rush of compassion.
"Let's go."

He looked startled. "Go? We came here to get some
answers, and she hasn't told us anything yet." He turned
back to Miss Terwilliger, but Jenna spoke again. There was
a finality in her tone.

"We've gotten all the answers we needed. Miss Terwilliger, you don't have to worry anymore." She reached out
finally, and touched the thin shoulder hesitantly. "We
won't bother you and Ziggy again."

There was no response, and Jenna let her hand drop. She
met Matt's annoyed glance directly, and her chin lifted defiantly, daring him to say anything more. For a moment
they stared angrily at each other. Then he shrugged slightly,
his expression softening as he searched her face.

"You're right. Let's go," he said. They started out of
the kitchen together, but they'd only taken a few steps when
the woman behind them spoke.

"Jenna." The normally harsh and authoritative voice
was barely above a whisper. Jenna looked back in surprise.

Sitting stiffly on the kitchen chair, Ziggy curled up in her lap, Miss Terwilliger's pale eyes met hers. "Please...call me Edna."

Jenna felt a prickle of moisture behind her own eyes but she summoned up a smile, knowing the value of the gift she'd just been given. "Goodbye, Edna. We'll see ourselves out."

Thankfully, the hallway was shadowy and when she and Matt got outside, the last of the daylight had faded. Jenna kept her face averted from his, feeling foolishly emotional.

"I know you're crying, and I know why." He unlocked the passenger door of the Taurus and held it open for her, but when she started to climb in he stopped her. They were under a streetlight, and he pushed her hair back from her face. His voice was gruffly uneven. "You did the right thing."

"She was scared, Matt. I think someone threatened to hurt Ziggy if she didn't lie about knowing me." She bit her bottom lip and looked up at him pleadingly. "All of a sudden it didn't seem that important to get the truth out of her. I just wanted to leave her in peace."

"Yeah." The streetlight, filtering through the leaves of a nearby maple, turned the flecks in his eyes to molten gold. His mouth was in shadow, but she could feel the warmth of his breath on her cheek as he bent his head closer to hers. "You know, I—"

"Wait!" The imperious cry came from the house they'd just left, and as Matt's head jerked up, Jenna twisted in his arms to look back. Raising her arm, Miss Terwilliger motioned at them and then marched decisively down the neat walkway of flagstones and started across the street.

"She's had a change of heart," Matt muttered, his gaze on the tall, thin figure coming toward them. "I guess her conscience wouldn't let her keep silent any longer."

A nebulous feeling of foreboding kept Jenna silent. Watching Miss Terwilliger's determined approach with growing unease, when she saw the headlights swinging around the corner of the crescent, her vague fear took sudden form. "Matt—that car! It's heading straight for her!"

He was already aware of the danger, and as he sprinted around the Taurus, calling out a warning to Miss Terwilliger, the older woman looked up in shock. Her hand came up to shield her eyes from the glare of the speeding vehicle's high beams, but even as Matt raced toward her the car made brutal contact.

"No!" Jenna didn't realize that the scream had come from her own throat. In the blinding headlights, she saw the silhouette of Miss Terwilliger's painfully thin figure flying through the air. She saw Matt's taller, bulkier shape knocked sideways as the front side fender of the car sped carelessly by him, its engine roaring. Then the harsh white glare was replaced by the red glow of taillights as the vehicle kept going, and in a second even those had disappeared.

Everything was the same as it had been a moment ago— except now on the quiet, darkened street lay the motionless, broken body of Miss Terwilliger. And beside Miss Terwilliger—

Jenna flew into the street, her heart contracting so painfully that the world around her faded, and a roaring sound filled her ears. She was sobbing, she was stumbling, and then she was falling to her knees, still trying to deny the evidence of her own eyes. But she couldn't.

Beside Miss Terwilliger lay the frighteningly still figure of Matt.

Chapter Six

"The old lady hasn't regained consciousness. I already called in my report to the director from the hospital."

Keeping his voice low as he spoke into the phone, Matt darted a look over his shoulder at Jenna, sitting stiffly on the edge of his recliner, her eyes downcast. Ziggy sat on her lap, ears laid flat to the delicate, triangular head, and Zappa perched on the arm of the couch nearby, intrigued by the new addition to the household.

"I know the Carling identification checked out, Jack, but do me a favor and take another look." Matt's mouth tightened and a muscle in his jaw twitched. He rubbed his face tiredly and closed his eyes. "I see. Yeah, that's about as conclusive as you can get. I wondered why Henderson didn't seem too interested in what I had to tell him." The silent woman in the next room hardly seemed aware of his presence, but he dropped his voice even further. "Listen, Jack, the doctor at the hospital insisted I take a few days off. Nah, just a torn muscle or something, but I need you to run a check on a Jenna Moon. She's not a suspect in anything, for God's sake. Just find out what you can about her. Yeah—totally unofficial. Thanks, buddy."

Hanging up the receiver, he hid a wince as he limped into the living room. At thirty-two, he was getting too old for this, he thought ruefully as he gingerly levered his protesting muscles onto the couch, taking care to hide the effort it cost him. Carmela would call it stupid macho pride, but at the hospital he'd refused to let the doctor do more than wrap a tensor bandage around his knee. Nothing had been broken, and he wasn't so decrepit that he couldn't handle a little bruising for a couple of days. Besides, he was damned if he was going to have Jenna worrying over him as well as over everything else that had happened to her tonight.

When the car had swerved at him, his reflexes had been a split second too slow to propel him completely out of harm's way, and its fender had clipped him solidly enough to knock him halfway across the pavement. The last thing he remembered hearing was Jenna's agonized scream, and for some reason her pain had been harder to bear than his own.

He'd blacked out for a few seconds. When he'd come to, there'd been about a yard of silky hair smothering him and his skin had been wet and salty from her tears. She'd been bending over him, and in a hoarse, anguished voice that sounded nothing like her, she'd been repeating his name over and over again, like a prayer.

Right, D'Angelo, he told himself roughly as he carefully straightened his injured knee and let himself sink thankfully against the sofa cushions. *You're the answer to her prayers, all right.* He stifled an oath as Zappa jumped from the arm of the couch and landed heavily on his bruised thigh. All he'd done for her so far was to stand by while a couple of con artists stole her apartment, scare her into living like a fugitive for a few days and let an old lady almost get killed right in front of her eyes. If he was the answer to her prayers then Sister Maria Theresa had been wrong all those years ago in parochial school. God *did* have a sense of humor.

"I'm responsible for what happened to her, aren't I?"

Jenna didn't look up as she spoke, but continued stroking Ziggy, her head bent over the cat and her hair falling forward in a curtain around her face. Matt glanced sharply at her, taking in the unnatural stillness of her slight figure and the way her legs were pressed tightly against each other, her feet straight and rigid on the floor, her ankles clamped together. She was just barely keeping herself from flying apart—and the only person around who could help her get over this was him.

Unfortunately, this newest information he'd just received wasn't going to be anything she'd want to hear from him. It could wait till tomorrow. Right now she needed reassurance and support, not another unwelcome shock.

"If anyone's responsible it's me." He shifted his leg and Zappa's claws pricked through the denim of his jeans. Grimacing, he placatingly scratched the Siamese behind one ear. "All I've been focusing on was what happened at your apartment, and I just couldn't see how the Terwilliger woman could have any part in that. It was easier to write her off as a forgetful old lady."

"I thought having you admit that Rupert Carling was alive and that I had to have seen him would be a kind of vindication," she admitted dully. "But I never wanted it to happen this way."

Matt's hand stilled on the cat's fur. Then he carefully started petting Zappa again, but it was too late. Jenna was watching him, her eyes wide.

"You do believe I saw him, don't you? For goodness' sake, Matt—what other explanation can there be for everything that's happened?"

"I asked a friend at the office to go over the report on

his death one more time," he said uncomfortably. "But he's not going to find anything suspicious, Jenna. Carling died in that explosion. Like I told you before, his own dentist verified that it was him."

"Then the man's lying, or he's being threatened like Miss Terwilliger was, or—or *something!*" she insisted, some of the frozen apathy thawing from her expression. "Why doesn't the Agency investigate *him?*"

"They have."

Why was he always the one who had to play devil's advocate for her? Matt thought in frustration. There'd been times when the two of them had briefly seemed to be on the same wavelength; times when, despite the differences in their outlooks, he'd let himself daydream a little about what it would be like to break out of the restrictive confines of the life he'd chosen and stop to smell the roses with Jenna Moon. But every time he did, something like this brought him to his senses. She lived in a world of her own that had nothing to do with harsh reality—and she thought he was too unimaginative to overlook the facts and go with his instincts.

Maybe he was. Facts and proof were what he worked with. The real world was made up of unpleasant facts and hard proof, and daydreams or wishful thinking wouldn't change that. It was a lesson he'd learned early on and once he'd learned it, he'd never let himself forget it.

"Dr. Borg is about seventy, a widower, with a spotless reputation," he said more brusquely than he'd intended. "He doesn't have any secret vices that he could be blackmailed over, and he doesn't have any grandchildren or cats or even a damn gerbil that someone could be threatening to harm. He's clean. If he says that according to his dental records it was Carling's body that was found, then you're going to have to accept it."

"Records." Jenna snorted. "Records are pieces of *paper,* Matt. They can be altered or *deleted!* People aren't records—people are flesh and blood and personalities, like Edna Terwilliger. I saw someone deliberately try to kill her tonight—a lonely woman who lived alone with her cat and who'd worked for the same firm for thirty years and who didn't deserve to be eliminated as if she was an inconvenient entry in one of those *records* you keep telling me about. I saw Rupert Carling alive—all the records in the *world* can't change that!"

"After the hit-and-run I was beginning to think you might be right, even with Borg's verification staring me in the face." He'd startled her, Matt saw. A faint spark of hope flared in her eyes and he looked away, knowing that his next words were going to extinguish it. "But fingerprints can't be altered, Jenna."

She stared at him, confused. "What are you saying— they found his fingerprints at the scene? For heaven's sake, Matt, it would have been suspicious if Carling's fingerprints hadn't been all over that car, or what was left of it. That doesn't mean he was in it when it—"

"Dammit, Jenna, they didn't just find a *print.*"

"What do you mean, not just a—"

In the powder-blue sweatsuit she looked as if the most pressing thing on her mind right now should be whether to go jogging or take a bike ride, but the dawning horror in her eyes revealed that she'd made the gruesome connection to what he'd left unsaid. She swallowed. "How much of him did they find?"

"The tip of his little finger. His prints are on file in several places, not least with the Agency itself. Carling was on a governmental financial committee a few years ago, and he required a security clearance." Matt leaned forward, ignoring Zappa's indignant protest and the throbbing of his knee. "It made sense to think he was behind all this, Jenna—he was wealthy enough and powerful enough to smash anyone who got in his way, and I know you need to find some reason for the way your life's been destroyed in less than a week. But it's dangerous to keep insisting on an impossibility. You've *got* to tell me if you can think of anyone else who might be out to get you."

"I was a junior records clerk, Matt, not Carlos the Jackal." The lush lips that he'd sometimes fantasized about were tight with denial. "Who else would be out to get me?"

"I don't know!" Goaded into forgetting his knee and the cat that was on it, Matt stood up abruptly and glared down at her in frustration. Zappa, who'd fallen asleep, yowled testily as he tumbled to the floor, and Ziggy, alarmed by the commotion, scooted nervously from Jenna's lap and fled under a chair. "The only person who might have the answer to that is you—and you can't let go of this crazy Rupert Carling notion long enough to help me out on this!"

Even as he finished speaking, his knee buckled and he nearly lost his balance. He grabbed for the back of the recliner to steady himself and she scowled up at him, startled.

"It's no use throwing your weight around and trying to *bully* me."

Matt could feel sweat beading on his forehead from the sudden pain, but she'd already switched her attention from him. Just as he regained his balance she flicked a lever at the side of the recliner and the chair leaned back slightly. His hand slipped off and another white-hot flash shot through his leg.

"Stop fooling around with my damn chair," he ground out, clutching at it for support like a drowning man with a life preserver. Jenna blew out her breath in an exasperated little burst, a stray red-gold strand of hair flying out of her eyes, and flicked the lever again. The back of the chair jerked into the upright position and she jumped out of it with exaggerated compunction.

"Oh, right—it's *your* chair." She stalked haughtily over to the fireplace as he fought back a ripple of queasiness and the room wavered before him. She gestured around her, her back to him. "And this is *your* house, and I'm supposed to accept *your* theories about this case. How retentive can a man get?"

All he could see at first was a powder-blue blur, but as the pain subsided and his vision cleared, Matt saw those stiff shoulders suddenly sag. Slowly she turned to face him, her gaze seeking his almost unwillingly.

"The—the tip of his finger?"

At his nod, a tremor ran through her and she took an involuntary step backward. She clasped her elbows tightly, hugging herself in an oddly defensive motion, her head dipping down as if to ward off a blow. As he instinctively started forward she shook her head in fierce independence.

She'd surprised him again, Matt thought, reluctantly keeping his distance. He'd assumed she wouldn't be able to take this latest bombshell he'd just dropped on her, but he'd overlooked the toughness he'd seen once before beneath that fragile and unworldly exterior.

For a long moment she was silent, and when she finally spoke, her voice wasn't much more than a murmur. She was talking to herself rather than to him, he realized.

"But I was so *certain*…" She raised her eyes and looked bleakly at him. "I've been wrong all along, haven't I? The man really *is* dead."

Out of the corner of his eye he saw Zappa join Ziggy, still hiding under the chair. The bigger cat settled companionably down beside the dainty little Siamese and started washing her ear as if to reassure her. The tension on Jenna's features eased for a moment as she watched, and then she turned back to him. "But if Carling's dead, then who tried to kill Edna Terwilliger?"

His only answer to that was something else he'd hoped to keep from her for as long as he could, but the time for shielding her was past. He met her gaze with equal directness. "The Agency's treating it as a simple hit-and-run, to be handled by the police. They're not investigating it further, Jenna."

"What?" The one-word question came out in an incredulous gasp. "A simple hit-and-run—when the woman was just about to come forward and tell you why she'd pretended she didn't know me at Parks, Parks?"

"I was told the evidence isn't convincing enough." Actually, what Henderson had said was that Matt was letting his hormones do his thinking for him, but Matt considered that comment classified information. He shrugged weakly. "The director thinks she's probably what I pegged her as at first—an older lady whose memory was starting to fail. There's nothing solid connecting her accident to anything more sinister."

"But it's all part of a pattern. How did he explain what happened to me at my apartment?"

Her voice had risen accusingly, and he knew she wasn't going to be satisfied with the Agency's verdict. He wished briefly that he'd let the doctor keep him in for observation. Even facing a needle-wielding night nurse would have been preferable to being responsible for tearing Jenna's world apart yet again.

"He said if I thought a damn cat hanging around a garbage bin was proof, then maybe I was the one who was crazy," he muttered. "Dammit, Jenna, he doesn't buy your story. Even if he did, he doesn't see how West and Janeway's little scam ties in with what happened tonight. Without Carling, there isn't a common denominator.''

"Oh, for goodness' sake—of *course* there's a common denominator. There's got to be." She let her breath out with sharp impatience. "And if the Bureau's not willing to investigate, then we're just going to have to find it ourselves. We can start by grilling that horrible Janeway woman."

"Good idea. I'll drive over to your old apartment, kidnap her and bring her back here while you're setting up the desk lamp so we can angle it into her eyes," Matt retorted. "She looked frail. It'll be a piece of cake." He raked his hand through his hair. "Hell, Jenna, that's just not the way things work in the real world."

He was doing it again, she thought, regarding him narrowly—treating her as if she was some kind of naive idealist, totally out of touch with the harsh realities of life. As if idealism, to him, was on a level with trusting in the tooth fairy, and eventually had to be left behind with other childish beliefs. Maybe she'd been wrong about him. Maybe the passion and commitment she'd thought she'd glimpsed in him once or twice had been an illusion.

"So you're just going to accept the official verdict instead of going with your own instincts?" she asked. "You're going to let whoever's behind all this walk away scot-free?"

"All I'm saying is that we should approach this thing logically and calmly, instead of—"

"Logically? What's logical about running down a defenseless woman?" Jenna's eyes flashed. "And how in heaven's name can you stand there and expect me to be *calm* when I've just witnessed an attempted murder?"

"Okay, poor choice of words—"

"On top of that, I thought *you'd* been killed, too. You

were lying there on the pavement, and I couldn't tell if you were breathing or not. Your leg was twisted under you in a weird position and—and—'' Her lower lip trembled. She swallowed audibly and blinked. "And I thought you were dead or unconscious or *something!* I was trying to remember how to do CPR, except then I wondered if that was just for drowning or heart attacks or—or lightning strikes…''

She sounded like a nitwit, she thought, her torrent of words trailing to a halt. Matt was staring at her with a half-wary, half nervously placatory expression on his face, as if he'd just walked in on her chopping up vegetables with a cleaver and been told that she was going through a possibly homicidal bout of PMS. It was an annoyingly male expression. Her incipient tears dried up, and embarrassed, she brushed past him on her way to the couch.

"Oh, don't worry,'' she muttered crossly. About to put her foot down on Zappa, who was stealthily heading for the recliner, she sidestepped and bumped Matt slightly. "I'm not going to go to pieces or anything. I might have known you'd come through it like the Bionic Man, but at the time I—I thought you'd been hurt.''

She heard a heavy thud behind her as she sat down on the couch. "And another thing,'' she said briskly, determined to demonstrate that she was in total control of her emotions again. "Zappa's put on about five pounds while he's been with you. The darn cat sounds like an elephant crashing around. Please stop feeding him snacks—I saw the pizza crusts in his food bowl in the kitchen.''

"Jenna.''

Matt's voice coming from behind her sounded strangled and hoarse. Obviously he was still afraid that she was on the verge of hysterics, she thought in annoyance.

"If you don't think grilling Mrs. Janeway is a good idea, what did you have in mind?'' she asked. "I'm willing to discuss this calmly and rationally, like you said. Just don't patronize me."

"I need your help, Jenna. I really, *really* need your help."

"I said don't patronize me!"

She folded her arms across her chest and stared straight ahead, more hurt by his sarcasm than she wanted him to know. Maybe she wasn't a professional investigator like he was, and maybe her idea about questioning the fraudulent Mrs. Janeway had been a little impulsive, but he didn't have to make it so apparent that she was way out of her depth here. That showed a streak of arrogance she hadn't suspected he had, Jenna thought, piqued. But she believed in karma—that kind of arrogance would prove to be Agent D'Angelo's undoing someday. If she was a more vindictive type of person, she seethed, she might almost wish that she could be around to witness Matt's inevitable fall when it came.

"Dammit, Jenna—I can't get up!"

For a split second Jenna wondered if Matt had been reading her mind.

Then she realized that the snarl had come from the level of the floor behind her, and she twisted her head around so swiftly that she felt a tiny crick in her neck. Matt was nowhere to be seen. She bounced up on the couch cushions and peered over the back of it, and there he was, sprawled out on the carpet with Zappa a few inches away from his head. She stared at him uncomprehendingly.

"Is this some kind of a joke?" she asked coldly. "What are you doing down there? Don't let him lick you right now," she added hastily as the cat bunted the top of his head affectionately against Matt's.

"You knocked me down when you barged into me." Furious gold-brown eyes glared up at her. "My muscle's gone into spasm or something. Can you kindly stop jabbering and help me get up?''

She gasped. Hanging over the back of the couch, she swiped impatiently at the mass of hair that had fallen forward and was obscuring her view. ''I don't jabber. And there's no way I knocked you over—I barely *touched* you.''

With her hair out of her eyes, she could see him clearly now. He had his patented resigned look on. Even as she watched, his eyes closed in long-suffering forbearance. Zappa took the opportunity to lean forward and lovingly sandpaper him with the tip of his tongue.

Matt jerked convulsively away, and as he moved she saw a muscle in his jaw tense and heard the suddenly indrawn breath that whistled past his clenched teeth.

His face looked pale. The man really *was* in pain, she realized in horror.

''You *are* hurt! Matt, I'm so sorry!'' Nipping around the couch and nearly tripping over his outsprawled legs, she fell to her knees beside him helplessly. ''What can I do to help? Where does it hurt?''

There was a faint sheen of sweat on his forehead and, pulling the tissue she'd been using earlier herself from the pocket of the blue sweat-top, Jenna dabbed gingerly at the moisture on his forehead.

''I had no idea I'd knocked you off your feet like that,'' she said, her eyes dark with contrition.

You better hope the johns like 'em a little chunky, Ginger...

Suddenly remembering Tiffany's sardonic comment, she flushed. Was it true? Ever since she'd embarked on this new life she'd been stuffing herself with all the deliciously sinful, nonhealthy foods that she'd never had the opportunity to sample on the communes—potato chips, processed-cheese spread, bread that wasn't whole-grain or stone-ground.

She bent over Matt worriedly, her hair tumbling around his face. "I'm going on a diet immediately," she promised.

He opened one eye and looked at her. "What?"

Jenna felt the zipper on the sweatsuit slip a couple of notches and she tugged at it ineffectually. "It's probably the sugar. I've never used anything except honey, and I guess I went a little crazy in the grocery stores the last week or so," she confessed reluctantly. "I've turned into a darn *whale*." His other eye opened and his gaze locked on hers, the ring around his iris molten gold and catching the glints from her hair. He was frowning. "I knocked you down and didn't even *realize* it. I didn't do it on purpose. You have to believe I would never hurt another human being deliberately, Matt."

"Jenna." He blew a strand of her hair out of his mouth and tried again. "Jenna—I fell down because I hurt my leg in that hit-and-run tonight. I've barely been able to put my own weight on it all evening. It wasn't your fault. You're perfect. I think I can get up by myself now. The spasm's stopped."

The muscle in his jaw was jumping again and he seemed to be having trouble breathing, but she ignored that. Two things stood out in her mind.

He'd said she was perfect. He was lying on the floor beside her, his mouth only inches from hers and he'd just said she was perfect. Despite everything else that had happened tonight, suddenly a rush of pure desire shot through her.

Except he'd also been hobbling around for hours insisting that he was fine, lying to her. She couldn't believe *anything* he said.

"I said the spasm's gone. I think we should get up off

the floor now." Matt's voice cracked and he cleared his throat. "Honestly, I'm okay now."

"You lied to me. How do I know you're not lying now?" Jenna's lips tightened as she hung over him. "How are we supposed to have any kind of a relationship—a working relationship, of course," she added hastily. "You don't even think I'm capable of dealing with the truth."

Matt sighed. "Look—I just thought you'd been through enough already without worrying about me. This kind of thing is my job, Jenna—but let's face it, the life you've led up till now hasn't exactly prepared you for—" He stopped. She pinned him with an icy gaze.

"For what?" she prompted.

"Well, you've been living in a kind of utopia," he floundered. "You've grown up in a world where everyone's kind and honest and so nonviolent that they won't even eat a damn hamburger, and now you've been plunged into the real—" He stopped again.

"The real world. That's it, isn't it—you think I'm some wide-eyed, incompetently childlike kook that you have to protect, right?" she said stiffly. "Admit it. Right from the start you've taken that attitude, and it keeps coming between us. The fact is, you seem to expect me to crumble every time your big, scary world throws another curve at me, and you're constantly surprised when I don't."

She took a deep breath, felt the zipper on her top give way another couple of notches, and went furiously on, her gaze lasering his with blue fire. "Get used to it. And start treating me like a grown woman, not a child, D'Angelo!"

Beside them, Zappa's ears pricked forward in interest. From her position under the couch, Ziggy poked a cautious nose out. Two pairs of crossed blue eyes stared unblinkingly at the scene: a man, lying prone and helpless on his back with an incensed woman half straddling him, her hair a crackling nimbus around her head and her bosom in danger of spilling completely out of her top.

The muscle at the side of Matt's jaw started to tense yet again. Then it relaxed.

"Oh, for God's sake," he said huskily. "I give up."

His hand reached up into a swath of her hair and then around the back of her neck and he pulled her to him.

Chapter Seven

Jenna felt immediately liquefied, as if she'd turned to clear water and could only mold herself to the implacable solidity of the man pressed up against her, could only open herself up to him as he moved into her. His mouth was hard, his hand around the back of her neck was hard, and beneath the crisp white shirt he was wearing his chest felt like a slab of granite crushing against her breasts. As Matt pushed her hair away from her face with an impatient gesture, the shadow of stubble on his cheek sandpapered the vulnerable corners of her lips.

"More," he murmured against her mouth.

Nothing like the Agent D'Angelo who always followed procedure and who never made a move he hadn't completely mapped out beforehand, Jenna thought incoherently, her fingers curling against his chest and clutching handfuls of his shirt.

His tongue penetrated her mouth fully, and immediately the taste, the scent, the *essence* of Matt D'Angelo ran through her, imprinting him on her senses as completely and indelibly as if she was being seared by a brand. He tasted dark and sweet and intoxicating, like chocolate liqueur spilling down her throat and splashing through her until even the tips of her toes felt as if they were melting.

His hand slid slowly down her spine to the small of her back, feathering lightly against every sensitive nerve, and then it slid farther, until those strong fingers were outspread and cupping the sensitive swell of her derriere. As if he was halving a peach, his hand slipped in between the twin curves and pulled her closer to him.

His lashes spiked against her cheek like tiny thick brushes. Somewhere deep in the back of his throat he made a soft sound; half growl, half purr.

He sounded like a tiger who was willing to play for a little while longer, but who wanted to move on to more serious business sooner or later. She hadn't been resisting, but at that purely male noise Jenna suddenly wanted to take him as much as he was taking her. Some basic, uncivilized female need in her wanted to imprint herself on him as he was doing to her, wanted to mark him as her own personal property—for tonight, at least.

"I can't do this."

His voice, ragged with frustration, penetrated Jenna's consciousness, and the erotically quivering nerve endings up and down her spine slowly stopped tingling. It was like coming out of the heat of a sauna and jumping into a snowbank—but the last thing she wanted to do was to let him know how she felt.

It happened to men sometimes, didn't it? she thought disjointedly, a last few tendrils of erotic haze still fogging her thought processes. She wouldn't have guessed that Matt ever would have experienced this particular problem, but perhaps it was a result of the stress he'd been under. Or the accident—what if he'd damaged more than just his *leg?*

For a moment there was silence. Jenna wondered if she should stand up—she was still lying on him, and there was something hard pressing into her thigh, but she certainly didn't want to make it look as though she was rejecting the poor man.

She moved her leg slightly. Then her eyes widened and she met Matt's quizzical look.

"Oh." Her voice was faint.

"Yeah." One straight dark eyebrow rose fractionally. "As far as I know, it's all there and working. It's just the audience that's throwing me off my stride."

He turned his head and, following his gaze, she saw what he was talking about. Zappa and Ziggy were sitting primly together less than a foot away, like disapproving statues, their electric-blue eyes boring into her and Matt.

"This must be why those giant pandas mate so seldom in captivity," she faltered.

"There's a door on my bedroom. I was wondering what that hair would look like spread out all over my duvet, anyway," Matt said in an undertone. He brought his hand to her mouth and traced the line of her top lip. "Hell, I was wondering what *you'd* look like spread out on my duvet. Wanna make a run for it?"

His finger slipped down to the fullness of her bottom lip, and Jenna felt the liquefying warmth return in full force. Suddenly she wouldn't have noticed if they'd been in the middle of a cocktail party. She closed her mouth on his finger and flicked at it with the tip of her tongue. The gold around Matt's irises glazed slightly and the hard pressure against her leg increased.

"No running," she said, releasing his finger and touching hers to his mouth. "You're incapacitated, remember? You have to take it very, very slow, Agent D'Angelo. Can you do that?"

"Not all the time." His voice was a raspy whisper. "You'd never know it to look at me, but sometimes I just lose all control. You're going to have to rein me in if that happens, Ms. Moon. Can you do that?''

Jenna rose to her knees, her gaze never leaving his. She let her hand run down the tanned column of Matt's throat to the knot in his tie. "Rein you in? On one of the communes we lived at they had horses, but I haven't gone riding for quite a while. They say you never forget how, though.''

"Yeah, it's one of those things that come back pretty fast.''

Rising with her slowly, one side of Matt's mouth quirked up in a half smile as she stood and pivoted, still holding on to his tie. As she started for the dimly lit hallway leading off the living room, a few stray tendrils of her hair floated back and he caught them gently, twining them around his fist. Feeling the soft tug, Jenna paused just inside the door of his bedroom and looked around inquiringly, her eyes velvety in the shadows.

"Did I tell you you're not my type?'' he breathed. Tugging again at her hair, he sunk his hand deeper into the fiery mass and pulled her closer.

"No.'' The lush lips parted. "But I could tell. You're not my type either. Too conservative.''

"You're too unconventional.'' He was so close that his breath fanned warm against her cheek.

"What are we going to do about it?'' Jenna let her fingers spread against his shirtfront. She looked up at him through her lashes.

"There's the bed. Let's start with that hair-spread-across-my-duvet idea and take it from there.''

He bent his head to hers and kissed her lightly on the corner of her mouth, at the same time nudging the door behind him closed with his foot. Jenna heard a muffled, indignant meow of protest coming from the hall and she smiled.

"There goes your last excuse, Agent," she murmured as he propelled her the few steps backward toward the bed. She'd caught a glimpse of his room earlier when she'd used the shower in its adjoining bathroom—had that really only been today? she thought with a little start—but now she realized just how perfectly it reflected the personality of Matt. His *real* personality, she told herself—the famous duvet he'd alluded to was a bronze-and-green velvet brocade, and the woven rug on the gleaming dark floorboards picked up the same richly primitive tones. The muted colors sprang into vibrancy as he bent to the night table beside the bed and lit the small and obviously old oil lamp that stood on its polished surface. The rest of the room receded into softly grayed shadows that melted gradually into black, but the warm flicker of the lamp encompassed the two of them in an intimate golden skein of light.

"The first time we met, you reminded me of warm caramel sauce and whipped cream." Taking her lightly into the circle of his arms, he looked down at her upturned face, his own expression wry. "I think you scared the hell out of me, honey."

"I scared *you?*" Jenna's mouth fell open inelegantly. "How?"

"Because all my life I'd operated on logic, played by the rules. But as soon as I saw you, I knew I didn't give a damn about the rules. There was nothing logical about the way I felt—I just wanted you." He shook his head slowly and touched a strand of her hair. "I kept reminding myself I was way out of line, but it didn't work."

"What are you telling me, Matt?" As his gaze held hers, Jenna felt intuitively that he was keeping up some last fragile barrier between them—a barrier that he was maintaining only through desperate effort. A terrible thought occurred to her and she drew back from him infinitesimally, a chill running through her. "It's because I'm really not your type, isn't it? I practically threw myself at you just now, and you didn't know how to get out of it, and now you're trying to let me down without—"

"Dammit, Jenna, shut up," he said mildly. "I'm trying to give *you* a chance to say no if you want to. And I'm trying to let you know that this isn't just some kind of a one-night stand for me. You drive me crazy, you make me laugh and sometimes you infuriate me. Then you look at me, and I feel like I've just been sucker punched in the heart. You take my breath away. But tonight's your choice."

His expression was easily readable even in the warm glow from the old-fashioned lamp. The humor that had lurked a few seconds ago in those amazing gold-brown eyes was still there, but now it was tempered with an ironic self-awareness. Matt D'Angelo was no saint, Jenna thought with a hidden little smile of her own, and the man wanted her— she'd felt the incontestable physical proof of that herself— but whether he acknowledged it or not, he would never completely discard the rules he set for himself. He wasn't about to take unfair advantage of what might have been an impulsively passionate reaction on her part. He wanted her to make a decision that she wouldn't regret later—even if that decision had him frustratedly stepping into a cold shower in the next few minutes.

Sweet, she thought in exasperation. But was the man crazy? Of course she wanted him—she'd wanted the intriguingly tight-assed Agent D'Angelo since the first moment she'd seen him checking his watch and trying to hide his poleaxed reaction to the slightly less than conservative hemline of her leaf-green dress. But if libidinous curiosity—as perfectly justifiable as it might have been—had been all she'd felt, she would have never have considered turning her R-for-Restricted daydreams into a night of reality, she admitted.

What in heaven's name was a sucker punch, anyway? she wondered, meeting Matt's waiting gaze. Whatever it was, it sounded exactly like the way she felt every time *she* looked at *him*—and making love was an integral part of what she wanted them to have together.

Of course, she mused, playing was an integral part of making love…

"I'm changing the plan," she said firmly. A shadow crossed his features and was instantly replaced by an expression of stoic understanding, but before he could speak she went on. "We're going to do this *my* way—the unconventional way, D'Angelo." Now he looked startled. She held back the bubble of laughter that threatened to escape. "That spread-out-on-the-duvet idea had possibilities…but *you* have to buff down first, Agent. And remember—nice and slow."

"Strip?" His eyes widened and then narrowed thoughtfully when she nodded.

He'd never do it—but there was something about him that made her want to shake him up, she thought impishly. It was the straight-arrow persona that he projected—any red-blooded female would be tempted to see if she could coax such a conservative man into being just a little bit bad once in a while.

Then he smiled at her…and all of a sudden Jenna realized she still had a lot to learn about Matt D'Angelo.

It was the slowest, sexiest, down-and-dirtiest bad-boy smile she'd ever seen. It was pure male, with absolutely nothing respectable or conservative about it at all.

Her throat was dry and, chagrined, she felt the hectic

color staining her cheeks. "On second thought—" She heard the nervous squeak in her voice and stopped. She swallowed. Matt gave her a gentle nudge toward the bed and grinned wickedly.

"Sit down, honey, before I make your knees go weak."

The challenging amusement in his eyes robbed his words of most of their arrogance, but enough brazen self-assurance remained that for the first time in her life Jenna realized how Little Red Riding Hood must have felt at the exact moment when the wolf had revealed himself.

Kind of jumpy, she thought. And kind of excited underneath the jumpiness. After all, Red Riding Hood hadn't screamed and run away, had she?

"Talk's cheap, mister." Sinking onto the velvet-and-brocade spread, she lay back slightly on her elbows in a deliberately appraising pose. She looked up at him in mock boredom. "Work it, D'Angelo. I'm waiting."

It was poker, with each of them pushing the stakes higher. But this time she'd called his bluff, Jenna thought smugly as Matt met her challenging gaze. Any minute now he'd cry uncle, join her on the bed and set about showing her how a conventional man indulged in foreplay.

With one hand he reached slowly for the knot in his tie and loosened it, never taking his eyes from her, and she felt her stomach turn over with a dizzying swoop, as if she'd just stepped onto a roller coaster in midride.

"Is it hot in here or is it just me?" he said in that melted-chocolate voice, his other hand raking a stray strand of dark hair from his face. He pulled at the knot in his tie until it came free from his collar, and then undid the first button on his shirt. "Maybe I'm overdressed."

He wasn't backing down. Jenna tried to control her racing pulse and match his casual tone. "It's getting a little warm, but it's nothing I can't handle so far."

Her hands, until now lying palm down on the bedspread, curled unconsciously into the deep nap of the velvet and tightened even more when the renegade strand of hair fell across Matt's forehead again. This time he ignored it, languidly undoing the second and third buttons on his shirt while still watching her through those sinfully thick lashes.

"Then it must be me, because I'm definitely feeling some serious heat, lady."

Working on the last couple of buttons single-handedly, he let his lashes drift to his cheekbones as he tipped his head back a little and ran his other hand down the strong column of his throat like a man who'd been working up a sweat under a hot sun. He opened his eyes to meet her mesmerized stare, and lifted one corner of his mouth in a grin as his fingers trailed past his collarbone and the noose of the tie he was still wearing, down his chest to the washboard flatness of his stomach.

Where had he learned *that?* Jenna thought in drymouthed fascination. The hazy light gave a golden sheen to his skin and drew attention to the tautly underlying muscle, and when he carelessly shrugged first one shoulder, then the next, from his shirt, her teeth caught and held her bottom lip.

"Still not feeling anything?" There was a hint of amusement in his voice but his expression was innocent. With his shirtsleeves straining tightly against his biceps he paused in the act of unfastening a cuff link. He fixed a wide-eyed look on his face. "I never would have suspected you were so cold-blooded, honey." His tie still in a sloppy half knot against the sprinkling of dark hair on his chest, he let the shirt slip slowly down his arms to the floor.

The man was sex personified, Jenna thought lightheadedly. Cold-blooded? If her temperature went any higher, steam would start rising from her skin—as it was, her face felt dewy and flushed and the soft velour top already seemed uncomfortably hot. Without conscious volition, she reached for the zipper on it.

"No audience participation," Matt said reprovingly without looking up, his attention seemingly focused on his tie. "Why don't you practice that deep-breathing technique of yours—you know, the one that gets poor defenseless males all hot and bothered?"

The last thin thread of Jenna's self-control snapped. She couldn't take any more of this, she thought, biting down hard on her lower lip, and since she'd set the rules for this game, she could break them. Sitting up suddenly on the bed, she reached out and grabbed the two ends of Matt's tie before he could release the knot. He looked up, meeting her heated gaze.

"You're a tease, D'Angelo," she said in a voice that sounded too strained to be hers. Slowly she pulled on the gray silk, bringing him closer to her. "And I doubt that you've *ever* been defenceless." She gave a little tug on his tie, releasing it finally and letting it slide to the bed. "You win."

Unresisting, he brought his face to within inches of hers, an infuriatingly amused light turning his eyes to pure amber. "It's only teasing if I don't follow through on it, sweetheart. And I'd call this a draw."

He obliterated the last minuscule space between them, pushing her gently backward, bracing himself with an arm on either side of her, and bringing one knee up onto the velvet-and-brocade-covered bed as his mouth came down on hers.

Jenna heard herself making a small incoherent sound, half moan, half satisfied sigh, as she opened herself to him, her lips parting and her hands outspread on his chest. Her tongue met his greedily and her fingertips dug into his hot skin, blindly clutching at the damp sprinkling of hair there and moving to the smooth masculine disks at the center of the well-defined pectoral muscles.

Matt lifted his mouth, his eyes concealed by his downcast lashes, and his breath catching audibly in his throat. His neck was corded and the muted light from the bedside lamp revealed a flush of color high on his cheekbones. Jenna looked at him and suddenly she felt an erotic thrill of control surge through her. *She* could make him feel like this. *She* could bring this sound of pleasure from Matt D'Angelo, could turn that normally cool gaze molten gold with need. Her touch, her scent...the *taste* of her on his lips had stripped away the civilized veneer of practicality and reserve that he usually wore. He was operating on basic male instinct, and she was the one who had brought him to this pitch of pure desire.

She ran the tip of her tongue along his bottom lip, rasped it over the shadowy stubble on his chin and followed the vulnerable line of his arched neck to the salty hollow between his collarbones...and then went farther. She could feel the heavy thudding beat of his heart against her lips as her tongue tentatively flicked against one taut male nipple, like a kitten sampling cream for the first time.

A shudder ran through him.

"Baby, better not," he rasped.

Still above her and keeping himself upright with one leanly muscled arm, Matt buried the fingers of his free hand into the tangle of hair at her temple, his grasp tightening convulsively. With what seemed like an immense effort he opened his eyes, but when he looked down at her, his gaze was glazed and unfocused for a second.

Jenna's lips felt moistly swollen. Reluctantly she drew away from him. A wry awareness gradually returned to his expression as their eyes met.

"Wasn't…wasn't it good?" she whispered.

He stared at her blankly, and then a slow smile lifted the corner of his mouth. "Good? Hell, no, honey, that was a bad, *bad* thing you were doing. You were driving me out of my mind. Now it's my turn."

In one smoothly impatient movement he reached for the zipper on the velour top and slid it all the way down, until the metal teeth parted at the bottom. Without a pause, he lifted Jenna just high enough to strip the garment off her completely, and then he stopped.

"I kept getting glimpses of these all night," he said huskily, tracing the curve of one breast with his thumb until he came to the whisper of pink lace that hid the rest of her from his view. "As sexy as the bra is, I'm in no mood to let lingerie get in my way at this point."

He didn't take the time to undo it, but simply pushed it up until her breasts slipped free. Jenna's limbs felt heavy and languid, as if she was powerless to stop him, powerless to protest against what he was doing. She didn't *want* to protest, she thought dreamily, her eyes half-closed and her lips parting on a sigh. She felt somehow more exposed like this, with the scrap of satin and lace still encircling but no longer concealing her, and the confusing mixture of shyness and wantonness that waterfalled through her was curiously erotic.

"Too much," Matt breathed. He was very still, the rise and fall of his chest and the pulse beating at the side of his throat the only indication of his state of mind. "Too much skin, too much of that gorgeous hair, too lush, too desirable…" His voice was slurred. "I want it all."

Through her lashes she saw him bend to her, and she felt the silky strands of his hair brush against her skin and his hand cup the tender undercurve of one breast. His mouth touched the straining peak of her nipple. Then his tongue and his lips were circling it until she could almost imagine that the rest of her body had drifted into nothingness and the only reality left was the whirlpool of sensation he was making her feel.

Her hands were in his hair, her fingers desperately entwined in the thick strands as she arched her back. She felt him pushing the elastic waist of the fleecy sweatpants past her hips, felt him pull the scrap of satin panties impatiently down her legs, and felt his strong, hard hand moving up the inner softness of her thigh to the secret thatch of fiery auburn curls there.

"You smell like cinnamon," Matt murmured against her skin. "I've got to taste you. I want your scent on me, honey."

His breath was hot on her rib cage, and then the sensitive skin of her stomach, but before he could venture any farther Jenna found her voice.

"Not yet," she managed to say, lifting her head from the bed and meeting his eyes. "You didn't keep your end of the bargain, D'Angelo."

He looked taken aback, and then his expression cleared. Sitting on the edge of the bed with his back to her, he crossed one leg casually over the other and untied the laces of his shoes, slipping his socks off with them. He looked over his shoulder at her as he completed his task, the corner of his mouth quirked up in a lazy half smile. Slowly he stood and faced her, his hands moving to the buckle of his belt, his gaze fixed on her. Undoing the belt, he drew it carefully through the loops and then he let the leather drop to the floor. His hands returned to the waistband of his trousers, and with excruciating deliberation he unbuttoned and unzipped them. Casually he slipped them down the length of his legs, along with the plain briefs he was wearing underneath, and stepped out of them.

For a moment he didn't move. With easy grace he stood in front of her, obviously aware that she was drinking in the sight of him and untroubled by her wide-eyed scrutiny.

"The knee doesn't work so good tonight," he said with a hint of wry laughter in his words. "But it could have been worse."

His skin was dark gold in the lamplight, shadows flickering lovingly over his body as the flame wavered slightly and then steadied. He was a big man, and more heavily muscled than she'd realized. He was big, he was gorgeous and everything he had, from the sexy curve of that bottom lip to those long lean legs, was hers for tonight.

Including, she thought breathlessly, all the equipment in between. As he'd reassured her earlier, it appeared to be working the way it should be—*exactly* the way it should be.

"I want it all, too," she said softly, her voice so husky it sounded like a purr. "Can the audience participate now, D'Angelo?"

"You can participate, honey." He knelt back on the bed, half straddling her. With unexpected gentleness he lifted the glowing mass of red-gold hair and spread it on the velvet-and-brocade cover around her head and shoulders. "You can participate all you want."

With a smoothly effortless movement, he scooped his hands under her hips and lifted her at the same time as he brought his mouth down. At the first touch of his lips, Jenna felt pure, elemental sensation spill through her. Her fists, blindly searching for something to hang on to, found and sank into the cool cotton of the down pillows by her head and she clenched them tightly.

She felt as though she was about to fall off the edge of the world, she thought disjointedly—as if the next shuddering wave that overwhelmed her would sweep her into a mindless, bodiless state of ecstasy. Against the tender skin of her inner thighs she could feel the harsh scrape of Matt's roughly stubbled cheek, and even that slight discomfort only added a rough urgency to the need building up inside her.

She didn't want to go there alone, she thought hazily. When she fell, she wanted him falling with her, holding her, crying out at the same time that she did.

Moving with dreamlike, underwater slowness, she reached up for him. "Everything." She could hardly hear herself, and at first she wondered if she'd even forced the word past her swollen lips. She opened her eyes and met Matt's inquiring gaze. *"Now,"* she breathed.

It was all she could manage, but it was enough. Through the veil of her lashes she saw him take something from the nightstand, and then he was holding himself, his hair falling across his forehead, his sure hands moving deftly until he was sheathed.

He wasn't the type of man to be careless about protecting the woman he was with, Jenna thought as he lowered himself to her. Which was good—this was their first time together, and it was something that she should have thought of herself. Why hadn't she?

He entered her slowly, but even so she felt a momentary panic. He was big. He was very big, and already it seemed as if he was filling her. She couldn't encompass him, she couldn't open herself any more for him, this wasn't going to work—

—except then it *was* working, and Matt D'Angelo was inside her as if the two of them had been made for this one physical joining. It felt *exactly* right. It was as if her body had waited all her life for this man to become part of her, Jenna thought as he began to move inside her. And that was why she hadn't thought of any kind of protection…because having everything this man could give her was what she eventually wanted.

"Is it good? Is it sweet, *cara?*" His voice slurred just a little. He withdrew almost completely and then entered her again, and her hips moved to meet his. His hair was in his eyes and he bit his lower lip as she tightened.

"Yes," she whispered dazedly, gasping as he filled her. "*Yes*. But I can't—I want—"

The muscles in his arms stood out like cords as again they came together and moved apart, came together and moved apart, his skin slick against the dampness of hers. It was like an express train going downhill, she thought; brakes off, speed building dangerously, and any control abandoned. The final fiery explosion was just around the next curve, and both she and Matt knew it and wanted it.

He thrust deeper and she met him completely, and then those gold eyes locked onto hers and he thrust again. "Hold me. Kiss me," he said in a drugged voice, the words matching the rhythm of his movements. "Come with me, *cara*."

His mouth covered hers desperately and then Jenna felt the dam burst inside her and a released flood of sensation pushed her over the edge. Matt's arms were tightly around her, but still it felt as if she were swirling through space, through inky blackness, weightlessness, her very consciousness a tiny, distant, receding speck.

And then she was tumbling earthward and behind her closed eyes she saw shooting stars, bushels of them, pouring through her like liquid light and tracing sparkling silver paths through her veins, her fingertips, each individual strand of her hair, until they softly burst, one by one.

She trembled as the last tiny star winked out. She opened her eyes slowly. Matt's face was inches away, and as she watched, he opened his, too, and met her unfocused gaze.

"Like I told you," he whispered huskily. "Right to my heart."

Chapter Eight

"I now pronounce you man and wife..."

That little dark-haired flower girl had to be one of Matt's nieces, Jenna thought as she slowly awoke, reluctantly letting the frothy yards of meringue-like white tulle she'd been wearing in her dream fade into insubstantiality, but fixing every last detail of its design in her mind for future reference. She stretched luxuriously and pulled the velvet-and-brocade spread up to her chin. Bars of buttery sunlight crossed the polished maple planking of the floor at right angles, and through the partially open bathroom door she could hear the roar of the shower.

Lifting her arms lazily above her head, she laced her fingers lightly together. Maybe in a couple of minutes she'd get up enough energy to join him...or maybe she'd just close her eyes, drift off again and wait for Matt to wake her for the second—no, the third time since this morning. They'd made love all last night, and finally she'd fallen asleep in his arms. Just as dawn had broken, they'd come together again in a sweetly slow and dreamlike joining. He'd stroked her hair afterward, his chin resting on the top of her head and the steadying beat of his heart the last thing she'd heard as her eyes closed, and a few hours later she'd woken once more, this time to the tantalizing smell of dark

Italian coffee as he'd set two mugs down on the night table beside the bed.

Too bad about the coffee, Jenna thought with a secret little smile. It had smelled fabulous—but somehow they hadn't gotten around to drinking it.

Matt D'Angelo hadn't been able to get enough of her. And she hadn't been able to get enough of him. Free spirit or not, last night had definitely been a first for her, she thought, a slight wash of color touching her cheeks—she'd *never* given herself so unreservedly to anyone. She'd had absolutely no inhibitions at all. Her toes curled as she remembered every delicious detail.

With Matt, she'd been—she searched for the appropriate word—*wanton.* An abandoned woman. Maybe even once or twice a *hussy.* And she'd loved it.

Which was just as well, because whether the man knew it or not yet, they were going to spend the rest of their lives together. Sometimes she read auras wrong, but although she'd only ever had a handful of precognitive dreams, they'd *always* come true.

Right from the start she'd felt a psychic link to him, as if they'd been lovers in another existence and had simply been marking time in this one until they found each other again. Of course, Matt's skepticism would never allow him to buy *that* theory, but she really hadn't expected him to accept karma, predestination *and* finding his other half all in one week. She wasn't an unreasonable woman. She'd give him a few more days to get used to it before she told him about the dream.

Straight to my heart.

He was the one, Jenna thought with absolute certainty. Even without the dream she would have known.

She let her glance move slowly around the room, realizing that she'd been right when she'd guessed that it revealed the essence of the man who lived here and who'd made it his own.

He'd been born here—had probably been conceived in this very room, he'd said with a wry laugh, although when Maria D'Angelo had moved into the condo in which she now lived she'd taken a few treasured pieces of furniture. The marriage bed she'd once shared with her Salvatore had been one of them. His mother had never hidden the fact that her marriage had been a passionate love affair, from the day she'd first met Matt's father right up to the moment when, stony-eyed with grief and dressed in black, the still-youthful Maria had tossed a handful of dirt and a single red rose on his casket as it had been lowered into the ground.

Her faith had sustained her, Matt had told Jenna quietly, his hand on her hair falling still and his eyes staring at nothing in the dark. After the construction-site accident, his father had been in a coma for eight months before death had belatedly taken him, and Maria D'Angelo had been at her unconscious husband's side every day during that long, futile vigil. When she hadn't been at the hospital or looking after her young son and three daughters, she'd been at St. Mary's, lighting candles and praying that the love of her life would be given back to her.

Matt and his older sister Carmela had prayed too—prayed with the faith and fervency of children who knew with unwavering certainty that miracles could happen. Hadn't their father himself been born in a city in Italy called Padua, where St. Anthony had once lived and performed miracles…the same St. Anthony who was venerated for recovering that which had been lost?

The Sunday after his father's funeral, Matt said quietly in the dark, he'd told Carmela he didn't believe in miracles anymore. He didn't believe in praying for impossible things, and he didn't believe in *anything* he couldn't actually see, touch or prove beyond a doubt. He'd continued accompanying the family to Mass, and he had sung in the choir for a few years after that. But he'd only made those concessions because he knew his mother would be heart-broken to think that her only son had rejected the unquestioning beliefs that meant so much to her.

She could picture him clearly, Jenna mused now, her expression clouding—a tough little boy not given to flights of fancy in the first place, choosing from that day on to confront the harshest realities face-to-face. She knew only too well how painful it was for a child to have to experience the death of a parent—but for Matt, even at that age stubbornly insisting that his world make logical sense, having his father hanging between life and death for eight long months only to finally slip away for good must have been devastating.

It explained a lot about the man he'd become. The adult Matt D'Angelo still preferred his world prosaically factual and clear-cut. She *wasn't* his type. With her unconventional upbringing among artists, dreamers, and…well, she had to face it, Jenna told herself—some of Franklin's friends had been downright *spacy*—she could see how she might try Agent D'Angelo's patience once in a while.

But that wasn't to say that the man didn't have his own brand of faith, his own set of beliefs. This room was evidence of that—this *house* was evidence of that. Family and heritage were what Matt believed in. His father and his uncles had built this house. His cousins had helped him renovate it when he'd taken it over from his mother, rather than let it fall into the hands of a stranger. There had been years of family dinners and celebrations in the cove-ceilinged dining room—Salvatore had insisted on doing the tricky plasterwork himself apparently, because Maria had always said she wanted a cove ceiling with a fancy Italian-glass chandelier hanging down from the middle. Although Matt had converted the room into an office, Jenna had noticed that the chandelier still hung over his work table, ready to be put back to its former use someday in the future.

The spread snugged under her chin had been made by Matt's long-gone but not forgotten great-aunt, Lucia, who'd painstakingly pieced the scraps of brocade and velvet together by hand. Even the small oil lamp beside her had been a valued possession of Maria D'Angelo's grandmother. She'd left her homeland and come to America in the 1920s, a lonely and frightened young girl carrying everything she owned in the world in one cardboard suitcase, but determined to make a new life for herself in this land of opportunity.

Picking up the lamp carefully and looking at it more closely, Jenna could understand why that original Maria had refused to leave the fragile item behind. Roughly fashioned out of clay, nonetheless it was beautifully painted, and although time had faded the once-brilliant colors the scene depicted still held the viewer's eye. It showed a small stream running through a rocky cleft. In the background were mountains, with a tiny castle nestled among the peaks.

She suddenly froze, her gaze fixed on the picture of the tiny castle and the mountain stream…

The next moment she flung back the covers, grabbed a shirt from the back of a nearby chair in a halfhearted attempt at decorum and charged into the bathroom, the tiny bells at her ankle jingling frantically.

She skidded to a halt, momentarily sidetracked by the sight of Matt, his hair wet and slicked back from his forehead like a swimmer's, and wearing only a skimpy towel tied loosely around his hips. *Dear God,* she thought breathlessly—the man was almost criminally sexy.

His eyes widened at her unconventional attire—his own shirt provocatively skimming her thighs, the cuffs flapping down well past her wrists, and the unbuttoned front not concealing a thing, but even as a slow grin lifted the corner of his mouth, Jenna found her voice.

"Matt—I know why someone's been trying to make it look like I'm crazy," she said in an unsteady rush. "And if I'm right, then—then I'm *next* on the list to be deleted!"

"CASTLE CREEK HOLDINGS?" Matt set a steaming mug of coffee on the round oak table in front of Jenna and pulled up one of the old pressback chairs for himself, impatiently straddling it backward and folding his arms along the top of it. He looked more worried than she'd ever seen him. "You're positive?"

He'd put on a pair of jeans, but there was still a beading of moisture on his unclad torso from the shower. She blinked and picked up her coffee mug.

"I'm positive. Even at the time, the name seemed kind of familiar to me, but it wasn't until I saw your great-grandmother Maria's oil lamp that I remembered where I'd heard it before. There was some big scandal a few years ago, wasn't there?" She took a cautious sip of coffee and her eyes widened. "This is wonderful! I'd never had anything but herbal tea until I worked at the diner, but Joe's coffee didn't taste anything like this."

"Joe's coffee was crap," Matt said shortly. "The secret is to mix in some ground espresso with the Colombian and then—"

He broke off in midsentence, and the muscle at the side of his jaw jumped. But as Jenna, her eyes blissfully and obliviously closed, took another appreciative sip, the tense set of his mouth relaxed and his gaze rested on her with rueful forbearance. He smiled faintly.

"You know, you would have liked my father, honey. He was a lot like you—he always found time to savor the moment."

She looked up, feeling as though she'd just received a precious gift. "You'd like—you would have liked Franklin too, Matt." Her voice wavered suddenly and she lowered her gaze, setting her mug down on the table with more care than the action warranted.

"It's only been a few months since you lost him. You still miss him, don't you?" His question was gentle. "If you ever feel like talking about it, I'm here to listen, Jenna. But right now it's important that you tell me everything you know about Castle Creek and its connection to Parks, Parks."

"But that's just it—I *don't* know anything more than I told you." Shoving her cuffs back from her wrists in sudden frustration, she turned to him. "I heard about it on the radio a few years ago, when it seemed that every politician in the state was being accused of having some connection to the company. It was some kind of massive investment scam, wasn't it?"

"It went further than that, but yeah." His eyes narrowed. "Careers went down in flames, a couple of people were whispered to have committed suicide rather than be exposed, and even the venerable firm of Parks, Parks, and Boyleston was rumored to have expanded their legal services to include money laundering and tax evasion for certain select clients who were being scrutinized by the authorities. But then Charles Parks—Senior, not the one you worked for—suffered a massive stroke in the middle of the investigation. A few weeks later the word came down that the firm had been exonerated of any connection whatsoever with Castle Creek."

"Except that can't be true—not if they have a file cabinet

full of documentation on the company,'' Jenna said. ''I had one of those files in my hand, Matt. I gave it to Miss Terwilliger myself with about a dozen others.''

''Did she realize what it was?''

''Of course. Miss Terwilliger wouldn't have let a batch of files go upstairs without vetting them first.'' The corners of Jenna's mouth drooped at the memory. ''She was pretty upset, in that icy way of hers, but at the time I thought it was just because I'd made a mistake—the requisition chit had said 'Castello Holdings.' She asked me where I'd found the file, and when I told her it had been in a separate storage room she practically took my head off. Apparently I'd somehow trespassed into an area of the archives that was off-limits and locked.''

''So how did you get in if it was locked?'' He looked confused.

''I don't know!'' She bent down and scooped up Zappa, who'd been weaving around the legs of her chair. She plumped him in her lap so firmly that he gave a startled meow and then the two of them stared accusingly at Matt. ''It was my second day on the darn job. I was lost in all those stupid corridors, and there was a passageway where the light had burned out and then I bumped into that exterminator and nearly had a heart attack.'' She stroked Zappa's fur agitatedly, and it crackled with the same electricity that was making a few flyaway strands of her own hair float around her shoulders. ''Maybe the room was supposed to be locked, but it wasn't when I blundered in there. I didn't unlock *anything*. And all the other files I got were the right ones,'' she ended miserably.

''I don't like it,'' Matt frowned. ''If you've discovered a connection between Castle Creek and Parks, Parks—a connection that your former boss swore never existed— then I think it's safe to say that a whole lot of attention is being focused on you. You've probably made some very dangerous people extremely nervous.'' His expression as he looked at Jenna was grim. ''You were right about one thing—for some reason it wasn't in their best interests to kill you when they found out you'd handled that file. That's why that charade was set up at your apartment to make it look as if you were crazy.''

''But how did anyone know I'd discovered the file in the first place? I can't believe that Miss Terwilliger would have told anyone—aside from everything I know about the woman's character, she obviously realized the implications of a link between Castle Creek and the law firm as soon as she saw what I'd found. Now I think she reacted the way she did out of fear.'' Jenna chewed distractedly at her thumbnail, ignoring Zappa, who was batting playfully at her hair. ''Maybe someone saw her putting it back...although I don't see how. Hardly anyone ever came down to the basement—and the partners *never* left their offices on the top floor. Besides, from the way she was questioning me, I don't think even she had a key to that room.''

''Let's start with what we do know,'' Matt said decisively. ''We have to assume that Parks is behind all this, since he's the controlling partner of the firm. Somehow he learned that you'd been in his private archives room, and it had to worry him that you might realize the significance of what you'd seen there.''

''But I *didn't*.''

''I know that. You know that. Even Miss Terwilliger probably knew that.'' He raked his hand through his hair and sighed. ''But all Parks knew was that the firm's most recent employee had discovered his closely guarded secret her second day on the job. He may even have thought you'd been planted on him to do just that.''

"Well, why didn't I get pushed down a flight of stairs later on that day?" Jenna said dismissively. She shook her head and gave him a slightly pitying smile. "Sorry, Matt, but you've got to start thinking logically here. Why didn't someone try to run me down on the street like they did with Miss Terwilliger?"

She froze, her hand suddenly clenching on Zappa's fur. The Siamese gave an annoyed squawk and jumped from her lap indignantly.

"What is it?" His gaze swept her still figure, her wide eyes, and he leaned forward urgently. "Something *did* happen, didn't it?"

"I knew there was a payphone in the restaurant across the street from my work," she said in a hollow voice. "That's where I was going—that's where I phoned you from that day. But while I was waiting at the curb for the light to change, somebody bumped into me from behind just as a bus went by. There was a man standing beside me. If he hadn't grabbed me I would have fallen right into its path."

"Did you see who pushed you?"

"No. There was a crowd of people waiting to cross—I never suspected it was deliberate, though it did shake me up a little. But by the time I thanked the man who'd helped me, the light had changed and everyone else was halfway across the street. A minute later I was on the phone talking to you."

"Did you find the number in the phone book, or did you ask the operator to connect you?" Seeing her look, Matt forestalled her. "No—it makes a difference, Jenna. Could anyone nearby have heard you asking to be put through to the Bureau?"

"Oh." Comprehension dawned in her eyes. "I *did* have to ask for the number. I suppose someone could have heard me, and…'' Her words trailed off and she looked at him, her expression uncharacteristically somber. ''If I hadn't made that call when I did they probably would have tried again, wouldn't they? I might never have made it home alive that night.''

Her voice didn't sound like her own, she thought. It sounded squeaky and high and as she reached for her mug of coffee, wanting something to counteract the sudden chill that she felt, she saw with dismay that her hand was trembling.

''Oh, this is stupid,'' she said with an attempt at a laugh. What came out sounded more like a shaky sob. ''Why am I falling to pieces now? At the time all I was worried about was—was getting back to work before—before—''

''Honey, don't.'' Matt was out of his chair and beside her even as the first tear landed on her bare thigh, and, pulling her to her feet, he crushed her to his chest. ''You couldn't have known the kind of danger you were in. You didn't even realize what you'd stumbled into. Don't forget, you phoned me to report that you'd seen Rupert Carling, not that you'd just discovered evidence in the Castle Creek affair.''

Gently he tipped her head back and met her flooded gaze. ''What's important is that you bought yourself time by contacting the Bureau. After you made the appointment with me, you couldn't be eliminated. Questions would have been asked, and the last thing Parks could afford is another investigation.''

''I know that, Matt.'' Jenna blotted her tears with the back of her hand. ''But I also know that the situation's changed again, hasn't it? What happened to Miss Terwilliger last night means that for some reason just discrediting witnesses isn't enough anymore. She was silenced—maybe permanently. I might have been safe for a while, but no longer.''

"When I called the hospital earlier, she was still holding her own, so don't give up hope on her yet. She's a fighter. And I'll talk to Henderson this morning and insist on protection for you," Matt promised. "When he hears what you have to say he'll—"

"For heaven's sake—you *know* the Bureau's going to think that since my first fantastic story didn't fly, the crazy Ms. Moon's just come up with a new one." Abruptly she drew away from his embrace. "I told you before not to sugarcoat things for me, Matt. Tell me the truth here—until Charles Parks is exposed for the criminal he is, my life isn't worth *spit*, is it?"

"I wouldn't put it that—"

"I've got a right to *know*, dammit!"

Blue eyes blazed out of a white face, the coppery mass of hair only making her pallor seem more pronounced.

She *never* swore, Jenna thought as she confronted him with her hands on her hips—but so help her, if the man didn't start leveling with her she just might toss in a couple of phrases she'd heard Tiffany and the girls use. She was in the process of choosing the most shocking one she could remember when he robbed her of the opportunity.

"You're a target, yeah," he said heavily. "And your assessment of the Bureau's reaction is probably accurate, too. I'm going to have to figure out some way of convincing Henderson to take you seriously enough to reopen the investigation against Parks, but short of breaking into the law firm illegally and going through the man's office, I don't see how that's going to happen." He frowned. "Unless we start with your original plan and have a little talk with West and Mrs. Janeway. Your ex-super looked like a man who'd run up against the law once or twice before in his career. He might make a deal if I present it to him the right way.''

"A small-time crook. I can't see your boss valuing his testimony any higher than mine,'' Jenna said dismissively. "No, you're right, Matt. We're going to have to break into Parks, Parks and look for that file.'' She tapped her teeth thoughtfully with her thumbnail. "It'd better be tonight— the sooner we can pin something on Parks the better. Does your niece have any black jeans or a black sweat suit I can borrow? Or maybe it would be better if you took me out today to get some clothes. I'll pay you back when this is all over, and I get another job.''

"Don't worry about it. Your basic break-and-enter outfit with a matching burglar's mask won't be that expensive. And after we get caught, we'll both be wearing prison-issue orange anyway. So your wardrobe problems will be taken care of for the next two to five years.'' Matt glared at her. "That's the most irrational scheme you've run by me yet. For God's sake, the damn cat could come up with a more sensible plan if I asked him.''

By his feet Zappa looked up with interest. Beside him Ziggy scratched in a ladylike way at her collar. Jenna tapped her bare foot in an exaggerated show of patience, the bells on her ankle bracelet tinkling merrily.

"Are you finished?'' she asked politely.

"No, I'm not.'' Matt looked down at her foot in irritation. "And stop doing that. I can't hear myself think with that jangling going on every time I'm near you.''

Carefully Jenna lowered her toes to the floor. Even that small movement brought forth one last silvery chime, and she looked up at him with a show of remorse. "Sorry, Matt. I jingled, Matt. It was your idea to break into Parks's office in the first place, Matt!''

Her last sentence came out in a drill sergeant's roar only inches away from his face.

She was too small to produce such a loud noise, Matt thought in aggrieved shock, taking a step backward before he could help himself. The woman had lungs like a mule skinner—it had to be those damn breathing exercises she did. With three sisters who weren't exactly shrinking violets themselves, he'd thought he knew what an angry female sounded like. He'd been wrong.

And it wasn't helping that all she was wearing while she was reaming him out was a pair of bikini panties and a man's shirt with only one button done up. Jenna Moon fought dirty. He forced himself to ignore the sudden memory of how she'd looked last night when they'd made love. Her lips had been soft and parted, her hair a tumble of gold and copper over her pale skin, her eyes so deep a blue that—

"It wasn't a serious suggestion," he said coldly, interrupting his own train of thought with an effort. "I assumed you would realize I was being sarcastic."

"Maybe Zappa caught your drift." She was tapping her foot again. "But then, he's more *rational* than I am, isn't he? He could come up with a more *sensible* plan than I could—isn't that what you said?"

"Okay, I was out of line there." His own voice was rising. "But dammit, Jenna—even if it wasn't completely out of the question to somehow get into Parks, Parks in the middle of the night, and even if the man kept incriminating evidence just lying around his office, there's no way I'd let you be part of such a dangerous scheme! Hell, even *you* have to admit it would be insane to let you get involved."

She glared at him. "I *am* involved! I have a vested interest in this whole situation. This is the twenty-first century, Matt—women don't stand around barefoot in the kitchen waiting for some darn man to take care of all their problems for them!''

"Good for you, honey—except the barefoot-in-the-kitchen line would have had more punch if you hadn't delivered it...well...barefoot in the kitchen. Hi, bro. I knocked, but I guess you two didn't hear me."

The stylish brunette standing in the doorway surveyed the scene for a second, and Jenna's mouth closed with an appalled snap. Beside her she heard Matt make a strangled sound.

"I'm Carmela, Matt's sister." The brunette stepped into the room and looked quizzically at Jenna. "You're not his type. This should be interesting."

Chapter Nine

"Matt, you're shedding." Turning to her brother, Carmela planted an abstracted kiss on his cheek while plucking a pale beige Zappa-hair from his jeans. Under strongly arched eyebrows her eyes were a warmer brown than his, and right now they were lit with a secret amusement. Matt saw it.

"Back off, *cara*," he said in an undertone as her lips left a faint carmine smudge just above his jawbone. He caught her gaze and held it defensively. "For your information, I'm thinking of becoming a monk," he muttered. He shot a frustrated glance at Jenna, who was hurriedly shrugging into the paisley robe she'd been wearing the day before and had left slung over a chair. "Preferably in a silent order."

His sister spared him a pitying glance. With one tanned thumb she rubbed perfunctorily at the lipstick print on his skin. "So handsome. So dumb," she said, shaking her head and smiling up at him. "Are you going to introduce us?"

"Jenna, this is my sister, Carmela Tucci," he said through gritted teeth. "Jenna Moon, Carm. She's…uh, staying here for a few days until she finds a new apartment."

He emphasized his last few words, but the only one paying attention to him anymore was Zappa.

"I'm glad to see someone using that robe." Carmela held out her hand to Jenna. "For some reason, my brother never wears it."

"It makes me look like Noel Coward," he muttered. "It's just not me, Carm."

"Of course." She let her glance dwell with sisterly appraisal on the discus-thrower shoulders, the washboard-hard torso, the well-worn jeans riding his hips. "You don't want to do anything to emphasize that effete powder-puff image you project."

No one seeing them together could doubt that they were related, Jenna thought. They both had the same thick dark eyebrows, the same strong cheekbones, and skin that still held the warmth of a Mediterranean heritage. But the real tip-off was the easy, teasing familiarity in Carmela's attitude and the slight, unwilling smile tugging at the corner of Matt's mouth. Despite the wicked gleam in Carmela's eye, the bond between the two of them was obvious. They'd grown up together. They'd always had each other. She felt a tiny, wistful pang of envy.

"What I really came by for was to remind you to show up for dinner on Saturday," Carmela continued. She made a small moue of resignation at Jenna as if she'd known her for years, and the wistful pang subsided a little as Jenna felt herself being drawn into the other's woman's hospitable orbit. "He's terrible at remembering family stuff, so I'm dumping this one on you, Jen. Seven o'clock and don't eat for at least twelve hours beforehand because it's the usual D'Angelo *famiglia* thing—Mom's making one of her massive lasagnas, Tina's bringing focaccia, Sophie's doing her weird eggplant dish and I'm baking a chocolate birthday cake for Stacey. My baby's turning sixteen," she explained wryly. "God, that makes me feel ancient!"

She looked anything but, Jenna thought as Carmela

swept past her brother, slipping off the buttery-soft short leather coat she was wearing and negligently handing it to him. Dressed in what had to be a cashmere sweater with a matching slim black leather skirt, Carmela looked more like an Italian movie star, supremely confident and elegantly sexy. She wasn't a tall woman, but the sheer black hose and the black heels she wore made her legs seem glamorously long.

Despite the heels, she whisked around the kitchen like a minor hurricane, pouring herself coffee, bending swiftly to scratch Ziggy behind one ear and finally settling herself at the table, her legs crossing with a swish of silk.

"You seemed to be losing when I walked in, bro." She darted a look through her lashes at Matt and raised her coffee cup to her lips. "So tell me, what was the argument about?" She smiled at Jenna disarmingly. "Not that it's any of my business, but I'm intrigued. I don't believe I've ever seen my brother do anything more drastic than raise an eyebrow, and there he was actually bellowing at you. You seem to know how to push all the right buttons with him. Oh dear." Her smokily shadowed eyes widened innocently. "Double entendre."

Jenna sat down herself, more abruptly than she'd meant to, her cheeks flaming but a surprised little snort of laughter almost escaping her when she saw Matt's thunderous expression. She liked Carmela, she thought, hiding her smile. What other woman could carry off walking in on her brother and a strange woman like this without feeling uncomfortable? Already Carmela had made her feel as if she was part of the family, and despite her inadvertent reference to the fact that Jenna and Matt had apparently spent an intimate night together, there was no awkwardness in her attitude. Carmela Tucci exuded a confident female sexuality of her own, she thought. It wasn't a subject she tiptoed around. It would be hard to, anyway, with Matt half-naked and the redheaded stranger practically spilling out of his robe.

Hastily Jenna cinched the silk belt at her waist more snugly.

"That's enough, Carm." Matt was looking down at the two of them with a slight trace of rebuke on his good-looking features. "What we were arguing—*talking* about—" he corrected himself in annoyance—"involves the Bureau. You know I can't discuss my job."

He was being pompous, Jenna realized in horrified amazement. The man who'd driven her crazy all night long, the man she'd driven crazy in turn, was turning into a stuffed shirt right before her eyes. She'd come into his life just in time, she decided. Without her, Matt D'Angelo might have eventually turned into a modern-day version of Calvin Coolidge.

"Shove it, Matt," she said rudely. "The Agency washed its hands of me and my problem, so I don't see why your sister can't hear about it. Maybe she might see something we missed."

"This sounds juicy." Carmela waved an expensively manicured hand at a white box on the kitchen counter. "Matt, I brought you some sweet cannoli from Forsini's. Be a darling and make more of your special coffee and we'll all have some." She turned back to Jenna. "So you met Matt through his work. Don't tell me—you're some kind of Mata Hari type femme fatale, right?"

"That would explain a lot of things." Matt stalked over to the coffeemaker, shrugging in defeat. "My career's down the tubes, my director's thinking of sending me to a shrink and a bunch of hookers downtown had a contract out on me. I think your work here is done, Jen. You must have other lives you're scheduled to destroy."

"He's bitter. Not attractive in a man," Jenna said carelessly. "That's because he knows I'm right. Okay—this is what happened. I came home from work four days ago, and this horrible old woman had taken over my apartment and confiscated my cat. It's a long story."

"Try the cannoli." Carmela shoved the box over to her and sunk strong white teeth into the creamy pastry. Powdered sugar drifted onto the black cashmere sweater. "Was she one of those old women who act sweet and frail, but you know they're really evil?"

"Evil—and a heck of a lot spryer than they let on," Jenna agreed, her mouth full. "What's in these? They're fabulous."

Jenna Moon had made a new best friend, Matt thought darkly—his own *sister*. He dropped a pinch of cinnamon on top of the coffee in the basket and propped his elbows despondently on the counter while he waited. In her irritatingly roundabout style of narrative, she was regaling Carmela with the whole story. He hadn't known that the hookers from the diner had actually offered to teach her the trade. At least she'd had the sense to turn *that* offer down. He closed his eyes in silent thankfulness, only to open them again as he heard her outlining her ridiculous plan to break into Parks, Parks.

"...and Matt said that even the *cat* could come up with a better idea, but the way I see it, until we get something solid on Charles Parks that we can take to the Bureau, I might as well be a *prisoner* here!" Sarah Bernhardt, watch out, Matt thought dryly. "And besides wanting to see daylight again someday, I've been wearing Stacey's blue sweat suit forever—I don't even have any clothes of my own. Please tell her I'll get it cleaned before I return it," she added, absently picking another cannoli out of the box.

"Well, that's one problem we can solve right now," Carmela said sympathetically. "I've got a couple of boxes of clothes in the back of the Ferrari that I've been meaning to take to the church—they run a used-clothing shop for charity. There must be a few outfits in there that would fit you. But Jen, though I hate to admit it, I've got to agree with Matt on the break and enter. There's already been one attempted killing. This Parks seems to have some pretty ruthless thugs working for him, and if you got caught going through his private papers…" She shuddered delicately, but real concern shadowed her eyes. "Why not confront your ex-super first? Granted, he's not the most convincing witness, but he may give you a lead you can follow to something more solid."

"Do you think so?" Jenna sounded dubious, but the intractability she'd shown toward him when he'd suggested the same thing was missing, Matt noted. "Maybe you're right, Carm. I guess it's worth a try."

Okay, he didn't get it. He brought the now-full coffeepot over to the table and set it in front of them with a thump. "So why did you ream me out half an hour ago when I told you it wasn't a good idea?" he asked bluntly. "You have cream all over your bottom lip," he added, reaching over and wiping it off with his index finger. He licked the cream from his finger, spooned sugar into his mug and suddenly realized that for the first time in twenty minutes both females had fallen ominously silent.

He looked up. Carmela was watching him with an oddly affectionate gaze, her head tipped to one side, her smile trembling at the corners. Jenna's eyes were very blue and almost as round as Zappa's, but as Matt, puzzled, met them, she looked away hastily.

"What are you two—"

Before his question was out, he realized what he'd just done—and the construction that Carmela would have put on it…the only construction that *could* be put on such a casually intimate and revealingly lover-like gesture. God help him, *he* was blushing, he thought, hoping desperately that his tan covered it. Ten to one Carm would be punching out Sophie's and Tina's numbers on her cell phone before she'd even left his driveway, he told himself with a sinking feeling. They'd be cruising Filene's for sisters-of-the-groom outfits before the stores closed today.

Well…so what? He suddenly grinned at Carmela and blew her a kiss.

"Siete troppo astuti per il vostro proprio buono, sorella mia," he said ruefully.

"Too smart for my own good? So I *am* right," his sister said softly. She held his gaze for a long moment, and then her smile widened and her carmine lips pursed teasingly back at him.

"Does she have pierced ears?" Jenna asked, looking up and frowning thoughtfully. Matt didn't have a clue what she was talking about. Carmela, however, didn't miss a beat.

"Stacey? Uh-huh. I drew the line at a belly ring, but her *nonna* insisted on getting Stacey's ears done when she was still little. All the D'Angelo girls get them done young." She shrugged. "Mom's pretty traditional in some ways, and as Matt knows, you might as well not even try to argue with her when she makes up her mind about something. Why? Oh—for her birthday present?"

"I'd forgotten." Matt raked his hand through his hair. "You think earrings are a good idea?"

"As long as you let Jenna pick them out. You'd probably buy something dull and conservative, like gold studs. But somehow I don't think you'd go that route, would you, Jen?" There was bland innocence in her question, but her eyes danced with amusement as she took in her brother's houseguest.

"Gold studs? Way too unimaginative," Jenna replied seriously. She bit her lip. "Something funky but pretty that she can wear with jeans if she wants to. Maybe silver with turquoise?"

"See, bro? The woman's perfect. Hang on to her." Carmela looked down and grimaced, dusting the powdered sugar from her sweater carelessly, and rose. "I have to hustle—I've got a lecture to deliver in forty minutes. Although I make a point of walking in fashionably late, I don't want Professor Beckstein to start thinking his guest speaker isn't going to show at all."

She caught Jenna's inquiring glance. "Quantum physics," she said absently, looking as if she had nothing more on her mind than an afternoon of shopping for a new pair of designer pumps. "I've come up with an interesting new theory that should rock those old fogies back on their heels. They'll try and disprove it, like they always do, but they won't be able to. Matt, come get those boxes out of the car for me. Jen—Saturday? And I'm warning you, you'll be expected to try some of everything."

Leaving a slightly overwhelmed Jenna with a quick hug, Carmela wafted out the front door on a scented cloud made up of a mixture of perfume, expensive leather and sweet cream-cheese pastry filling. As she stood by and watched Matt lug two enormous cardboard boxes spilling over with last year's fashions onto the porch, the smile she flashed at him held a hint of mischief.

"She's the first one you ever brought home who doesn't look like an ice princess. You better not mess up, bro. Jenna might just be the best thing that ever happened to you— and that retro-male junk you pull sometimes could make her walk real fast out of your life."

"Retro-male?" Matt retorted as he opened the car door for her. "For crying out loud, you heard what she was proposing, Carm. I'm trying to protect her, that's all."

"I know, sweetie." Her eyes darkened as she searched his worried expression. "She's in real danger, isn't she?" At his slow nod, she reached impulsively for his hand, her grip tight and warm. "Matt, she's right on one thing—she won't be safe until you get that *bastardo* put away. Can you do it?"

"Yeah." He held her gaze. "I can do it, sis. I've got a personal stake in this. I guess that was obvious, though, right?" He mustered a grin and her tense grip relaxed slightly. She managed a laugh.

"Matthew Salvatore, when I walked into this house you two were in the middle of the kind of argument that either ends up with a vase flying through the air or fabulously hot make-up sex." She tossed her purse on the passenger seat of the low-slung Ferrari, lifted herself on tiptoe and kissed him perfunctorily on the mouth. "And Jenna didn't have a vase in her hand when I interrupted that extremely interesting little scene."

She wiggled her fingers at him as she got into the Ferrari, the black skirt hiking halfway up one curved thigh, but just before she started the ignition she paused, as if making up her mind about something. Suddenly she lifted the shining blunt-cut swath of hair at the back of her coat collar and fumbled with the catch of a thin gold chain she wore tucked under her sweater.

"I know you turned away from this long ago, Matt." Her words were uncharacteristically tentative, her gaze uncertain as she pressed the fine chain, warm from the touch of her skin, into his hand and closed his fingers over it. "But keep it for a while. I'd feel better if you had it."

The next moment she'd closed the car door and started

up the engine. As he watched, wincing, she pulled out of the driveway with a faint squawk of protest from the Pirelli tires, and drove off just a little more sedately than Mario Andretti.

Curious, Matt opened his palm. The chain was so delicate that it looked like one of Jenna's hairs curled against the tan of his skin, and on it was a small disk of the same precious metal, worn smooth over the years.

Even before he could make out the image stamped into the gold he knew what it was. Carmela had worn this for as long as he could remember, not even taking it off all those years ago when Zia Francesca had gathered them into her arms and told them that their father had been lost to them forever.

She'd given him her St. Anthony's medal. With a mixture of emotions that he couldn't quite define, Matt stood there for a moment, looking at it, his expression unreadable. Then he closed his palm carefully and slipped it into his pocket.

"HE'S HERE ALMOST every night—I heard him mention the place to another tenant." Jenna looked around the smoky bar with an air of repressed excitement. "How are we going to handle this, Matt? Maybe you should stay out of sight. When he comes in, I can pretend there's no hard feelings and kind of flirt with him until he's drunk and ready to spill the beans. I'll pour my drinks into a nearby plant." She wriggled uncomfortably on the red vinyl seat of the booth they were in, tugging at the hem of the black, formfitting dress she was wearing. "I'm a little taller than Carmela. Does this fit all right?"

"Just barely. And forget about drinking West under the table and then prying his secrets out of him, Jenna." Matt glanced over at the entrance and then back at her. "The man didn't look like the type to get giddy after a couple of Pink Squirrels. He's a professional drinker.''

Morosely he swallowed a mouthful of what the bartender had laughably called scotch. He repressed a shudder and wondered briefly what was happening to the lining of his stomach. Across from him, Jenna happily lifted a bright pink concoction festooned with paper umbrellas, cherries and garishly colored citrus slices to her lips.

The Liffey Tavern was an Irish-themed bar—what part of Ireland, Matt couldn't imagine. Polynesian Irish, maybe. Along with the hokey shamrocks and the shillelaghs nailed to the walls, dotted here and there were gaudy plastic leis, and the illumination in the room came from a series of electrified tiki lamps with orange shades. Jenna, in the slinky number she'd chosen from Carmela's grab bag of designer outfits, with her legs bare and her feet shoved into a pair of strappy Ferragamo sandals, didn't fit in any more than he did.

Left alone with his thoughts a few minutes later while she checked out the ladies' room, it occurred to Matt that he'd actually never seen her fitting in anywhere, so perhaps that wasn't the fault of the Liffey Tavern. But there was no denying that the other women in the place were, for the most part, older than she was. In fact, most of the patrons seemed to be on the far side of fifty, he realized as he looked around. The Liffey was obviously where the bifo-cals-and-dentures crowd went when they wanted to have a good time.

But that wasn't it. Jenna never fit in anywhere because she was a complete original, he thought suddenly, and when she was sixty herself she'd still be drawing attention. It was her attitude. *Everything* was interesting to her. Heck, she'd even gotten a charge out of that inane paper umbrella, and had actually eaten the lurid cherries, poking down into the ice of her drink with her straw to retrieve the last one.

He had to admit it, he thought as he saw her returning to their table—she looked *extremely* sexy in the black dress, even lurching as she was on the unaccustomed heels of Carmela's Italian sandals. He found himself smiling as he watched her approach, her attention distracted by the dancers who had taken to the floor when the green-vested Irish band—surprisingly good, given the rest of the bar's amenities—had started the evening's entertainment.

The band changed tempo in midsong, and a ragged round of clapping arose from the tables nearer the dance floor. Big excitement, Matt thought curiously. He caught the eye of his neighbor, a stout and balding older man wearing white patent shoes and a plaid sports jacket, and raised a questioning eyebrow.

"Maureen's going to do a number." The man nodded and Matt saw that the couples on the dance floor were slowly moving off, leaving a clear space. Jenna was craning her neck at the edge of the crowd, he noticed. "Now we'll see some dancing—she's a regular here, and she always puts on a little show for the rest of us. It's almost as good as that thing we saw on the television, right, hon?"

His wife had a severe perm and a mouth like a bear trap. She opened it just wide enough to let half a glass of beer slide down her throat, swallowed and flicked a glance over at the clapping crowd. "*Riverdance*. Maureen certainly thinks she's pretty hot stuff, but I notice she always borrows someone else's husband when she wants a partner."

Matt hid a smile. West hadn't shown, but perhaps the evening wouldn't be a total bust. Even if Jenna had been ready to leave, he would have insisted on staying a few more minutes, if only to see with his own eyes the notorious Maureen, jig-dancer and husband-stealer extraordinaire; and just then a couple returned to their table, leaving a gap in the crowd and enabling him to get his wish.

In the middle of the pocket-size dance floor stood a buxomly attractive middle-aged woman wearing a flounced electric-blue silk dress. She was about fifty-five and holding, he thought with wry amusement, though he'd be willing to bet she never admitted to it. Her hair was carefully coiffed and its copper hue had to have come out of a bottle, but as she put her hands on her hips and inclined her head to her audience it was obvious that bear-trap woman's assessment had been right—she *did* think she was hot stuff. As an expectant hush came over the crowd, she stamped her foot on the floor as if she was testing it, and Matt saw that she was wearing what looked to him like tap shoes.

''It's *you!* You—you *fraud!*''

The accusing voice rang out just as the band launched into the first bar of their song, and Maureen's opening flurry of clattering tap steps faltered and died.

Oh. My. God. A sense of impending doom fell over Matt. He knew that voice. He could see Jenna, pushing her way through the startled crowd like a linebacker, her hair crackling angrily around her head. As if he were having a bad dream, he rose to his feet and started trying to make his way through the onlookers, but by now everyone was standing and staring.

''Shouldn't you be in a *walker* or something?'' From around Matt came an audible gasp as Jenna's furious voice rang out again. ''I mean, we both *know* that you can hardly shuffle across the floor, don't we? We both know that you're too decrepit to hobble to your apartment door without assistance, so you're obviously not capable of *dancing,* are you—*Mrs. Janeway?*''

Matt was hemmed in by a solid wall of people, their faces avidly turned toward the dance floor, but he was taller than most of them and he saw that Jenna had broken through the crowd and was now confronting the woman in the blue dress. Her opponent's boldly lipsticked mouth was thinned into a contemptuous line.

"Challenging Maureen—the last woman who did that never showed her face here again," a gray-haired man beside Matt muttered worriedly. "The girl doesn't know what she's getting into."

"I don't know what you're talking about, dear."

Maureen gave Jenna a saccharine smile, the contemptuous expression no longer in evidence on her carefully made-up features, and Matt froze.

Jenna was right! He could hardly believe it, but the tone of the middle-aged redhead's voice, the sweetly poisonous inflection, even the words she'd just spoken—he'd heard them all before, in Jenna's apartment, delivered by the frail and tottering Mrs. Janeway.

"I don't know anyone called Janeway, and as for not being capable of dancing—well, that's just ridiculous. I could dance even a young chit like you into a corner." Penciled eyebrows lifted in amusement and Maureen, aka Mrs. Janeway, graciously acknowledged the ripple of laughter that greeted her sally by nodding to the audience. She suddenly dropped her arms straight to her sides and Matt heard the staccato flurry of heel-taps as she executed an admittedly impressive series of lightning-fast steps.

"Dance-off! *Dance-off!*"

The unfamiliar phrase ran through the packed room like a brushfire racing through dry grass, and apprehensive, Matt tried to get to Jenna, only to have a well-corseted matron turn and glare at him through rhinestone-rimmed glasses.

"Stop shoving, handsome." She jabbed her elbow in the ribs of the meek little man standing beside her. "Harold, they're taking bets at that table over there. Get a twenty out of my purse and put it on Maureen. Go on!''

''I don't think so, you—you apartment-thief! Take *this!*''

Jenna's face was pale and set and her hands were clenched into fists. For one terrible second Matt thought she was planning on decking Mrs. Janeway. Already he could see the headlines—''FBI Agent Charged in Brawl at Senior's Bar!''—but then he realized that she was holding her arms straight down at her sides the way the other woman had.

The designer pumps weren't tap shoes, but that didn't matter. Jenna's feet moved so fast that they turned into blurs, and it sounded as if she had firecrackers rigged to their heels. Her knees rising and falling like pistons, her body held rigid and her back like a ramrod, she moved closer to Mrs. Janeway, forcing the other woman to take a step backward.

''Harold, wait—put the twenty on the girl!'' Matt's neighbor commanded, her eyes wide behind the rhinestones. ''Put *fifty* on the girl!''

''Very—very impressive.'' Mrs. Janeway's arch tones lacked some of their former confidence, but then she rallied. ''For a novice. And for your information, dear, I didn't steal your dumpy, low-rent apartment. *Hornpipe!*''

For a plump woman she was certainly light on her feet. The electric-blue dress swirling around her raised knees, her hands resting on her hips and a few rigid curls bouncing down onto her perspiring forehead, Mrs. Janeway advanced on Jenna, stopping only inches away from her.

''I'm not only a dancer, but I've been on the stage as well,'' she said, panting a little from exertion. ''I was hired for my acting abilities that day at your apartment—and I might say, considering the short notice I had, I felt I pulled it off quite convincingly. But you'll never be able to prove anything."

"You're out of breath," Jenna said scornfully. "Who paid you to pretend you lived there?"

"I don't get it." The woman with the harlequin glasses looked up at Matt. "What are they talking about? Is this what they call performance art?"

"I'm Italian. It must be an Irish thing," he said shortly. "Here—ask Harold to put a ten on the girl for me too, will you?" He fished a bill out of his jeans' pocket and handed it to her.

"Sorry, dear—part of the deal was keeping my mouth shut." Mrs. Janeway smiled. "Tell me, did you ever find that stupid cat?"

Jenna's eyes blazed. Slowly she brought her hands to her hips. She tossed her hair back from her face.

"His name is Zappa." She stamped the heel of one foot hard. "And yes, I found him." She stamped her other heel. It sounded like a gunshot. "And I'm going to dance you into the ground if you don't tell me who hired you! *Blackbird!*"

It had to be the name of the dance she was performing, Matt thought. He watched awestruck as Jenna, moving with precision and grace and astounding speed, the short black dress climbing up those satiny thighs, came closer and closer to the older woman.

"Who hired you?" she barked. One leg flashed behind the other, her foot pointing straight down. Except for a dewing of moisture on her top lip, she seemed utterly at ease. Mrs. Janeway hopped up on her left foot a little awkwardly, raising her right foot.

"St.—St. Patrick's Day!" she puffed.

"St. Patrick's Day?" Jenna whirled like a dervish around her. "That's a beginner's dance! Who hired you?"

"I don't know his name! I never met him—he contacted me by phone and sent a messenger over to deliver my payment." As she rose again on her left foot and attempted to bring her knee up, Mrs. Janeway stumbled. A shocked gasp ran through the onlookers.

"What did the messenger look like? *Garden of Daisies!*"

On the dais behind her the fiddler changed tempo, his bow frantically scraping faster and faster, like a man playing the devil for his soul. Jenna's hair, the only part of her not under complete control, flew madly about her shoulders in an arc, nearly scything her opponent.

"*Job of Journeywork!* What did he look like?" She was inches away from Mrs. Janeway, and every time her knees flew up and her heels stamped down, she advanced a little closer. Abandoning any attempt to hold her own, by now the other woman obviously had all she could do to keep from losing her balance completely.

"I can't remember!" Mrs. Janeway had reached the outer edge of the dance floor. Behind her was a wall. Her breath was coming in gasps and she was fanning herself with her hand. "I can't remember. All I can remember is that he wore—he wore—"

She wasn't exhausted, Matt thought, narrowing his gaze. It was worse—Mrs. Janeway had been humbled before her audience, and all the bluster had gone out of her.

"He wore what?" Jenna's heels came down in one last resounding crash and suddenly she was standing stock-still in front of Mrs. Janeway.

"He was young, and he was wearing a flowered tie. That's all I can recall." Her back against the wall, Mrs. Janeway looked up at Jenna with an expression of impotent rage on her plumply feminine face. "Dammit, I wanted

West to drown that stupid cat, and he wouldn't. I should have done it myself, just to spite you.''

''I knew you were a horrible woman the first time I laid eyes on you, Mrs. Janeway. I just didn't know how horrible.'' Jenna flicked a cold glance at her defeated opponent and then turned to walk off the dance floor, but before she'd taken three steps the entire room burst into loud applause.

Watching her make her way through the congratulatory crowd, Matt felt a wad of bills being pressed into his hand, and looking down, he saw the woman in the cat's-eye glasses, her mouth pursed in a sour smile.

''We doubled our money, handsome. Guess Maureen will have to find somewhere else to strut her stuff—oh, come on, Harold.''

''Matt!'' Jenna was beside him, her face pale with excitement and her hair curling damply around her forehead. She grabbed his arm. ''Matt—we've found the link between Parks, Parks and what happened to me at my apartment. The young man in the flowered tie who paid off Janeway and West—his name's Jeffrey Barkin, and he's one of Charles Parks's junior partners!''

Matt's eyes narrowed. Glancing past her to the hastily retreating figure of Maureen, aka Mrs. Janeway, he drew Jenna to him. ''Looks like you got everything she knows out of her, but if we do need to pick her up she shouldn't be too hard to find. We'll let her go.'' His gaze hardened. ''Now that you've discovered the Barkin link, I think we just might have the bait to catch the big fish—Charles Parks.''

Chapter Ten

Waking up beside Matt D'Angelo was getting to be a habit, Jenna thought drowsily, opening one eye and peering through a tangle of hair at his sleeping face, only inches from hers. It was a habit she was quite willing to get used to. His arms were a solid weight around her, and as she shifted slightly they tightened and he murmured something in his sleep. It sounded...it sounded like "Blackbird."

She stifled a surprised snort and gently started to disentangle herself from his unconscious embrace. Her method of interrogating that horrible Janeway woman last night *had* been unorthodox, to say the least, but at the time even Matt had admitted that the result had seemed worth it. They'd come straight home, and he'd been on the phone to a friend in the Bureau within minutes, asking him to run an address check on Barkin. Moments later, he'd hung up the phone and was staring frustratedly at her.

The Barkin lead was a dead end, he'd told her—possibly a literal one. Jeffrey Barkin had been reported as a missing person by his girlfriend a few days ago, and he hadn't been seen since.

As far as she was concerned, that left only one last avenue of investigation open to them. Sliding stealthily from the warm bed, Jenna padded noiselessly out of the bedroom. As she carefully closed the door behind her, she looked back. Matt was smiling in his sleep.

She couldn't see why he was being so infernally stubborn about breaking into Parks, Parks, she thought in exasperation, plugging in the electric kettle and rummaging around in the cupboard for the box of chamomile tea bags she'd spotted yesterday. Well, to be honest, he hadn't *completely* dismissed the plan, but he'd made it pretty plain that even if *he* was contemplating a highly illegal operation that could lose him his job, *she* wasn't going to have any part in it.

She darted a look down the hall at the silent bedroom and took her tea over to the kitchen table, uncomfortably aware that her righteous indignation was more than a little forced. *Maybe he's excluding you from his plans, but isn't that exactly why you're sneaking around right now—to make sure he doesn't find out what you're doing?* she asked herself guiltily.

Jenna sighed. No, she *couldn't* share this with anyone, not even Matt—not yet, at least, even though keeping it from him was the hardest thing she'd ever done. She chewed nervously at her lip and reached for the phone. She'd grown up among people who were open and honest with one another, people who had discarded lies and pretense along with everything else that they couldn't accept about mainstream society, and ever since she'd met Matt she'd been living a lie. If he knew, he'd never be able to trust her again.

She couldn't let it go on much longer—not if she wanted any kind of future with him. Her hand shaking slightly, Jenna glanced over her shoulder again and then punched out a number that she hadn't needed to remember in years.

"Hello?" She spoke in an undertone, shielding the receiver with her palm. "Is this—is this the Sunflower Commune?"

"YOU MAY NOW kiss the bride..."

Matt bent toward Jenna as she tipped her head back, those lush lips trembling with emotion. *God*—she looked like an angel in that antique satin-and-lace wedding dress she was wearing, and the cornflowers strewn throughout her fabulous hair echoed the starry, intense blue of her—

—her *crossed* eyes?

"Ahh!" Coming to with a horrified start, he gave a shocked yell as he found himself nose-to-nose with an affronted, brown-masked face. He shot backward, trying to put as much distance between himself and the apparition as possible.

"Waaahh!" Zappa's fur bushed out and he let loose with his patented banshee wail as his cozy little nap was so rudely shattered.

"What do you do with a drunken sailor, what do you do with a drunken—"

He hadn't had a heart attack, because it was still smashing away like a pneumatic drill against his chest wall, Matt thought sourly, glaring at Zappa, who was glaring back at him. Meanwhile, Jenna was happily and discordantly singing in the shower, totally unaware that her damn cat had nearly put him into an early grave—not to mention that he'd almost gotten up close and way too personal with a Siamese—

He wasn't going to go there, he told himself firmly. It had never happened, the memory was wiped, he didn't want to think about it ever again. Zappa jumped haughtily off the bed, sat down and stuck his back leg up into the air.

Matt shuddered. Getting out of bed and detouring stiffly around the cat, he stalked to the bathroom. Billows of steam enveloped him as he entered, and behind the frosted-glass shower doors he could see a curvy silhouette moving under the spray of hot water.

"Her name was Baaaa-bra Allen," Jenna warbled. Her singing voice was nothing like the honey-and-cinnamon tones of her speaking voice, and the thought suddenly occurred to him that if that dream of his had meant anything at all, it was quite possible that he would be hearing Jenna Moon's incredibly bad singing every morning for the rest of his life.

He smiled slowly. He *did* know how to distract her, he told himself. And there were times, like when her eyes were half closed and she was holding on to him and whispering into his ear, that her voice turned him inside out.

He opened the shower door. "Shut up, honey, and stop hogging all the hot water."

With a choked-off squeak she whirled around, almost knocking him flat with the object she was holding. Her hair had been pinned to the top of her head, but it hadn't escaped the steam. Like pavé diamonds, tiny beads of moisture clung to the precariously-balanced mass of hair.

"Is that a loofah in your hand, or are you just happy to see me?" Matt drawled, knuckling his eye where a flying blob of soapsuds had landed when she'd turned around.

"I could ask you the same thing." Her body was slickly wet and flushed from the heat, but as she raised an eyebrow and looked him up and down, her appraisal was exaggeratedly dry. "Hmm...*not* a loofah. You'll have to use this one then. I can't reach my back."

Slapping a hard sea sponge into his outstretched hand, she presented her back to him; but, being Jenna, she started talking.

"I love this shower—I've never seen one so big. The acoustics make me sound like Whitney Houston!"

He opened his mouth and then closed it again. She went on.

"Just about halfway down my spine, Matt. I can reach

the top, and if I switch hands I can scrub lower, but I keep missing the middle.''

He batted her lightly on the derriere with the loofah.

''Ow.'' An astonished eye blinked at him over her shoulder.

''Honey, I'm naked in the shower with a woman. I think I can figure out what to do without the manual. Stand still.''

He grabbed the liquid soap dispenser from the hanging caddy and, shielding her from the brunt of the shower's blast, ran a line of pale green pine-scented soap down the delicate ridge of her backbone. Slowly he started to move the loofah in small circles around her shoulder blades, noting with interest that her skin immediately took on a rosier hue.

''Lean forward,'' he said, keeping his voice professionally detached. ''No, a little more and lift your arms. Yeah. That's good—don't move.''

Moving the loofah in an ever-widening circle, he brought it under the curve of her upraised arm, braced against the white-tiled wall, and traced the full swell of her breast. Creamy lather ran in slow rivulets to the tip of her nipple and dripped to the floor.

Jenna made a tiny sound of pleasure deep in her throat.

''Don't distract me, lady.'' Beneath the foamy soap her breast was pink, as if she was blushing all over, Matt saw. He took a deep breath and gently scrubbed the loofah lower. ''You needed a job done, and you came to the right man. I take my work damn seriously.'' With his other hand he held her firmly against the length of his body, the wet strands of that ridiculous topknot just brushing his jaw, and he reached around her farther, feeling the silky-soft skin of her belly.

''All work—all work and no play, though...'' Jenna's

murmur was interspersed with a little gasp. "Isn't that kind of boring?"

"Nope. I love this job, lady."

Ain't that the truth, Matt thought, sinking his teeth into his bottom lip and wondering just how long his willpower could hold out. He slipped the loofah between her open legs and scrubbed the top of her inner thighs, the pine-scented lather running all the way down to the tips of her toes.

In the enclosed shower, with water drumming all around them, it was as if they were in a steamy, torrid universe of their own. The needlelike spray pulsed hypnotically against his back, an erotic contrast to the smooth curves of Jenna's derriere snugged tightly up against his groin. As Matt let his gaze linger on those ripe curves, he felt the last of his control slip away.

He let the loofah drop to the floor.

"Are you finished?" she asked faintly.

"Just starting." His voice was hoarse and slightly strained. Did she have any idea how much she affected him? he wondered. He placed his hands on her slick wet shoulders and turned her around to face him. "Unless you had something else planned for this morning," he murmured.

She was looking up at him the way she had in his dream, but instead of flowers, glittering drops of water shimmered in her hair and there was nothing concealing those lush breasts, the flare of her hips, those legs that seemed to go on forever.

"I just want a day with you," she whispered. Even though he was standing between her and the shower, water had beaded on the tips of her eyelashes like tears. "I just want an ordinary day with you, Matt. Just for today I want to pretend that I never heard of Parks, Parks, or Castle Creek or—or *any* of it.''

He could give her that, he thought. He had some calls to make, arrangements to set up, but she didn't have to know about them. And a day with her was something he wanted, too. He touched one of the crystalline drops of water on her bottom lashes with a light finger and made it disappear. ''Forsini's for coffee and cannoli. Then we'll go for a walk this afternoon on the Common. I'll get the ingredients for my world-famous sauce, a bottle of wine, and impress the hell out of you tonight with my culinary skills, okay?''

''Okay.'' She smiled slowly. ''But feel free to impress the hell out of me right now with any other skills you might have, D'Angelo.''

Their eyes locked and time stopped. Then Matt bent his head to hers. Even as he kissed her, he was lifting her lightly off her feet, and those long, incredible legs were wrapping themselves around him...and he was moving slowly into her, all coherent thought breaking up like static on a receding radio station. Pure sensation flooded in to replace logic. He was hers. He had been made, shaped, designed...he'd been *destined* for this woman, this act, this moment. Everything that was basic male about him fitted with everything that was female about her. He felt as if he was being wrapped in silk. Tight silk. Jenna's arms were around his neck, her head was thrown back and water was running down her face, her breasts...crazily he wondered why it didn't sizzle when it finally reached the fiery tangle of curls he could feel pressing against his own dark thatch.

''Matt...I *want* you.'' The thready command was barely intelligible, but the plea in her voice was an urgently erotic signal.

He was moving with her, was part of her, he was flying,

he thought hazily as the sweet pressure built inside him; he was a burning Pegasus with her riding him straight to the core of the sun. He was...he was *shattering*...

...and an incredible eternity later each individual shattered piece of him was melting, running back together. He'd seen the heart of the sun, Matt thought disjointedly. It was Jenna. Jenna was the heat, Jenna was the light, Jenna was...

He held her to him, feeling the triphammer rhythm of his heart begin to steady and slow to something approaching normality. Her head was tucked into the curve of his shoulder, and tiny spasms were still running through her.

...and Jenna was a liar. She'd been lying to him since the day they'd met.

IT HAD BEEN as close to perfect as a day could be, Jenna thought, standing in front of the closet in the spare bedroom and riffling through the outfits she'd gotten from Carmela. Perfect would have been if she'd found the answer she'd been looking for from the Sunflower Commune, but although that hadn't happened, at least she'd been given a lead. She intended to follow it up sometime tomorrow. But right now she had other, and equally clandestine, plans.

She paused, her gaze narrowing critically on a long-sleeved black sweater. Beside it on another hanger was a pair of black linen slacks. She pursed her lips and shoved them aside. The sweater was mohair. She'd boil in it. And the pants looked a little too tailored for what she had in mind.

Aside from that furtive early-morning phone call, the rest of the day had been heaven. Her eyes softened and she leaned against the frame of the closet door, her lips curving in a reminiscent smile. When she and Matt had made love this morning...water pouring over them as if they were standing under a steamy waterfall, the way he'd so effort-lessly lifted her and held her against him, the slick hardness of his arms clasped around her hips and of his chest against her breasts…there'd been an element of sensual urgency in their joining, as if neither one of them wanted to take the time to choose a more convenient trysting place. She'd been all wrong about the man—in some areas Matt was *extremely* unconventional.

And in others he was a complete throwback to the Victorian era. She straightened and started flipping through the rest of her new wardrobe.

They'd gone out afterward as he'd promised, and she'd managed, just barely, to control herself at Forsini's, where Matt had had strong black espresso and where she'd taken ten minutes to decide on which pastry to have, while he chatted with the old Italian men who were playing checkers at one of the tables—friends of his father's, he'd told her later. They'd eyed her appraisingly from under bushy gray eyebrows, and then the strong, tanned faces had broken into smiles and they'd shaken her hand. One of the men had actually pressed her palm to his lips, and when Matt had said something in Italian, the whole table had chuckled knowingly.

"What did you tell him?" she'd asked through a mouthful of almond cream after they'd sat down. "Everything in Italian sounds so romantic and exotic, Matt."

"I told him that I'd known him all my life and I respected him like an uncle." Matt had stirred his coffee. He'd looked up blandly. "Then I said that if he didn't stop putting the moves on my woman I'd tell his wife, and he'd be sleeping alone on the sofa for the next month."

At that, she'd almost choked on an almond sliver, and he'd ended up pounding her on the back, both of them laughing.

They'd laughed a lot today, she thought, remembering. They'd gone shopping together—they'd chosen a pair of earrings for Stacey, and Matt had insisted on buying Jenna some sneakers since Carmela's care package had only included heels, heels and even higher heels—and then they'd just wandered aimlessly and happily around for the rest of the afternoon.

But even when they'd been walking through the Common, even when he'd been smiling at her attempts to coax a squirrel to eat out of her hand, she'd sensed that he hadn't lowered his guard completely. Some part of Matt D'Angelo was still on duty, and watching out for her safety.

It had been a tiny shadow on their day. She didn't want that shadow dimming even one more *hour* of their time together, Jenna told herself, pushing yet another outfit aside with more force than was necessary. After that fabulous dinner he'd made, Matt had told her he intended to run some checks on the missing Barkin himself at the office—there was still a possibility that the man had disappeared voluntarily, and if he had, Matt intended to track him down.

But for heaven's sake, she thought in frustration, zipping disconsolately through the collection of clothes—doing it Matt's way could take *days. Weeks.* She wanted this over with *tonight.*

She stopped suddenly and stared at the shapeless one-piece garment hanging in front of her. Pulling it off the hanger, she tugged experimentally at it. It was stretchy. It looked as if it might be kind of clingy. When Matt had seen her unpacking it yesterday, he'd raised an eyebrow and made some comment about Carmela obviously not having the nerve to wear her Emma Peel catsuit again after nearly sending a visiting professor from Oxford into cardiac arrest at a faculty banquet.

Jenna couldn't imagine what he'd been talking about, or

who Emma Peel was—television again? she wondered dubiously—but the term *catsuit* made her think of daring jewel thieves and cool-headed female spies. It was *exactly* right for a break-and-enter job, she thought with satisfaction.

Except she didn't even have to break into Parks, Parks. Because in the pocket of her leaf-green dress this morning she'd found she still had the back-door key to the firm's basement archives room...

FORTY-FIVE MINUTES later she was staring with impotent hatred at that same key. The stupid thing wasn't working. The stupid key wasn't working and the dumb catsuit was riding up her behind and the knitted ski-cap she'd filched from Matt's bureau so that she could tuck her hair under it had fallen off somewhere in the bushes a few minutes ago. Okay, that wasn't a bad thing, Jenna thought. It had had a goofy little bobble on the end of it and Matt was better off without it. Why did perfectly sane men seem to lose all sense of style and dignity when it came to sporting headgear?

She was standing in a sunken stairwell that smelled of leaf mold, sodden newspapers and—she wrinkled her nose suspiciously—and she was pretty darn sure somebody's dog had been down here recently, although it was pitch-black in the stairwell and she couldn't be positive. A second later she was positive.

"My new runners!" she wailed softly to herself. The key slid in smoothly and turned. "Hey!" she added in surprise.

This was the point of no return, she thought nervously, scraping her shoe against a pile of dry leaves. Up until now she hadn't done anything too illegal, and she still had the option of turning around, sneaking back home before Matt got there, and—

"—and living in fear for the rest of my life," she muttered. "I don't *think* so. All I need is one scrap of evidence tying Parks to the Castle Creek scam, and he'll be behind bars with the rest of those crooks."

Quietly she nudged the door open, waiting for alarms to go off. Nothing happened, and she let her breath out slowly. She'd thought there was a good chance that despite the security on all the other entrances to the building, this one might have been overlooked, and she'd been right. The spacious lobby, the marble staircase, the panelling in the reception areas of Parks, Parks—they were all designed to impress clients and provide a fitting setting for the upper echelon partners, like Charles Parks. But the employees' areas, where the monied clients and the bosses never went, were much more utilitarian; and the archive room in the basement was the poor relation of the building. Miss Terwilliger had given the impression that she was quite content that her little kingdom remain forgotten and undisturbed, and right now Jenna felt the same way.

"Please, God, let her pull through," she said under her breath. "Edna, I wish you were here with me right now. I bet you'd be able to put your hands on that file in two seconds."

Except she didn't have Edna Terwilliger's unerring sixth sense when it came to locating a particular file, Jenna thought despondently an hour later. She'd searched under 'Castle', she'd searched under 'Creek', she'd found Miss Terwilliger's keys and unlocked a drawer labelled 'Private and Confidential-Do Not Open'. In that last she'd found a fossilized banana and a nibbled and dessicated sandwich.

Somewhere along the way she'd also found a flashlight. She was just about to slam the drawer shut again when she saw, right at the very back, a gleam of metal.

It was a huge, old-fashioned key—obviously fitting one

of the original locks in the basement. Her heart beat faster. There was one last room down here in the basement that she hadn't searched, and it was the one she was pretty sure she'd gotten the Castle Creek file from the day her life had started to unravel. She'd tried the door—unlike the rest of them, which were beige-painted metal, this one was heavy oak—but it had been locked. Scuttling down the passageway again, she tried the key she'd just found, and the massive lock clicked open.

She stared around her in disbelief.

The room was empty—*completely* empty. All along the wall squares of less dusty areas on the floor showed where filing cabinets had stood until recently, but now there wasn't even a scrap of paper left behind. This *had* been the room where she'd found the Castle Creek file, Jenna thought, and the cabinet she'd found it in had been in that little alcove over there, where the ceiling pitched steeply down at an angle. She'd caught her hair on a nail there, she remembered.

"This room was *overflowing* with file cabinets and boxes of documents that day." Bringing the weak yellow light closer, she saw that one thing hadn't changed, at least. The dangerously protruding nail still stuck out about half an inch from the slanted ceiling, and twisted around it were two or three red-gold hairs.

"Well, that proves it." Somehow she didn't like to think of any part of herself staying in this empty, eerie room. Unwinding the fine hairs from the nail head and tucking them into her pocket, Jenna made her way back out into the passageway, carefully closed and locked the heavy oak door again.

For some reason the empty room had unnerved her. It had been too reminiscent of what had happened at her apartment and that terrible night she'd spent at the bus station, wondering if she'd fallen victim to the same delusions that had dogged Franklin for all those years. Somebody—probably Charles Parks—had the power to reshape her reality, to change her world around until she didn't recognize it anymore, to make her doubt her own perceptions.

She knew what she had to do next. She had to make her way through the darkened building, up through the lobby and the impressive marble staircase, until she reached the third floor where Charles Parks had his office. She had to go through his desk, his papers, his personal files. The chances were slim that he would have left anything out in plain sight, especially since he'd obviously made a whole roomful of documents disappear as if they'd never existed, but if there was even a faint possibility that she might find something that Matt could take to the Bureau she had to try.

Jenna took the stairs two at a time, not daring to look back over her shoulder. She knew she was being ridiculous, but even at the best of times the offices of Parks, Parks had an oppressively intimidating atmosphere. In the middle of the night, with the only sound her own footsteps squeaking along the marble floor, it was easy to let her imagination take foolish flight and imagine that he was working late in his office.

She forced herself to go on. Gathering her courage, and making her way swiftly to the third floor, she sped nervously down the long carpeted corridor to Parks's office. Covering the last few feet to his office, she silently turned the ornate brass knob and pushed the door open.

It was hard to believe that this enormous room and Miss Terwilliger's cramped quarters down in the basement could both exist in the same building, she thought, taking an awestruck step forward and looking around her.

The setting was one of solid worth. For the first time

since she'd slipped into the building, Jenna felt like an intruder. She had no right to be here. What she was doing was illegal. This was the office of Charles *Parks,* for heaven's sakes—the senior member of one of Boston's oldest and most distinguished law firms.

"It's the office of a *crook.*" Thinning her lips, she strode across the priceless Oriental rug to the desk. She'd give herself fifteen minutes and no more, she thought, flicking a glance at the polished cherry-case clock in the corner. Despite her bravado, she felt a flutter of apprehension as she hesitatingly pulled open the first drawer and shone her flashlight on its contents.

"What the heck?" Her jaw dropped in astonishment as she saw the dozens of amber plastic bottles with their white plastic caps packing the drawer. She picked one up and glanced at the label. " 'For stomach upset.' "

"The man's a hypochondriac," she muttered.

Among the litter of prescription containers were luridly packaged over-the-counter remedies for everything from hemorrhoids to skin rash, and with a disdainful sniff, Jenna slammed the drawer shut and opened the next one.

It seemed more promising at first, but after flipping for a solid five minutes through the files she found there, she sat down despondently in Charles Parks' carved and upholstered chair. Oh, for goodness sake—the man had a lumbar pillow attached to the back of it, she thought in disgust, pulling the thing out and tossing it on the floor impatiently.

As far as she could tell, the files she'd found so far contained nothing that had the remotest connection to Castle Creek Holdings. Maybe they were evidence of other shady schemes he was involved in, or maybe they were simply what they appeared to be—files that for one reason or another he took a personal enough interest in to want easily to hand.

There was a slim sheaf of papers on a newly created company—E–Z Corp.—but the names of its officers were unfamiliar to Jenna and the details of its incorporation seemed mundane and aboveboard enough. Aside from E-Z Corp., there were assorted deeds, agreements, legal memos and a couple of investment profiles on companies that Charles Parks obviously had money in.

"Matt was right. How could I have been so stupid as to think the man would keep incriminating evidence sitting in plain view on the top of his desk?" she asked herself out loud. "All I've learned is that he's stressed-out enough to have flaky skin and acid indigestion."

She picked the lumbar pillow off the floor and replaced it. She had three minutes left of her self-allotted time limit, but really, what was the use? She supposed she could look behind all the framed engravings and the oil paintings on the walls for a safe.

"And then what? Concoct some kind of explosive with Mr. Parks's laxatives, a few antacid pills and a paper clip? Maybe it's time to consider the possibility that you're not just a little offbeat and free-spirited, Jen," she muttered to herself. "Maybe you really *are* completely out of touch with reality. This whole *plan* was crazy—the best you can hope for now is that you can get out of here without getting caught."

She got out of the chair and shoved it back into position. Getting out wouldn't be hard. She was leaving everything exactly the way she'd found it, so no one would ever know that she'd been here at all. She straightened the edge of Charles Parks's appointment book and stood back, surveying the desk. Yes. He would come in tomorrow morning, sit down, jam his stupid lumbar pillow behind his back and flip open his appointments calendar, never even guessing that—

She stopped in mid-thought. Glancing over at the clock, she grabbed the black-bound daily planner and hastily flipped through its pages, scanning them too swiftly to assimilate much detail. She had a minute left. If there was any reference at all to Castle Creek, she could only pray that she'd catch it.

"Doctor's appointment, doctor's appointment, chiropractor..." Jenna's finger ran down a week's worth of dates and then jumped to the next page. "Planning commission, another doctor—yuck, proctologist—dental appointment with Dr. Borg, bar association meeting—"

She froze.

She'd found a link—but it hadn't been the one she'd been expecting. And someone had just switched on the lights in the hall outside.

Chapter Eleven

Dammit, that had been *too* close a call. Melting into the shadows, Matt backed away from the fire escape he'd been about to climb and ran lightly down the alleyway at the side of the building to the back. He ducked down behind some concealing bushes, berating himself under his breath.

He had to be losing his mind. If he'd shown up here ten minutes earlier, he would have been inside Parks, Parks right now, going through the private papers of the senior partner—who'd just walked in the front door with a couple of burly thugs who didn't look as if they were there to help him research the finer legal points of torts and contracts at this time of night.

They were muscle. Hired muscle. And both they and Parks had been in a hurry to get into the building.

If he'd even managed to jimmy open a window, Matt mused, he'd be worrying right now that he'd inadvertently set off some kind of silent alarm and that for reasons best known to himself, Charles Parks was on his way to deal with the intruder without alerting the authorities.

He closed his eyes, imagining Henderson's reaction to a phone call informing him that one of his agents had been arrested as a common thief. He would have been fired, of course. Probably he would have ended up having to ask

Jimmy, the security guard from the doughnut shop, if his firm was hiring.

Jenna was like one of those large, unstable planets that threw everything else in their vicinity wobbling out of orbit. He didn't think straight when he was with her—he took chances, he ran insane risks, he ignored his common sense. Tonight was just one example. This morning had been another.

He'd hopped into that shower with her like a damn *jackrabbit,* he thought in chagrin, and he'd checked his brain at the bathroom door. It hadn't been until later that he'd suddenly realized he hadn't even given a thought to protection.

She could be pregnant right now, carrying your child, D'Angelo, he told himself.

Jenna…pregnant with *their* child, he mused in the dark.

Who had the cradle? Carm had used it for her two, when they'd been babies years ago, and then it had been passed on to Sophie when Joey was born. Tina would have been the last to need it, he thought. When her twins had outgrown it, she must have put it back into storage to await the next D'Angelo baby. He'd ask her when—

What was he *thinking?* Matt reined in his thoughts sharply and replaced the slight smile on his face with a hasty frown.

How could he even daydream about her when he knew in his gut that she wasn't being honest with him? She was keeping some secret from him. It was obvious—as transparently open as she was most of the time, once or twice in the last day or so there had been an evasively guilty air about her. She didn't trust him. Why would he imagine, even for a moment, that there could ever be anything lasting between them?

Still preoccupied, he started to make his way around the

back of the building in a cautious half crouch. There was a fence between this property and the next, and when he'd scouted the perimeter earlier he'd seen that there was a handy gap in the boards that he could slip through if necessary. It would be better to go that way rather than risk walking into Parks and his muscle on their way out of the law firm.

There was something draped on the scrubby bush beside him. It looked like a knitted ski hat—a darn nice one, too, by the looks of it, he thought judiciously, picking it off the bush and examining it. Why would anyone toss a snappy-looking hat like this away? It had a jaunty bobble on the end of it, just like the one he had at—

Aw, hell.

"Jenna, I'm going to wring your *neck!*" he hissed, his blood congealing to ice in his veins. She'd gotten in down there, he guessed swiftly, glancing over at the half-hidden stairwell. She was in the building—most likely in Charles Parks's own private office…and any minute now Parks and his goon squad would be walking in on her.

"THERE'S NO ONE in the basement, there's no one in the lobby or in reception, and we've searched all the offices. Nada. Zilch."

From her hiding place behind the silk-covered sofa in Charles Parks's office, Jenna listened to the harsh voice. She felt light-headed with fear. There was a creaking noise and then the sound of a drawer being pulled out.

"Where's my inhaler, for God's sake?" It had to be Parks himself. She held her breath. There was an unpleasant snuffling sound and then the drawer closed again. "I'm telling you, I got the call from the security company at home. Someone's been in the building," Parks huffed in irritation. He gave a slightly British intonation to his words.

It sounded off-kilter, like an affectation he put on to impress, and behind the sofa Jenna curled her lip.

What a *fake* the man was. Everything about him was phony: from his reputation and his imaginary ailments, right down to the way he talked. He didn't even seem to have any real authority over the two men he was trying to control. She wondered how long he was intending to stay here. With any luck his less-than-enthusiastic minions would persuade him to leave in a few minutes, and after waiting a safe interval, she could go, too. She'd probably set off those darn invisible sensors again on her way out, but by the time Parks raced back she'd be long gone.

And then the only one she'd have to face was Matt.

She shifted uncomfortably. He was going to be furious, but when she told him what she'd discovered he'd be forced to agree that her caper had been worth it. On top of that, he'd have to admit she'd been right from the very start—Rupert Carling *was* alive. She *had* seen him that day in the basement of this building. Somehow Dr. Borg had falsified the identification of the body found in the wreckage of Carling's car. She didn't know yet how to explain away that tip-of-the-finger thing, except that it had to have been a mistake on the part of the Bureau.

Because nothing else made sense. Charles Parks probably *had* been involved in the Castle Creek Holdings scandal—after all, she'd seen the file, and now it had disappeared—but all that meant was that the man had a secret that made him controllable. He was the type who worked behind the scenes, who fiddled financial records, who cheated small-time investors out of their life savings...but he didn't have the bold ruthlessness to have masterminded what had happened to her these last few days.

He was Rupert Carling's puppet.

And since he was Carling's puppet, then all she and Matt

had to do to find Carling was to follow the strings that led from Parks to his master. The first place those strings led was to Dr. Borg, the dentist with the spotless reputation.

Huh! She narrowed her eyes skeptically. Despite what Matt had been told, kindly old Dr. Borg had to be in this up to his incisors—

"You know, Mr. Parks, we haven't searched this office." It was Rough-Voice, and he sounded thoughtful. "Maybe we should, just in case. Wilkes, you take the kitchenette and I'll have a quick look in the sitting room and the bathroom."

"You mean you think whoever it is could have been right here all the *time?*" The desk drawer slid open and Jenna heard Parks using his inhaler again. "My God, yes— by all means, search the adjoining rooms. Hold on a minute! The drapes—check behind the drapes, man!"

"There's no one behind the drapes, Mr. Parks. It's a damn kitchen, Davis—whadaya want me to do, look inside the refrigerator?"

Wilkes, the one with the sarcastic tone, sounded almost bored, but Jenna knew she couldn't take any reassurance from that. Charles Parks wouldn't rest now until every square inch of this office had been searched, and it wouldn't take a fine-tooth comb to find her crouched behind the only logical hiding place in the room.

Once she'd been found, she had the distinct impression that her fate would be taken out of Parks's hands. Davis and his companion weren't working for the lawyer—their lack of respect for him made that plain. No, they answered to the same boss as Parks himself, and she was pretty sure that Rupert Carling would make one of his ruthlessly swift decisions when his thugs delivered her to him.

She was going to die. Rupert Carling was alive, but nobody would ever know it, because she wasn't going to be around to tell anyone.

And she was never going to see Matt again, never going to be able to tell him that she loved him and that she'd had a dream foretelling their marriage, never going to—

Wait a minute! She sat bolt upright, drawing her legs up beside her.

Her dreams were *never* wrong. She'd dreamed of her wedding day to Matt, right down to that adorable dark-haired little flower girl. And that meant...

Well, obviously, I'm not going to be killed, Jenna thought with relieved certainty. Something was going to happen in the next few minutes to save her, or somehow she was going to escape, but she just wasn't *fated* to die tonight. It was as simple as that.

She heard Parks's wheezing into his inhaler again, and then she heard him sniffing loudly. He must drive his wife crazy, she thought in disdain. He sniffed again...and then she realized why.

"Wilkes! Davis! Get out here!" His voice had an edge of hysteria in it, but this time it was understandable. "I can smell *smoke!* Someone dial 911—there's a fire in the building!"

"Aw, for the love of... Jeez, he's right—the whole damn hallway must be on fire!" Wilkes didn't sound bored anymore, he sounded nervous. "There's smoke coming from under the door!"

"It's a setup."

Edging out around the edge of the sofa a fraction, Jenna saw the man called Davis stride over to the bank of windows and look out. He was thin, and his mouth was bracketed with two deeply grooved lines. "The damn fire trucks are outside already."

"Setup or not, that's real smoke, for God's sake. I—I've

got a phobia about fire, man. We've gotta get out of here before we burn!''

"You've got a phobia about fire." Davis's voice was flat. "That's something I'll have to keep in mind. But right now you're going to cut the hysterics and stay cool, understand? Somebody set this fire, and one reason they might have for doing that is to give the authorities an excuse to come in here without a warrant. Mr. Parks, is there anything on the premises that our…our *friend* might not want the cops knowing about?"

"Our friend." *Carling,* Jenna thought, sinking down closer to the floor. She pulled some of her hair across her mouth and her nostrils to filter the smoke that was already making it hard to breathe in the room.

"No! No, everything that could tie Car—"

"Mr. Parks." All of a sudden it was obvious that Davis was in charge. "No names. He wouldn't like it if you used his name. We're going to try to get down the hall to the fire escape. If we can't and the heroes in the big red hats have to send up a ladder, you're going to tell them that you came back to the office tonight to get some work done. Wilkes there is your driver, I'm security for when you're in the building after hours, and everything's kosher, get it? We don't want to tell them you got a call from the alarm company tonight and didn't notify the cops, because then they're going to think you've got something to hide. And you don't have anything to hide, do you, Mr. Parks?"

"No. No, I came here—I came here to get some work finished up. Please—can we just *go* now?"

"Sure. Wilkes, open the door. Mr. Parks—" Davis had slipped back into a spurious respect again. "Mr. Parks, don't forget your inhaler."

"I can't see out here! Where's the fire escape?"

Wilkes's voice was already receding, but Jenna waited a

few seconds longer before she peered tentatively around the sofa. The room seemed to be empty, but it was hard to see anything very clearly. The door to the hall stood open and in the last minute or so the smoke had thickened. Billows of it, thick, greasy and dark gray, roiled in through the open door.

She stood up, and immediately sank to the floor again, choking.

Feeling along the wall with her hand, she tried to orient herself in the foglike smoke, but with only her sense of touch to guide her, she wasn't positive she was heading in the right direction. Where was the *door?* It was getting almost impossible to breathe now, and suddenly a panicky sliver of fear ran down Jenna's spine. Had she pinned her faith, like Matt once had, on a miracle that didn't exist? Had she relied on a fantasy to protect her—a fantasy that was no protection at all against hard reality?

She heard a tiny jingling noise, and realized that her bracelet had slipped out from beneath the leg of the catsuit. All at once, along with the acrid odor of smoke, she could smell something else—a sweet, exotic scent that was at the same time familiar and reassuring.

Patchouli. Sara Moon had always mixed her own fragrances, and no matter what else she'd added to them, their base had invariably been oil of patchouli. Years after her death her favorite fringed shawl had still held the lingering perfume, evoking her presence for Jenna whenever she'd needed the comfort of the mother who'd been taken from her too soon.

Sara's here. She's here, and she's trying to tell me it's going to be all right, she thought tremulously. *She's telling me not to lose faith.*

"Jenna!"

Even as she heard the hoarse shout, the smoke started to

dissipate as if someone had turned off a switch. Just as immediately, an eddy of clean, untainted air wafted by her. It was like stumbling onto an oasis in the middle of a desert, and greedily she gulped it down, filling her lungs thankfully. Her eyes were watery and stinging from the smoke, but as she rubbed them, the world around her solidified again, the bulky shapes of chairs and tables and bookcases looming out of the last wisps of smoke like reappearing landmarks.

A pair of black rubber boots under bright yellow waterproof pant legs became visible a few inches from her nose. Before she could look higher, a pair of soot-grimed yellow-slicker arms reached down and the firefighter swung her up in his arms.

Beneath the red hat furious golden eyes blazed out of a grimy face.

She gave Matt a narrowed bloodshot glare. "You *lied.* You said you were going to the Bureau, but all the time you were intending to break into this place and look for that file without me."

"That was the plan, yeah." The relief that flickered momentarily in the back of his eyes didn't match the grim line of his mouth. "Thanks to you I had to change it at the last minute—and let's not forget you lied to me, too. Cover your face with this blanket so I can get you down the fire escape without Parks and his boys recognizing you if they're still hanging around."

"They wanted to get out of here without being seen as much as I do," Jenna said. The last part of her sentence was muffled as Matt flung the end of the silvery heat-resistant cover he had with him over her head and started down the hallway impatiently. Jenna flipped the blanket back again. "And you're wrong," she continued. "They aren't Parks's men, they're—"

"Look, I'm supposed to be a firefighter and you're sup-posed to be unconscious," he snapped, jerking the blanket into place again. "For all I know, the damn media's outside already. We don't need a News at Eleven shot of you being carted out of Parks, Parks following a mysterious fire, so stay covered. My car's just around the corner, but my cousin Vito's got an ambulance standing by to make it look good if anyone's watching."

Jenna felt him turn slightly and push open a door with his shoulder. Even under the blanket the cool night air was a welcome relief, and as she heard his boots clattering on metal she realized they were on the fire escape. She felt them descending.

"Hey, Matt—you get her out? Is she okay?"

The speaker was obviously waiting for them at the bot-tom of the fire escape, and his query was voiced in an undertone. Matt's reply was loud enough to carry.

"I found a kid up there—he musta run in to grab what he could and then the smoke got to him." Their descent ended, and Jenna realized that they had reached the ground. Matt lowered his voice as the other man had done.

"Yeah, I got her. Jenna, meet Vito, my cousin. Vito, the lump under the blanket is Jenna Moon. So what the hell happened? I said I only wanted a *little* smoke."

"For crying out loud, Matt, you call me up at the station house telling me it's life or death and you need the trucks out *immediatamente*—oh, and by the way, there's no fire yet so can I arrange one—and now you've got the nerve to complain because the *smoke* got a little out of hand?" Matt's cousin's voice held an edge of explosive anger. "If we weren't *famiglia* I'd—"

"Dammit, Vito, she was in the middle of it!"

Even through the bulky slicker the tension in Matt's mus-cles was apparent. Jenna felt his pace slow as they turned a corner and then his grip relaxed. Setting her lightly on her feet, he let the blanket fall away, keeping one arm protectively around her. With the other he lifted his hat and wiped his forehead, taking a deep breath. He shook his head and sighed wearily. "Hell, you're right. You put your butt on the line for me tonight, no questions asked. I owe you."

The family resemblance between them was in the dark hair, broad shoulders and firm jawline, but Vito was a few inches shorter than Matt and a couple of pounds stockier. His eyes, when he flashed a glance over at Jenna and then back at his cousin, were a milder brown. He looked at Jenna a second time and lifted an eyebrow, a slow smile replacing the frown on his face.

"Okay, I get it now. You're the one Tina phoned Carol about yesterday. Carol's my wife," he added, holding out his hand to Jenna. She took it, a little confused. "Tina said Carmela invited you to the birthday tomorrow night. Carol can't wait to meet you—in fact, they're all dying to meet you."

Leaning against his car, Matt was stripping out of his borrowed gear, and as he bent over to pull off one of the heavy boots, he grunted shortly. "Great. And just what did my darling sister tell everyone in this marathon of phone calls?"

"I didn't understand most of it." Vito shot Jenna a teasing glance and took the heavy slicker from his cousin. "Something about you standing in the middle of your kitchen half undressed getting reamed out by a gorgeous redhead."

"I wasn't reaming him out," Jenna protested. "And he had his *jeans* on."

"See? I told Carol there had to be some perfectly ordinary explanation for the whole story."

Vito looked over his shoulder, still grinning. The commotion at the front of the building wasn't visible from the alleyway, but the sweeping arc of the fire truck's red light flashing on and off illuminated even the concealing shadows surrounding Matt's car. He clapped Matt on the shoulder.

"You didn't need me to start a fire, *compare*—not with all these sparks flying around between you two. I'd better get back to the truck. Jenna, I'll see you tomorrow night at the party." He winked. "And hey—save room for the tiramisu Carol's bringing. You never tasted anything like it."

With a casual wave that encompassed the two of them, he trudged down the alleyway in his bulky gear, a solid silhouette against the swinging reflections of the red lights.

"You could have been killed. If they'd discovered you in that office, this time Parks wouldn't have stopped at just trying to discredit you, Jenna." Matt's voice held no anger. He sounded empty, as if the last hour had exhausted his emotions. "When I saw them arrive and realized that you were somewhere in the building, I nearly went out of my mind. I knew if I went in there after you there was a good chance Parks would panic and kill you before I could do anything."

In the shadows his eyes were dark, and the garish lights from the emergency vehicles threw the strong lines of his face into bleak relief. She'd put him through hell. The unwelcome revelation swept through her, followed by a rush of appalled compunction as she gazed at the closed-off expression on his face.

"Matt, I—" she began, but he continued tonelessly.

"You should have trusted me with the truth."

For a long moment they faced each other, Matt's posture stiffly unapproachable and Jenna, stricken with remorse, wanting to reach out to him but suddenly uncertain of his reaction. Then, turning from her, he started to open the car door.

"Come on, we'd better get out of here."

At the remote finality in his words, something inside her snapped.

"But I *did* tell you I wanted to search for the Castle Creek file—and you wouldn't even *consider* my plan. You made it clear that you thought it was just another one of kooky Jenna Moon's irresponsible ideas, so in the end I decided to handle it myself. And as for trusting you with the truth—you told me you were going to run some computer checks for a few hours at the Bureau, so what the heck were *you* doing here tonight?"

"Saving your sweet ass, that's what!" As if she'd goaded him beyond endurance, at her accusatory question Matt turned back to face her, his hand still on the car door. Although his voice was pitched low enough not to carry beyond the two of them, it was charged with the emotion he'd been repressing earlier. "Coming up with a hare-brained, spur-of-the-moment scheme to get you out of there *safely,* that's what I was doing!"

"But you came here in the first place to look for the file. Admit it—you were intending to do *exactly* what you'd told me not to do, D'Angelo. Why?"

"For God's sake—because I knew it was too damn dangerous. I didn't want you involved!"

His hair falling into his eyes, he glared at her with exasperated impatience—as if he was stating an obvious fact and couldn't understand why she didn't agree, Jenna thought, her sharp annoyance changing to a slow burn of fury. Raking his hair back he went on, not noticing her ominous silence.

"Hell, I *knew* Parks wouldn't have left anything incriminating lying around, but you were so damn sure that the only way we could catch him was by breaking into his office that I decided I'd better search it myself, just so I could convince you there was nothing—''

''Manly-man,'' Jenna said in a clipped tone, cutting through his tirade.

Caught off guard, he frowned suspiciously. ''What?''

''Manly-man,'' she said again, staring up at him coldly. She folded her arms across her chest and her expression hardened. ''Or at least, that's what I thought at first. But now I'm beginning to think it's more than that.''

''What are you talking about?''

''I'm talking about the way you seem to think I can't handle my own decisions, Matt—the way you seem to think you have to *shield* me from everything. I'm talking about the way you think you have to come riding up on a white charger to *save* me all the time. Some part of you still thinks of me as spacy and out of touch with reality, just because I don't look at life the way you do.''

''That's just crazy. Why the hell do you think I fell in love with you?'' Matt hissed angrily. ''Yeah, you see the world in a kind of a naive way, but that's endearing. It's refreshing. Sometimes I catch myself wondering what it would be like to see things the way you do.''

''I know what you mean. Sometimes I wonder what it would be like to be Zappa, and experience the world through a cat's eyes,'' Jenna said flatly. ''I'm not a darn *pet,* Matt. And I've fallen in love with you, but right now I'm beginning to think that was a *big* mistake.''

''Okay, tell me one thing,'' he demanded. ''Did you find anything at all tying Parks to Castle Creek when you were going through his files? You didn't, did you?''

''No, but—''

''That's all I'm trying to get at here, Jen.'' His voice softened. ''You see things in such a simple way, and most

of the time that's fine. It would be great if the whole world
was as direct and uncomplicated as that...but it's not.'' He
shrugged helplessly. ''Parks is dangerous and devious—far
too devious to have left evidence around for you to stumble
upon. From the start you've operated solely on instinct and
intuition.''

''But I *was* right!'' Her voice rose in outrage. ''I found
Parks's desk diary tonight. Dr. Borg is his dentist!''

''Parks has a connection to Borg?'' Matt froze, his eyes
locked onto hers.

''That's right.'' She made an impatient gesture. ''And
despite the hard proof you think you have of Carling's
death, my intuition tells me that's one coincidence too
many. Carling was hiding out in the basement of Parks,
Parks. His body was identified by Dr. Borg. Borg is linked
to Charles Parks.''

''You found all that out tonight?'' There was a strange
note in Matt's voice.

''Not only that, but I'm sure that those two men with
Parks are Carling's hired guns. Parks might think he gives
them orders, but they're definitely keeping an eye on him
to make sure he doesn't crack.'' Jenna took a deep breath.
''I'm checking out Dr. Borg tomorrow. Do you want to
work with me?''

''If I asked you to let me handle it, you'd go ahead and
confront the man on your own, wouldn't you?''

''Well, this time I'd tell you so you wouldn't come racing after me with the whole darn fire department, but yes.
Borg's the key, Matt. I'm going after him.''

''Borg's the key, and Rupert Carling's alive. But then
how did the tip of his finger—'' He shook his head. ''I
know. I've got to start thinking outside of the box. I have
to start trusting my instincts, using my intuition. Have I
been coming off like a patronizing stuffed shirt?''

"Yes, you have," Jenna said promptly. "It's endearing, as long as I don't let you get away with it for too long. So tomorrow we tackle Borg as a team?"

"That appears to be the plan." He opened the car door for her, his expression glum. "But I still don't feel good about letting you in for the real ordeal."

She glanced up sharply. "I told you, I'm perfectly capable of handling—" She saw the wry smile at the side of his mouth and stopped. "Oh. The D'Angelo gathering of the clan. Now *that's* got me nervous."

"If my mother pulls out a photo album, we're outta there," Matt said firmly as they got into the car and he started the ignition. "If my sisters start telling you the story about me on the garage roof with the balloons and a lawn chair, don't believe a word they say."

Beside him she laughed. "You thought you could fly?"

"I was a pretty naive kid." Instead of putting the car into gear, he turned to her, taking a strand of her smoky hair between his fingers and raising it to his lips. "I didn't know I'd have to wait a few decades before I met the woman who could take me to the stars." His finger moved to her mouth, tracing its outline softly. "When you were giving me hell a couple of minutes ago, did I hear you say something about falling in love with me?"

She looked at him innocently. "Would that have been just after you told me that I was crazy and that *you'd* fallen in love with *me?*"

Chapter Twelve

"Jamie O'Hara's the financial writer for the *Globe*." Pulling into the parking space that he'd spotted from half a block away and that Jenna was frantically gesturing at, Matt continued. "He's got a sixth sense about these things—he says if he held stock in any of Rupert Carling's companies he'd be on the phone to his broker right now telling him to unload."

They were on a quiet street. Midmorning sunlight warmed the brick facades of the elegant old buildings and picked out gleams of gold from polished brass mail slots and door knockers. Most of the buildings also had discreet brass plaques affixed beside their doors.

"So the Carling financial empire is tottering?" Smoothing down her skirt and impatiently shoving a renegade bobby pin into the unfamiliar and uncomfortable chignon at the back of her head, Jenna frowned. "I don't get it, Matt—why would he fake his own death when he knew it would bring everything down? That doesn't make sense."

"It would if everything was about to fall anyway. Carling's no fool, especially when it comes to money. He probably read the writing on the wall months ago and decided he wasn't going to go down with the ship." His lips tightened as he opened the car door and glanced over at her.

"A numbered account in Switzerland, a new name and identity—over the last year he must have been setting everything into place so that he could discard his old life and walk into a new one."

Despite the warmth of the day, Jenna shivered slightly as she got out of the car and joined Matt on the sidewalk. "He's been deleting himself," she said softly. "And when I recognized him that day in the basement, he knew he'd have to delete *me*."

"You and Miss Terwilliger and anyone else who gets in his way. I wouldn't want to be Charles Parks right now." Matt's voice was grim, but as he saw the shadow cross her features he put a hand on her shoulder. "Edna's going to make it, Jen. She's been moved to another room under an assumed name. Even if someone comes looking for her they won't find her."

"Another deletion. Another person who's been forced to give up their identity because of him." She looked up at him, her usually uncontrolled hair neatly hugging the shape of her head, but her eyes glowing with the commitment and the passion that Matt had come to recognize as an integral part of her. "How many lives has he erased in the past? How many people have had everything they care about snatched away from them by him? He's *got* to be stopped before he manages to disappear into another life."

They had reached the shallow stone steps leading up to the old Federal-style building that housed Dr. Borg's practice. Matt stopped, his hand on the black wrought-iron railing.

"You might have hit on something," he said slowly. "Why did Carling choose that particular method to discredit you? He's got Parks in his pocket—it would have been a whole lot easier to have planted stolen money on you and have you arrested at work. If you'd come forth with your story about seeing Carling in the firm's basement at that point, you'd just have been written off as a dishonest employee trying to make trouble for the employer who'd fired you. Why concoct this elaborate scheme to take your life away from you and make you look crazy? It's almost as if he's done something like this before.''

"Reality check, Matt," Jenna said kindly. She took his arm and nudged him toward the steps. "Like you said, it was an elaborate scheme, but it wouldn't have held up forever. Sooner or later someone would have looked into my story, but obviously Carling wasn't planning to be around by then." She raised the brass knocker and let it fall. "I was speaking metaphorically. There's no way he *literally* could have ripped someone's identity away from them before—for heaven's sake, that would mean that his victims would have spent their whole lives under assumed names, forced to—''

"Are you here to see Dr. Borg?"

The woman who opened the door was young, no more than twenty or twenty-one. Her hair was a streaky blond with darker roots, scraped tightly back and springing from the crown of her head in what looked to be a painful ponytail, secured with a purple scrunchie. Her bangs had been teased and gelled into a frozen uplift. At Matt's assenting reply she turned and trudged ahead of them into a reception area, taking her place behind an incongruously modern office module, complete with a computer, printer and telephone, which she picked up.

"I gotta go, some patients just came in. I'll call you back." She replaced the phone on the receiver and looked over at Matt. "It's an emergency appointment, right? Toothache?"

"We phoned this morning. We've just moved here and we don't have a regular dentist yet, but a friend of ours—

Charles Parks—told us Dr. Borg was one of the best, and old-fashioned enough to still see patients on a weekend.'' Jenna took the clipboard the girl handed her. "My husband was up all last night, which meant of course that *I* didn't get any sleep either. With the pain, I mean," she added, carelessly ticking off the boxes in the list of questions the receptionist had given her. Looking over her shoulder, Matt reached for the pen, but before he could change anything the blond girl had taken the questionnaire back.

"I'll buzz Dr. Borg. He should be out in a minute."

"Bladder control problems? Why would a dentist need to know that? And why did you check off yes?" Matt hissed as they sat.

"Did I? Sorry. I wasn't really paying attention to the questions." Absently Jenna picked up an outdated copy of *Field and Stream* from the table and leafed through it. "Look, Matt, it's a magazine about deer—oh no!" Hurriedly she snapped the magazine shut and tossed it back on the table.

"I'll steer the conversation around to Carling while I'm in with Borg and watch his reaction," he said in an undertone. "It's not common knowledge that he ID'd the dental work, so he won't suspect that I know. I'll just mention that the newspapers are speculating it might not have been Carling in the explosion."

"But what if he doesn't react at all?" Jenna argued. "Does that mean we just drop it? He's probably a pretty cool customer if he's tied up with Carling and Parks, and you're going to be at a disadvantage anyway. He'll have one of those big lights glaring down into your eyes—listen, if he even *looks* like he's going for the Novocaine take him down before—"

"No, Dr. Borg, this way." The receptionist grabbed the arm of the elderly man who was heading for the front door, and steered him toward Matt. "Mr.—" She peered at the clipboard. "Mr. Angel's your patient. He has a toothache." She spoke loudly, giving an exaggerated enunciation to each word. The old man in the white coat looked over at Matt and Jenna.

"Thank you, Cindy." He nodded in a courtly fashion. "Good to make your acquaintance. Mr. Angel, if you'll follow me we'll take a look at that tooth right away." He beamed vaguely at them, not noticing Matt's appalled expression and Jenna's suspiciously narrowed stare, and started shuffling out of the reception area.

"I know what you're thinking, but don't forget Mrs. Janeway," Jenna said in a low tone, watching the old dentist's excruciatingly slow retreat with a steely gaze. As soon as he and Matt were out of sight, she turned to the receptionist.

"Your boss—he doesn't go dancing at a place called the Liffey Tavern, does he?"

Cindy looked at her as if she was crazy. "Hardly. He had a hip replacement last year, and he's going in to have the other one done soon." She pulled a package of gum out of her desk drawer. "Want a piece?"

"Sure." Jenna popped a stick of sugar-free gum—it would be, since they were in a dentist's office, she thought disappointedly—into her mouth. "Maybe he just said he was going in for a hip operation," she persisted, chewing thoughtfully. "Maybe he really took off on…oh, I don't know—a Caribbean cruise or something. He probably has this secret life that nobody knows about." She laughed, as if she was joking, but her eyes were fixed appraisingly on her companion. She leaned confidingly closer, her arm bumping lightly against the computer.

Chewing her gum, Cindy picked up the little stuffed pig that had fallen from the top of her monitor and put it back.

"I wish he did have a secret life, or at least some fun once in a while. He's a nice old guy, and I'll be sorry when he retires and I have to look for another job. But since his wife died he hardly gets out at all. I guess I shouldn't say it, but if you and your husband are looking for a permanent dentist, you might want to find someone a little younger. Dr. Borg's just not up to it anymore." She glanced swiftly at the door to the surgery. "He's pretty deaf, and he's starting to forget things. You saw what he was like."

"Yeah, I saw," Jenna said woodenly. This had been a big fat waste of time, she told herself. What had Freud said? Sometimes a cigar was just a cigar? It looked as though the phrase applied here. Dr. Borg was nothing more sinister than what he appeared to be—a kindly old man who was overdue for retirement and who had coincidentally provided dental care to both Rupert Carling and Charles Parks. The operative word being *coincidental,* she thought glumly.

The little stuffed pig rolled off the monitor and fell at her feet. She picked it up and handed it back.

"He's always falling off." Pulling a length of tape from a dispenser, Cindy strapped the pig's trotters to the top of the monitor. "That should keep him there. I call him Fred," she added.

"Cute." Actually the pig was one of the least attractive toys Jenna had ever seen. It was a brilliant pink, and it had mean little eyes. Piggy eyes, she thought. But Cindy was stroking the velvet ears as if it was one of her most prized possessions.

"My boyfriend gave him to me, so I named it after him. His name was Fred, too."

What the heck was taking Matt so long? There was a hairpin digging into Jenna's scalp, and she tried unobtrusively to discover which one it was, wishing she could just unpin the whole thing. She'd only dressed up like this in case Borg had heard about her from Carling or Parks, she thought in frustration, pulling out a pin and sliding it back in again. She'd attempted to look as little as possible like her normal self, but after meeting the old dentist it was obvious her precautions hadn't been needed.

"And—and I think something must have *happened* to him, and it's all my fault!"

Shocked, she yanked her attention back to the girl in front of her. Cindy's eyes were red-rimmed and overflowing, and even as Jenna's mind scrambled guiltily to put together the conversation she'd been tuning out, the blond receptionist unpeeled Fred the pig from the top of her monitor and pressed him to her cheek.

"He just fell on the floor a couple of times," Jenna ventured nervously. Where was Matt when she *wanted* him to rescue her? she thought. "He's not broken."

The purple scrunchie shook in denial. "Not *this* Fred. My *boyfriend*." Cindy raised her head and plucked a tissue from the box on her desk. "He took off a couple of weeks ago without telling me, and I went to his place and everything's gone. My friend Tara's like, 'Girlfriend, that man's not *worth* it,' but I *know* he wouldn't have just walked out on me." She blew her nose loudly.

Putting her hand on Cindy's shoulder, Jenna sat on the edge of the desk, feeling a pang of compassion for the unhappy girl in front of her. Bright pink polish covered the bitten nails digging into the stuffed pig, and although she was wearing white, vaguely nurselike shoes, in the corner by a plastic carrier bag and a glossy magazine sat a pair of pink-laced sneakers. She took public transit, she had to work on Saturdays and she was still trying to look pretty for a man who'd dumped her, Jenna thought. She looked closer. It was a bridal magazine.

"Your friend's probably right, but if you're worried, you

should go to the police. Or you could check with his work. He wouldn't have quit his job, would he?''

She'd meant it as a helpful suggestion, but for some reason, at her words Cindy darted a frightened glance up at her, dabbing hastily at her red eyes and putting Fred the pig back on the top of her monitor.

''I can't go to the police and I don't—I don't think it would be such a good idea to try to get in touch with his work,'' she said, shaking her head firmly. ''I don't know why I told you all this anyway, Mrs. Angel. You must think I'm some kind of weirdo, unloading my problems on a complete stranger.''

''Call me Jenna. And I don't think you're weird at all— who wouldn't be upset, losing someone they cared about? Maybe you don't want to hear this, Cindy—but have you thought that he might have been in a car accident? Or something might have happened to him on the job—that's why you probably should contact his employer.''

Again, the reaction she got took her by surprise. The blood draining from her face, Cindy jerked her head up and stared at her, her uplifted bangs a jaunty contrast to the fearful expression in her eyes.

''Who *are* you? Who sent you here? Look—I haven't told anybody what I did, and I won't. You don't have to worry about me, okay?'' Her fist went to her mouth suddenly. ''What you just said about a car accident—it *was* him, wasn't it? Oh my God—I helped you people *do* it!''

''It could be bruxism. That's grinding of the teeth, especially while you're sleeping.'' Dr. Borg's mildly lecturing tone drifted out of the surgery as the door opened. ''It can cause an ache. If you find yourself clenching your jaw a lot, you may be carrying that tenseness over into your sleep, Mr. Angel.''

''Please—I *promise* I won't go to the police,'' Cindy

said in an undertone. "I don't really know anything anyway, right? I mean, I got a couple of patients' charts mixed up, big deal. It's not something I'm going to report, and if I did I'd probably be charged as an accessory or something, so I've got just as much to lose as anyone. I just want to know for sure—was it him in that explosion?"

"The *bodyguard!*" Jenna stared at Borg's receptionist in shocked comprehension. "He was Carling's *bodyguard,* wasn't he? The one who disappeared after the bombing— he was your *boyfriend!*"

"For a young man you do seem far too tense. The body is a delicate instrument, Mr. Angel—every component affects the whole. Your teeth are in superb condition, but..."

Jenna spoke quickly. "Cindy, I'm not from Carling and I'm not here to threaten you—but if you had anything at all to do with this you're in danger. People are disappearing. My—" she decided not to take the time to explain their subterfuge "—my husband's with the FBI. He can help you, but you have to tell the authorities what you did. We'll take you to the Bureau right now and you can give a statement."

"You're not one of *them?*" Cindy shot an apprehensive glance toward the door to the hallway where Dr. Borg and Matt could be heard slowly approaching. "He's with—he's with the FBI?" She swallowed. When she spoke, her voice was an anguished whisper. "Fred had a record. I knew that, and I didn't care. But when the thin man showed up and told me Mr. Carling wanted to help Fred get a clean start, I thought—I thought..." She broke off, her eyes squeezing shut and the purple scrunchie shaking. "He was going to give him a whole new identity—new driver's license, new social security, new everything. He said Fred was a good employee and he shouldn't have to pay the rest of his life for a few mistakes he'd made when he was a crazy teenager. It seemed kind of odd, wanting to change even his dental records, but I told myself they were just being thorough. The thin man—Davis, he said his name was—he told me that the plan wouldn't work unless there was nothing left to identify Fred at all. So I stayed late one night and switched all the information from Mr. Carling's dental chart over to Fred's, and then about a week later Dr. Borg was called in to ID the—the—"

She stopped, unable to continue. Jenna put her arms around her. "And Dr. Borg relied totally on the charts," she hazarded, finishing the other woman's confession for her. "They knew he wouldn't suspect anything as long as the paperwork matched up. We need you to give a formal statement, Cindy."

"I know. I guess I've always known I'd have to tell someone sometime." Her voice was dull and lifeless. "Dr. Borg closes at noon on Saturday. I could meet you outside in about half an hour."

"…and of course, flossing is our number-one weapon against gingivitis. The war against plaque never ends." Dr. Borg had finally made it to the reception area, Matt beside him looking numb. Cindy bent her head over the computer keyboard. "Just our usual examination fee, Cindy," the old man said. "Mr. Angel's teeth are in perfect condition. Do we have any of those sample toothbrushes left?"

"That's okay, I've got—" Matt sighed as Cindy pushed a cellophane-wrapped toothbrush across the counter at him. He handed her some bills and waited while she silently counted out his change. "I'll remember what you told me about the grinding, Dr. Borg," he said through gritted teeth. "Honey, shall we go?"

His grasp on her arm as they made their way to the door was like a death grip, and once outside he hustled her down the shallow stone steps at a trot.

"God, I feel like scarfing down a couple of caramel apples and a quart of chocolate milk and then going to bed without brushing," he muttered. "Here, put this in your purse."

He thrust the complimentary toothbrush at her and Jenna took it automatically. It was a child's brush, with a smiley-face on the handle. On the back it said, I'm a Member of the Happy-Tooth Club!

Matt didn't look as if he'd joined the club. "There's no way he's in cahoots with Carling. I'm sure he was a top-notch dentist once upon a time, but he just kept going on and on about teeth and gums and then he brought out some pictures of periodontal disease." He winced. "I've seen my share of crime-scene photos, but nothing as gruesome as—"

"The receptionist's boyfriend was Carling's driver and bodyguard," Jenna said. "Borg wasn't in on it, she was. She's agreed to give a statement."

He stared at her, his keys in his hand. Then he shot a quick look down the street. "Get in the car. We can't talk out here on the sidewalk."

As soon as they were in the Taurus, Jenna kicked off her shoes and started pulling the bobby pins out of her hair.

"She's got this stuffed pig on her monitor," she mumbled around a mouthful of pins. "His name is Fred. He's really ugly but—"

"Just the facts, Jen." Matt's jaw tightened.

"No, *not* just the facts, Matt." Pulling the last pin from her hair and shaking it loose, she turned to him. She could feel a prickle of tears behind her eyelids. "The facts don't tell the whole story. There are real people involved in this—people like that poor girl in there with her *Modern Bride* magazine and her purple scrunchie and her stupid pig and—and—"

He gathered her into his arms and pulled her to him. She pressed her face against his chest. "It's like what he did to Miss Terwilliger—what he did to *me*. We're just ordinary people, Matt—our lives aren't glamorous and exciting, but we *like* our ordinary lives and our daydreams and the work that we do or the friends that we have. And he rips it all away from us because he's wealthy and he's corrupt and he—he's—" She raised her tear-stained face, her sobs subsiding and the soft cornflower blue of her eyes suddenly hardening to a brilliant sapphire. "He *destroys* people. I'm going to destroy *him*."

"We'll bring him down, Jen." His hand, roughly tender, smoothed her hair and his gaze searched her face. "We'll get Cindy to the Bureau and they'll take it from there."

"That's not *good* enough. Even if the Bureau believes her, even if they find Carling and bring him to trial, what then? He'll end up hiring lawyers a lot slicker than Charles Parks and keep throwing money at them until he walks away a free man. He deserves—he deserves to be *deleted*, Matt." She saw his expression and flushed defensively. "For the first time in my life I'm facing facts. You can't fight someone like Rupert Carling with your eyes blissfully closed!"

"Yours were *always* wide open, Jen." He contradicted her without a second's hesitation. "You saw everything and everyone. Nothing escaped you—not a lonely waitress in an all-night coffee shop, not a couple of tough working girls who became your friends, not Cindy just now. You saw them—really *saw* them—and they knew you were seeing deeper than anyone else had ever bothered to before. You saw what they wanted to be, what they could be." He cleared his throat. His eyes were brilliant with emotion. "You saw that in *me*."

"But you said it yourself—the way I was brought up

didn't prepare me for real life. I've got to toughen up, become harder.''

"For crying out loud. I've been wrong about everything else so far, Jenna!'' he snapped, his tenderness suddenly turning to irritated chagrin. "I was wrong about that, too. Under that cream-and-caramel exterior you're as tough as rawhide, and I've got the scars to prove it.''

She stared at him, taken aback by his sudden outburst. "Tough? Like in I push you around? That's just not—''

"Please. Carmela knows it. Vito knows it. My whole damn family must know by now that Matt—the conservative one, the cautious one, the slightly stuffy D'Angelo— went out and found himself a wildcat who tells him off and drives him crazy and who's the best thing that ever happened to him.''

A corner of his mouth rose in a reluctant smile. The golden-brown eyes met hers. "Don't think you have to change to take on the world, Jenna. Don't let Carling do that to you.''

"That's what Franklin used to say,'' she said softly. "He always told me that love was the strongest weapon and the surest shield. I'm—I'm glad you didn't let me forget that, Matt.''

"He sounds like he was a great guy. I wish I could have known him.''

She gave an odd little shrug, and turned her gaze to the brick building where the old dentist had his office. "He was an ex-hippie. He also used to tell me that velvet Nehru jackets were a groovy look for a guy. Isn't it noon yet?''

Her question was abrupt, as if she wanted to change the subject. He looked at his watch with a frown. "It's quarter past. Borg's probably just puttering around in there, but where the hell's—''

"Cindy! Matt, something's *happened* to her!'' Without

taking the time to put on her shoes, Jenna leaped out of the car and sped down the sidewalk and up the steps, her linen skirt hiked up high enough for her to run, Matt catching up to her as she burst through the brass-trimmed front door and into the reception area.

There was no one sitting at the desk, and as Jenna rounded the corner of the module she saw that the magazine and the sneakers were gone. The white nurse shoes looked as if they'd been hastily tossed under the desk in their place.

She turned to look at the monitor, knowing what she'd see—or what she *wouldn't* see, she thought with a sinking heart.

"The stupid pig's *gone*. Cindy's skipped out on us!"

Her appalled gaze met Matt's, and for a moment she had the ridiculous notion that *he* might vanish at any moment. Everything and everyone else had, she though fearfully. Why not him?

He'd stood beside her from the start, whatever his opinion of her theories had been. He'd been the one constant reassurance throughout this whole nightmare—and suddenly Jenna realized that she could bear losing anything else, as long as he never disappeared from her life.

"She can't have gotten far." There was raw frustration in his tone, but as his keen glance searched her features he covered the distance between them and tipped her chin up, his face only inches from hers. "Don't look so worried, Jen—it's not the end of the world. We've finally got some solid information to pass on to the Bureau, and with any luck Cindy'll be picked up at the nearest bus station or—"

"It's like I said." Her voice rose, a thread of panic pervading her words. "Carling makes people disappear. He doesn't even have to try—they just aren't *there* anymore. When is he going to take *you* away from me?"

"He's not. He can't." Matt gave her a little shake. "If that's what's frightening you, forget it. All the Rupert Carlings in the world couldn't make me walk out on you, Jenna."

"But—"

He laid a warm finger against her lips. A corner of his mouth lifted wryly. "God, you're an argumentative woman. Don't you get it? The only person who can make me leave is you. So unless you're getting tired of me, I'm afraid you're stuck with me." He kept his eyes on hers a moment longer, as if to make sure her concerns had been allayed, and then he slipped his arm around her shoulders. "Come on, let's get out of here before Borg hears us and dashes in."

His feeble joke had the desired effect, and as Jenna proceeded him down the steps to the car her spirits lifted and she felt her earlier irrational fear subside. If the only person who could make him walk away was *her,* she thought, then she had nothing to worry about.

Nothing, she told herself firmly, at *all.*

Chapter Thirteen

"And so I'd like to propose a toast."

Carmela and Frank Tucci's massive mahogany dining table, candles and flowers grouped along its damask-draped length, had finally been cleared of the numerous chafing dishes and platters and tureens that had covered every inch of it during dinner. In the warmth of the room, filled with D'Angelos and assorted relations, Matt had long since shucked the jacket to the lightweight gray suit he was wearing, but even in shirtsleeves and suspenders there was an air of traditional formality about him as he stood at the head of the table and raised his glass.

"To Stacey—yet another gorgeous D'Angelo heart-breaker. I hear your papa's going to let you start dating in another four or five years, right, Frank?"

Carmela's husband shook his head firmly and the whole table laughed. Matt went on.

"Stacey, *cara,* you've just turned sixteen...but you've been sweet since the day your mama brought you home from the hospital and let your uncle Matt hold his very first niece in his arms."

"To Stacey!"

"To Stacey!" Jenna echoed the toast a little shyly as everyone touched glasses and drank.

"And since we're all together tonight, it's only right we also toast the whole family. *A la famiglia!*"

Once again the table enthusiastically joined in, but before anyone could raise a glass, Maria D'Angelo, trim and attractive in a dark silk-knit suit, a fine gold necklace and a wedding band her only jewelry, tapped her glass with the back of a dessert spoon imperiously.

"*Silenzio!* Silence!" The room fell quiet. She smiled, her still-beautiful eyes flashing. "It occurs to me that Jenna doesn't speak Italian—my son, I'm sure, has whispered a word or two in her ear at appropriate times—"

"*Sì*, Mama—I'm male, and a D'Angelo. What do you think?" Matt, still standing, shrugged as knowing laughter greeted his words. His grin, as he met Jenna's gaze, was wry.

"But she may not understand how we translate *famiglia*—family," his mother said in a softer voice. She looked across the table at a slightly pink-cheeked Jenna. "*Famiglia* is the family, but to us it's more than that. It means the ones we love, and the ones we hope will be with us for many family celebrations to come. When we make a toast *a la famiglia*, you are part of that, too, Jenna. So—to family!"

Glasses were raised all down the length of the table, and in the hubbub of talk and laughter that followed the toast Jenna looked up and saw Matt watching her. He smiled and reached for her hand.

"Overwhelmed?"

"A little." She liked the unselfconscious way he was touching her. "But it's nice. You're lucky, Matt."

He didn't pretend not to understand her. "Growing up a part of all this? Yeah, I'm lucky and I know it. Sure, we have our fights and our disagreements, but nothing ever breaks that bond of total trust. Any one of us knows that we're all here for each other, no questions asked.''

Total trust. She raised her wineglass and took a hasty sip. Around them a wave of laughter swept the table as Vito told a joke.

''Your boss, Henderson—he doesn't intend to throw a lot of manpower into finding Cindy, does he? Not on my word alone,'' Jenna asked. Matt had told her on the drive over to Carmela's house that Henderson had grudgingly sent an agent to check the bus terminals after Matt had reported Cindy's hasty disappearance. A woman matching her description had been seen boarding a bus bound for Albuquerque, but that lead hadn't been followed up yet.

He looked away uncomfortably, his strong fingers tracing the rim of the delicate crystal. ''He's told me to drop what he calls this 'Carling obsession.' He asked me if I wanted another couple of weeks off—unpaid.'' He saw her stricken expression and shrugged. ''I told him I had some personal time coming to me anyway. It was the apartment thing, Jen. He's never been able to see past that, and he still thinks you're some kind of—''

''Kook,'' she finished for him flatly. ''Carling's plan to discredit me worked perfectly. I guess all we can do now is try to trace Cindy ourselves and hope that he doesn't vanish for good before we find him.'' She saw the shadow that crossed his face, and her own fingers tightened on the stem of her glass. ''What is it? What haven't you told me?''

He sighed. ''Jamie phoned me while you were getting dressed this evening. I was going to tell you tomorrow. It seems that when he was supposedly killed by that car bomb, Carling's software company was in the middle of negotiating a merger. It's been delayed, but now that things have settled down it should be going through early next week. I don't know how he's rigged it, but I'm guessing he's waiting for the deal to be finalized so he gets one last massive influx of currency to take with him. With Parks on board, he's probably set up some phony investment company as a front, but the actual money will go into his own pocket in the end. We don't have much time, Jenna."

"He's going to pull it off. He's going to get away scot-free, and he's never going to stand trial for his bodyguard's murder or the attempted murder of Miss Terwilliger or what he did to me." Jenna's face looked frozen, her lips hardly moving as she spoke. "And you've been labeled as the agent with the 'Carling obsession'—Matt D'Angelo, who tossed away his career for a crazy woman."

"And who'd do it all over again tomorrow without a second's thought," Matt said seriously. He reached over and cupped her chin, running his thumb along the corner of her mouth. "*Cara,* we've got a couple of days, at least. Don't give up hope just yet, and don't let that bastard overshadow everything good that we have. Tomorrow we'll be back on his trail, but let's reserve tonight for ourselves. Deal?"

It took a moment, but finally the troubled look faded from her eyes and her lips curved into the ghost of a smile. "You're too much, D'Angelo," she said softly. "What exactly comes with the deal?"

"Me." He looked affronted. "What more could a woman want?"

"Some of Carol's tiramisu, for a start," she said promptly. "Although that birthday cake Carmela's bringing in right now looks fabulous. Do you like your women a little chunky, Matt?" she asked with a sudden frown.

"I like my women luscious," he said, a trace of huskiness in his voice. "That's why I had to wait until I found you."

"Good. That means she can try a little of both, bro."

Looking up, Jenna met Carmela's amused gaze, and she felt herself blushing. "I was just saying it all looks so good I don't know what to try first," she said weakly.

"Funny, I thought that's what my brother was saying." Carmela's eyes danced, and then she relented. "Look at the birthday girl over there. She hasn't taken those earrings off since you two gave them to her."

"I'm glad she likes them. The silver looks pretty against her hair." Jenna smiled as she glanced over at Stacey, who was cutting a slice of cake for a cousin and licking chocolate frosting from her fingers. "That's Tina's son, Domenic, right?"

"He's a handful. In a month or so he'll be a teenager, too." Matt's sister laughed. "Over there's my Marco, the taller one in the suit—he's going to make some hearts flutter in a few years, isn't he?" She beamed proudly and then went on. "The little guy with the big plate of ice cream is Sophie's Joey, and sitting there on Vito's lap is Trish, the only blonde in the group. Carol says all the females in her family are born with that pale wheat-colored hair."

Jenna drew her brows together in a crease. "But isn't there another girl? Doesn't Matt have a niece with dark hair and big brown eyes?"

It was silly, she knew, but all of a sudden she felt a tiny, unsettling doubt. The little flower girl in her dream—the dream she'd been so sure had been a glimpse into her future—where was she? *She's not here,* an unpleasant voice said inside her head. *She's not here because she was only a figment of your imagination—and the dream was only a dream, not a premonition. It was what you want to happen, not necessarily what will happen.*

She reached up and laid her hand on Carmela's arm, the diamond-studded bracelet the other woman was wearing feeling cold to her touch. "Carmela, am I right? Doesn't Matt have another niece?"

"Domenic's sister, Diana." Carmela smiled. "She must be who you mean—she's a charmer, big eyes and curls past her shoulders. Tina asked Mrs. Natale to stay with her tonight. She's just getting over the flu, and Tina thought the party would tire her out too much."

A ridiculous feeling of relief swept through Jenna, and as Carmela moved away and Matt refilled her wineglass, she let herself forget everything else and enjoy the unfamiliar but warmly welcoming feeling of being part of a large and loving family. Stacey, alight with excitement and happiness, hugged them once again for her birthday present, Carol promised to give her the recipe for the tiramisu and hours later when the party was breaking up and everyone was clustered by the front door saying their goodbyes, Maria D'Angelo took the opportunity to draw Jenna aside.

"Carmela told me I would fall in love with you at first sight. She was right," she said simply. As elegant as her daughter, her patrician features might have seemed slightly intimidating but for the affectionate gleam in her eyes and the fine laugh lines that accentuated her smile. "I always hoped my son would someday find a woman who could give him the same fire and passion that his father and I had in our marriage. Now I think he has."

Swiftly she leaned over and kissed Jenna on the cheek, and then, looking down, she broke into a delighted laugh. "All night I've been hearing little bells—I thought it sounded like angel music. It's your ankle bracelet."

"My mother's. I've worn it since she died," Jenna said, feeling as if she could tell this woman anything.

"And this was my Salvatore's." Matt's mother touched the gold chain around her neck, and for the first time Jenna noticed the slightly darker gold medallion strung onto it.

Maria saw her glancing at it. "St. Anthony. He finds what has been lost."

"Yes. Matt…Matt told me," Jenna said hesitantly.

"Ah. Then he must also have told you he believes St. Anthony failed him when his papa died." A shadow crossed the elegant features. "Perhaps one day he will understand, as you and I do. The angel bells you wear—they remind you of your mama, *sì?*"

"They bring her close to me every time I hear them," Jenna said softly. "They make me feel as though she's still with me, even though I can't see her."

"And she is. As my husband is with me always." Maria gently touched the medal with a perfectly manicured fingertip. "You see, St. Anthony didn't fail. My Salvatore was never lost to us—not as long as we still love him and remember him." Despite her smile there was a shimmer of moisture in the velvety brown eyes. "But I still miss him very much. He was my *destino*—my destiny."

Their gazes locked in a moment of perfect understanding. Impulsively Jenna reached out and gave the older woman a hug and for a second they embraced, the fiery-red mane of hair spilling against the smooth brunette chignon.

"I understand that, too," Jenna whispered.

"*Nonna,* I want a hug!"

Little blond Trish was scowling drowsily up at them like a disgruntled angel, her arms held out and her face creased from where she'd been sleeping against her father's shoulder for the last hour. The two women looked down at her, laughing, and then Maria stooped down and swung the little girl into her arms.

"And one from Jen, too!" Trish added firmly.

Amid laughter and hugs and with every member of Matt's family coming over to Jenna to give her a warm goodbye kiss, she and Matt finally made it to his car. Jenna

waved to the gathered D'Angelos in the driveway until
Matt finally turned the corner of the quietly monied avenue
where his sister and brother-in-law lived and the luxuriously sprawling Tucci residence was out of sight. Sitting
back in her seat with a sigh she looked over at him in the
dark as he drove. The headlights from oncoming cars illuminated the relaxed set of his mouth and emphasized the
tough angles of his face.

He was right, she thought, letting her lashes drift down
onto her cheeks and feeling a pleasurable weariness steal
over her. Finding Carling and bringing him to justice was
important, but it couldn't be allowed to overshadow everything else in her life. She could smell the faint scent of the
pine soap that he used, and suddenly she didn't feel ready
for sleep at all. For *bed,* maybe, she thought. Snuggling
under Great-Aunt Lucia's velvet-and-brocade spread with
Matt and feeling his hands on her and his mouth covering
hers would be a perfect way to end the evening.

Rupert Carling had tried to destroy her life. Instead, he'd
inadvertently helped her find the other half of her soul. If
she ever met the man again, Jenna decided, she would tell
him that. She would let him know that even with all the
power of money and determination behind the darkness he
had taken for his creed, love had proven to be the stronger
force by far.

The universe is unfolding as it should. Sara Moon's favorite expression held an indestructible truth; one that no
Carling could ultimately subvert. Jenna could even find it
in herself to feel faintly sorry for the man. Had he ever
known love? she wondered idly. Had he ever looked up
from his pursuit of fortune and domination long enough to
connect with another human being? Perhaps he had, she
thought, frowning a little. When he'd encountered her in
the hall that one time, for a split second there had been an

oddly incredulous look on his face—incredulous and somehow searching, as if she reminded him of someone he'd known and lost long ago.

And now she really *was* going crazy. She pulled herself up sharply as Matt swung the Taurus onto his street and looked over at her with a smile. Rupert Carling's softer side, if he'd ever had one, certainly hadn't been roused even momentarily by running into her. Within hours he'd attempted to arrange a fatal accident for the stranger he'd run into in the basement of Parks, Parks.

"Midnight snack time," Matt said as together they walked companionably to the front door and he fished his house keys out of his pocket.

Jenna looked at him, appalled. "Honestly, Matt, I'm stuffed! I won't even be able to look at a darn grapefruit for a couple of days, at least."

"Not for us. For them." Pushing the door open and standing aside to let her enter, he lifted a resigned eyebrow as Zappa and Ziggy, their meows sounding more like sobs, stampeded down the hall to meet them.

"I'll open up a can of tuna feast—but I'm well aware you guys are blackmailing us." Slipping off her shoes, she padded ahead of him into the kitchen. She shot the two brown-masked faces at her feet a dirty look. "You're perfectly capable of keeping us awake all night with that noise, aren't you?"

"Actually I was planning on keeping you awake myself." Matt tossed his jacket over the back of a chair and stood behind her as she reached on tiptoe for the can of cat food in the cupboard. His arms went around her waist. "I thought maybe it was time for another Italian lesson, *cara.*"

Jenna leaned back against him and then gave a little jump as the phone rang on the counter beside them.

"It's probably Carmela, making sure we got home all

right.'' Matt reached for the phone with one hand, the other still lightly clasped around her holding her close. ''She's a worrier.''

As he picked up the receiver and spoke into it, Jenna smiled to herself. Dexterously she positioned the cat-food can in the electric opener and watched it neatly cut through the lid. She was getting good at this, she thought smugly. She no longer felt like a temporary guest in this house— she felt as if she'd come home.

''Yeah. But, Jack, are you—''

On the phone behind her, Matt fell silent, releasing his hold on her and raking his hand through his hair. It obviously wasn't Carmela, Jenna thought, glancing over at him. He flicked an unseeing look at her and then spoke again.

''Well, run it again, dammit!''

His voice was harsh. Swiftly she set the plates of food down for the cats and watched him apprehensively, a feeling of foreboding uncurling slowly in the pit of her stomach. He closed his eyes and rubbed his temples as if he was in pain.

''Sorry, Jack. It—it came at me from left field, that's all. Yeah, definitely not something I was expecting. Okay. Thanks.''

Slowly he hung up the phone. Without looking at her, he simply stood there for a moment, his head bowed. A muscle twitched at the side of his jaw.

''I knew you weren't being honest with me. But when I realized you'd intended all along to break into Parks, Parks, I thought that had to have been your secret.''

His words were barely audible. In fact, he sounded as if he was talking to himself more than to her, Jenna thought. He certainly didn't seem to expect a response, and when she spoke he didn't even look up.

"That was someone from the Agency, wasn't it? You had them check into me."

She felt behind her for the edge of the counter and grasped it tightly. She was finding it harder to breathe here in this quiet, familiar room than she had in the midst of Parks's smoke-filled office, she thought light-headedly.

"I'd forgotten I'd even asked Jack to run your name." Matt gave a short laugh that held no humor. "It was just after the Terwilliger incident, when I'd learned that the Bureau had clinched the identification of Carling's body. I thought the more information I had on you the faster I could figure out who was targeting you and why."

He raised his head. The golden-brown eyes were unreadable. "Why did you lie to me? Was *anything* that you told me true?" His mouth tightened. "My God—Henderson was right all along. I fell for this whole Carling wild-goose chase, hook, line and sinker, didn't I? Tomorrow we were going to scour the city looking for the elusive Cindy, who so conveniently confessed everything to you, and *only* you."

He was looking at her as if he didn't know her at all, and Jenna's heart sank. She *had* lied to him, and right from the start she'd been afraid he'd find out. *Total trust.* She recalled his words from earlier in the evening and closed her eyes, squeezing back the tears that threatened and desperately searching for a way to make him understand.

He'd found out that Franklin was alive, of course.

"I wanted to tell you, Matt—" she began. He cut her off impatiently.

"No more lies, okay? Just tell me *why*. Are you running some kind of scam yourself—is that it?"

She'd known if he ever found out, he'd feel betrayed that she hadn't told him the truth, but there was something disproportionate about his reaction, she thought. He didn't even *want* to hear what she had to say.

"Of course I'm not running a scam," she said with a trace of defensive heat in her voice. "And you *know* the Carling investigation isn't a wild-goose chase—just what kind of a person do you think I am?"

"I don't know." He looked at her emotionlessly. "Ten minutes ago I would have said I knew you inside out— who you were, what you cared about, everything about you. Now the only thing I can say for sure is that I never knew you at all."

"But you *do* know me! I'm still the woman I was ten minutes ago, Matt!"

There was something terribly off-kilter about this whole scene, Jenna thought fearfully. They were standing there, facing each other—close enough to reach out and touch each other—and yet it was as if a chasm was opening up between them, widening faster and faster.

They were *losing* each other, she thought with a flash of pure terror.

"I admit I lied to you—"

"I could have accepted one lie! But why the hell did you have to carry it so *far,* Jenna? *Why did you pretend to fall in*—" He stopped suddenly, an expression of self-disgust flickering across his features. "I keep forgetting—even the name's false, isn't it? There *is* no Jenna Moon. I just about fell in love with a woman who doesn't exist."

Chapter Fourteen

Agent Matt D'Angelo was back on track, but no one at the Bureau field office was foolhardy enough to ask him any questions about the Carling fiasco. One look at his grim face as he strode from Henderson's office to his own was enough to daunt even his closest acquaintances.

"No calls, Pam," he said to the secretary as he passed by her desk without slowing down. "And I mean none, *capisce?*" He disappeared into his office, slamming the door behind him.

Half an hour later Matt tossed the Bradley file over his shoulder and called up the solitaire game on his computer. After losing six games in a row he switched to Sub-Hunter and bleakly watched his destroyer sink beneath the waves without a trace.

She'd looked at him with those fabulous blue eyes, and those lush lips had kept on insisting that she had no idea what he was talking about. He grimaced. When he'd arrived this morning Jack had unobtrusively handed him the printed-out results of the check he'd run—the four checks he'd run, Matt corrected himself. There was no doubt about it—he could put Jenna's name through the system himself a hundred times if he wanted to, and the results would come back the same.

She didn't exist. She'd never existed. There never had been a woman called Jenna Moon.

At one point he'd thought she was going to come clean—hell, she'd gone so far as to *admit* that she'd lied. But then she'd started playing games again; feigning complete bewilderment, telling him that there had to be some mistake, and finally telling him that he was the one who was crazy. She'd almost convinced him, too.

Almost, but not quite.

Why had she done it? Obviously he couldn't rely on anything he'd thought he'd known about her, but he was willing to swear she wasn't what he'd thought at first—a complete flake with no grasp on reality. No, Jenna Moon—aka probably a dozen other aliases, he thought in frustration—was as sane as he was. Maybe saner, he admitted. He was about to go out of his mind trying to figure out what had been behind her little charade.

And of course, you're still in love with her, D'Angelo, he told himself drearily. *All you have to do is close your eyes and she's there—walking around in your shirt with that gorgeous butt hardly covered, lying on your bed telling you to take your clothes off, laughing at something those goofy cats did.* Pain swept through him, fresh and bright and unbearable, and with an abrupt movement he pushed himself from the chair, needing to do something—*anything*—to take his mind off her. He walked over to the window, his hands jammed into his pockets and his shoulders set.

If the family wasn't here in Boston he'd ask for a transfer, he thought, staring out at the familiar skyline. He wouldn't ever be able to go walking on the Common without remembering her spilling peanuts all down herself while she was trying to feed the squirrels, wouldn't ever want to drop into Forsini's again after watching the pleasure she'd taken in meeting his father's friends, couldn't sit at Carmela's table without seeing her beside him, blushing and laughing and looking as if she'd always been a part of his family.

"God, honey—why?"

His question came out in an anguished whisper. He hadn't even realized he'd spoken aloud until he felt his throat close in pain and the skyline in front of him blurred and wavered. He closed his eyes and rested his forehead against the coolness of the window.

After a moment he straightened. He turned back to his desk and saw that he still had seven hours before he could decently leave the office, go home and sit around in his empty house. He felt something unfamiliar in his pocket and with no real curiosity he pulled it out.

It was the St. Anthony's medal that Carmela had given him. He held it to the light, one corner of his mouth lifting wryly as he opened his desk drawer.

"You're zero for two, Tony," he said in a normal speaking tone. "Hey—pitch me another one of those killer fastballs of yours. I just love to watch them whiz by me while I'm still swinging."

The worn embossing was hard to make out, but Matt knew what it depicted—a seemingly frail figure holding a lily in one hand, the other arm clasped protectively around the Child. He felt suddenly contrite, and instead of tossing the medal into the open drawer, he closed his palm around it uncertainly. Then he dropped it back into his pocket.

"Not your fault, Tony," he murmured. "I can't lose something I never really had."

After occupying separate rooms last night—he hadn't actually slept—they'd confronted each other with stiff formality this morning. She'd insisted that she wouldn't stay another night in his house, even when he'd offered to take a motel room himself for a couple of days while she looked for a place to rent.

They'd been like a divorcing couple, Matt thought—a couple who had nothing left to say to one another but who still needed to cooperate on the logistics and mundane demands of carving out separate existences.

He'd been afraid that she wouldn't take the money, and it had been something that he'd been prepared to insist upon, if necessary. No matter what had happened between them or who she really was, he didn't want her out on the street again, looking for any kind of job and not having a place to stay. To his relief she'd taken the money with distant courtesy, telling him that she considered it a loan and would pay him back as soon as possible.

She'd asked him if it would be possible for Zappa and Ziggy to remain with him until she'd found an apartment that allowed pets. He'd agreed. He'd told her where to leave the key when she left. She'd nodded.

Maybe they should have thrown plates at each other, he thought. Anything would have been more bearable than that cold and eminently logical discussion between two people who only recently had brought each other to gasping, incoherent ecstasy.

"Matt, I'm sorry to bother you, but—"

Pam's tinny voice on the intercom broke off in midsentence, and with a muttered oath Matt snatched the phone up.

"I said no calls—"

The door to his office flew open. The man who burst in was no one he knew, and behind the unfamiliar visitor Pam threw him an outraged look.

"I tried to stop him, but he just *ignored* me." She was holding a sharpened pencil point-first in her hand, and looked flustered enough to use it. "Should I call security?"

Through narrowed eyes he studied the intruder. Although

the stranger looked slightly eccentric he seemed harmless enough, and the last thing Matt wanted was to cause a stir on his first day back on the job. Having security called to remove this oddball would make him look foolishly incompetent.

Been there, done that, he thought.

"I'll handle it, Pam," he said tersely.

As she reluctantly closed the door behind her, the stranger looked at him, his pale blue eyes steady behind round gold-rimmed glasses. Despite the fact that he had to be in his mid-fifties—his neatly trimmed blond beard was streaked with silver—there was a quality of youthfulness about him. The impression that he'd somehow held back time was reinforced by his anachronistic attire.

He was wearing faded blue jeans—normal enough, except for the tattered peace symbol embroidered on one knee. Scuffed boots covered his feet, and over a well-worn chambray shirt he wore a fringed suede vest. One tanned wrist was encircled by a leather thong with an indigo bead strung on it, and another thong held back the ponytail that brushed the back of his collar.

"You've got three seconds to explain why you forced your way in here before I escort you out," Matt said, controlling his anger with difficulty. He placed his hands on his hips, exposing his shoulder holster. "It better be good."

"Violence doesn't solve anything, Agent D'Angelo." The older man shook his head, still fixing him with that oddly assessing stare. "Besides, now that I'm finally here, the Bureau wouldn't thank you for letting me go. Your people have been looking for me for thirty years."

Ignoring Matt's skeptical expression, he extended his hand toward him. "I'm looking for my daughter. My name is Franklin Moon."

THIS WAS ALL *WRONG*.

Jenna sat up on the edge of the bed with a shuddering sigh and wiped her eyes with the heel of her hand.

She was all cried out, she thought shakily. Her body felt as if every last molecule of moisture had been wrung out of it, leaving her empty and brittle—but also more clear-headed than she'd been since last night when Matt had first confronted her with his crazy accusation. Zappa jumped lightly up on the bed beside her, bunting her in worried affection with the top of his head, and distractedly she stroked his creamy fur.

"I thought he'd found out about Franklin, Zap—and if he had I would have been able to make him see that I didn't have the *right* to go back on my promise and tell anyone that he was still alive. Not until I'd located Franklin and told him what I intended to do, at least."

Zappa folded his paws underneath his chest and started purring. Greatly daring, Ziggy leaped up beside them, and Jenna rubbed the smaller cat's ears with a gentle finger.

"It's not my secret to tell. Matt eventually would have understood that—I *know* he would have." She frowned. Her father's fears might well be based on paranoia and fantasy, but to him they were real—real enough so that he'd asked her never to reveal his existence to a living soul.

"It's the only way, Jen," he'd told her the night before she'd left for Boston and her new life. Looking at his drawn face, she'd felt the pang of concern that had kept her from striking out on her own in the past—the worry that his delusions might get worse in the future without her constant presence. But before she could speak he'd gone on, his voice charged with desperation.

"You'll just have to trust me on this. The danger's real, and my biggest fear has always been that they'd try to get to me by harming you. That's why I've never told you any more about what happened in the past than I absolutely had to—because the less you know the safer you are.'' He'd leaned forward, twisting the indigo bead around his wrist in an unconsciously familiar gesture. ''You deserve a life of your own—but as far as the outside world's concerned, Franklin Moon is dead. *Promise* me that, Jen. It's the only way I can be sure that you'll be safe.''

''How was I supposed to know that within a week I'd find the one man I wanted to share everything with?'' she asked Ziggy helplessly. The small Siamese looked up at her with round blue eyes. ''If *only* I'd managed to track down Franklin in time. At least then I would have been able to defend myself.''

Which didn't change the fact that there had to have been some mistake with the report itself, she thought impatiently. Of course there was a Jenna Moon. She *existed,* didn't she?

Not to Matt you don't, the dire little voice inside her head piped up. *Not anymore. All he knows is that you betrayed his trust. It's all over between the two of you.*

Except…except it *couldn't* be, she thought with dawning hope. Her dream had been proof of that. She and Matt had a future together, and no matter how bleak things looked right now, somehow everything was going to work out. How could she have forgotten?

But just because it was fate didn't mean she could sit around on her duff waiting for her life to sort itself out all by itself, she thought with sudden determination. That just wasn't the way things worked. She had to take matters into her own hands—and the sooner she got started the better.

''I'll have to leave him a note,'' she said, chewing her lip thoughtfully. ''Then I'll phone the bus station and pack a bag.''

She jumped to her feet, her ankle bracelet ringing softly and both Zappa and Ziggy giving her startled and disgruntled looks. Padding purposely out of the bedroom and down the hall, she sped into Matt's converted dining room and went straight to the large desk under the old chandelier, noting with interest the framed photos grouped where he could look up and see them as he worked. She sat down, found a blank sheet of paper and a pen in the top drawer, and began to write.

"Dear Matt—" She frowned, scratched that out, and began again.

Darling Matt,
You were right last night. I have been lying to you, but not about what you thought. By the way, tell your friend at the Bureau to run his dumb computer check again—he has to have made a mistake about me not existing. I never heard of anything so ridiculous. Anyway, like I said, I haven't told you the truth, but only because of a promise I made to someone else. I have to find Fr—

She'd almost written "Franklin," she thought, exasperated. She scored that part out.

...to find this person and tell him I can't keep his secret anymore. When I do, I'll come back and tell you everything.
With love,

your Jenna.

She added a P.S.

That *is* my real name.

She started to fold the paper, and then added a second P.S.

Please do *not* let Zappa have pizza like you did before.

Kathy Fish at the Sunflower Commune had told her that Franklin hadn't called in for messages lately, but that when she'd last spoken with him he'd mentioned a possible visit to Maine, and mutual friends they had there. It was just like Franklin, Jenna thought, neatly folding her letter and rummaging around in Matt's desk for an envelope, to have made it almost impossible for even his own daughter to discover his whereabouts. But she'd spent a lifetime with him. If anyone could locate him, she could.

She was positive he would release her from her promise when she told him she'd met the man she was going to marry, but even that certainty wasn't enough to allow her to divulge his secret without first warning him. She found an envelope and slid the letter inside, her expression troubled. The need for concealment and the possibility of instant flight had been so ingrained in her from childhood on that even now she couldn't lightly disregard Franklin's fears.

"I never should have made that promise. I hated having to lie to Matt," she murmured unhappily, her wistful gaze taking in his collection of photos.

There was Carmela and Frank with a younger Tommy and Stacey, in a picture that had obviously been taken a few Christmases ago. In a silver frame was a much older photo—a formally posed wedding picture of a stunningly vibrant and beautiful Maria D'Angelo. The man beside her had to be Salvatore, Jenna thought, studying the strong face and the broad-shouldered figure of Matt's father. She smiled a little mistily. Maria's *destino*—the man she'd always been meant to love and marry...just as her son was Jenna's destiny.

Blinking rapidly and letting her gaze settle on the next photo, she studied it with curiosity. It showed Matt's sister Tina and her husband, Nick, with a boy and girl so identical that they could have been twins. She picked the picture up and looked at it more closely, puzzled.

The boy was Domenic. She recalled Carmela's laughing comment the night before—*"He's a handful, and in a month or so he'll be a teenager."* But who was the pretty dark-eyed girl who, except for her long curls, resembled him so closely? And where was little Diana—the tiny flower girl from her dream?

She turned the frame over in her hands, confused. The photo looked recent—why had Diana been excluded from the family portrait? Who was the older girl in her place? With suddenly shaking fingers she started prying at the back of the frame, grappling with the minute hinges that held it in place. One of her nails broke off. Shoving the small hinges sideways, she pulled urgently at the thick cardboard support until it came free, and then she released the decorative mat that backed the photo, letting it fall to the surface of the desk, unheeded.

The photo fluttered onto the floor, faceup. Jenna grabbed it and turned it over.

To Matt with love on his birthday—from Tina, Nick, and the "terrible twins!"—Dom and Diane

"No! No, she's supposed to be a little girl—she's supposed to be much younger!," she whispered, her face ashen. "She was about five years old in my dream, and she was carrying a basket of petals almost as big as she was and if she doesn't exist then that means—"

It felt as if a giant hand was squeezing her heart.

"—then that means it was only ever a *dream*," Jenna finished numbly, her hand going to her mouth as if to silence the terrible words. "It was only a dream—it meant nothing. *Nothing.* I can lose him—I could have lost him *already.*"

Ziggy ran into the room, her ears laid flat to her head. She disappeared behind the floor-length drapes that covered the nearby window, but Jenna's eyes were staring blindly at the photo, the almost inaudible words forced out from between frozen lips.

"He's *not* my destiny. *Anything* could come between us. Anything could *happen!*"

Zappa backed into the room, his tail bushed and his back arched. She closed her eyes and the photo fell from her stiff fingers.

"Even if I find Franklin and tell Matt the truth, he still could—"

Zappa screamed, a bloodcurdling yowl that tore across Jenna's whisper. Her eyes flew open and she spun around, but before she could scream herself, a strong hand was gripping her, a sickly-sweet smell was overwhelming her, and Zappa's terrified yowls were following her down to darkness and oblivion.

LIKE DAUGHTER, like father, Matt thought, unconsciously rubbing his temples and staring at the man who claimed to be Franklin Moon—and that had only been one small part of his incredible story. Franklin met his gaze calmly, but when the phone on Matt's desk shrilled through the silence he gave a slight start.

You're not as Zenned out as you're pretending to be, are you? Matt thought, keeping his own features rigidly impassive. *You've painted yourself into a corner, buddy, and this is the moment of truth. Either your whole damn tale was a lie, in which case you're in big trouble, or—*

Or the man was Jenna's father, and really *had* been running from the authorities for years. And in that case he was in even bigger trouble, because the crime he was wanted for was murder—of an undercover agent. He reached for the phone and picked it up.

"Agent D'Angelo? Patching you through to Agent Hendricks." The voice of the switchboard operator was brisk. "Go ahead, Agent Hendricks."

"D'Angelo?" Gravelly tones that obviously belonged to an older man came on the line. "I hear you've got word on a ghost from my past, calls himself Franklin Moon?"

"That's right." Matt's lips tightened. "He said the Agency's been hunting him for thirty years for a murder he didn't commit. The victim was one of ours—Maggie Dawson, a female agent who was working undercover."

"That was a crazy time," Hendricks said. "A lot of unrest, a lot of social upheaval—and along with the legitimate reformers there was a dangerous fringe element that we kept a close watch on. I knew Maggie. She was one of the best. She managed to infiltrate a radical group that had us worried, and shortly after that she was found dead in her apartment, strangled."

"I see." He kept his tone neutral. Out of the corner of his eye he saw Franklin turning the indigo bead on his wrist over and over, but aside from that, the man gave no indication that the conversation might concern him. He had to have nerves of steel, Matt thought incredulously.

"Moon—he wasn't going under that name then—was our prime suspect right from the start. Ironically enough he had nothing to do with the radical group. He lived in the apartment below, and only knew Dawson as a neighbor, but there wasn't any doubt that he'd killed her." Hendricks broke off suddenly. "Hold on a minute—is he actually with you right *now?*"

"Yes, that's right." Matt's hand crept unobtrusively toward his shoulder holster. "Listen, perhaps it would be best if I called you—"

"Wait—you've got to hear the rest," Hendricks interrupted. "No—*he's* got to hear the rest. Put me on speaker, D'Angelo. It's important!" he snapped as Matt hesitated.

"He wants you to hear what he has to say, Moon." He reluctantly hit the speaker button with his thumb, not taking his eyes from Franklin's. A flicker of confusion passed swiftly over the ex-fugitive's features before he nodded. "But what he's told me so far has me pretty nervous, so don't make any sudden moves, understand?"

"Franklin?" Hendricks voice, slightly distorted, sounded excited. "Franklin, why the hell didn't you turn yourself in ten years ago, dammit?"

"You know why, Hendricks." Moon frowned. "You were the one who said you'd never rest until I was tried and convicted, remember?"

"Yeah, and you're lucky I was so obsessed with your case." The older agent gave a short laugh. "So obsessed that when DNA testing became possible, I pulled strings and got a sample from a hair of yours we had—and it was run against the DNA from the killer. Maggie put up a fight. There was skin under her fingernails."

Franklin Moon's face was white, and all of a sudden he looked his age, but his voice was steady. "I've always said I was innocent, Hendricks. Are you trying to tell me that you finally believe me?"

"I've believed you for ten years, dammit. I've kept your file open hoping that someday we'd pick you up just long enough to let you know you could stop running!" On the other end of the line Hendricks cleared his throat. When he spoke again his voice was husky. "Franklin, welcome back to the world."

"Moon!" Matt leaned across his desk, his eyes burning with a golden intensity. "Moon—does Jenna know any of this?"

Franklin was polishing his glasses rapidly. Without them his face looked strangely vulnerable. "No." His voice cracked and he kept his head bent to his task. "No, she—she doesn't. It was a burden I never felt she should have to carry. And—"

"Does she even know what her real name is?" Matt demanded urgently. "She's been as invisible as you've been all these years, hasn't she?"

"Officially she doesn't exist." Franklin looked up at him, once more under control. "It was the only way I could keep her safe."

"For God's sake, man—you couldn't have thought we would have harmed your *daughter!*" Hendricks, over the speakerphone, sounded outraged, and Jenna's father reacted with the first hint of violent emotion that Matt had seen in him.

"You still don't get it, do you? I wasn't just running from the Agency all these years—we were being tracked by the killer!" His eyes no longer looked mild. "I was supposed to pay for his crime and then the file on Maggie Dawson's murder would be closed. But when I ran, he knew the Bureau would keep the case active until I was found. He couldn't *afford* that! He couldn't take the chance that someday some overlooked piece of evidence might come to light and implicate him! He had to *delete* me!"

Matt felt a roaring in his ears. Slowly he rose to his feet, feeling strangely disconnected from the room around him. "What was his name?" he asked in a voice he hardly recognized as his own. "You knew who the real killer was, didn't you? *What was his name?*"

The pale blue eyes suddenly took on a deeper hue. For

a moment Matt felt he was looking into Jenna's eyes, and his heart contracted painfully.

"His name was Rupert Carling," Franklin Moon said flatly. "Why?"

Hendricks answered before Matt could. "Rupert Carling? Son of a— Franklin, this must be your lucky day. If it's the same Carling, then the man who's had a contract out on you for the last few decades died himself not a week ago! Tell him, D'Angelo!"

Matt grabbed the phone, his hand so clumsy he almost dropped the receiver. "Hendricks, I can't go into details, but listen carefully—*Carling's not dead.* I need to make a call. If I don't get back to you in the next few seconds contact this office again right away and tell them what I told you. Get them to send backup to my house—they'll know the address."

He broke the connection, cutting off the other agent's shocked questions, and dialed his own number.

"She left word for me at the Sunflower Commune. She mentioned you and said that she couldn't hide the fact of my existence much longer. I assumed the worst—that the Bureau had somehow found out who she was and was using her to get to me. I couldn't let her go through that. But I was on the wrong track, wasn't I, D'Angelo? Just how close *are* you to my daughter?" Franklin was standing now, too, his gaze fixed on Matt. "If she's in danger I need to know that you're as committed as I am to keeping her safe."

She wasn't answering, Matt thought numbly. Logic told him that could mean any number of things—she'd already left the house, she wasn't expecting the call to be for her, she was in the shower.

He'd already lost Jenna once by relying on logic and proof. He *knew* she was in trouble—bad trouble. He slammed the phone down and met Franklin's eyes.

"She's my *destino*. I'd give my life for her." His mouth was grim. "Moon, I'll explain on the way—but right now we've got to get over to my house. I think Jenna is Carling's latest target. I'll call down for my vehicle to be brought up from the underground garage."

"Forget that." Franklin was already heading toward the door, the fringe on his suede vest flying out behind him. "I'm parked right outside. We'll take my van."

At any other time the sight of Franklin Moon's ancient Volkswagen van might have given him pause, Matt thought a few minutes later, wrenching open the passenger door and jumping in as his companion gunned the engine. Right now it just seemed another part of the nightmare. Huge psychedelic flowers in pop art primary colors adorned the side panels, while a massive peace symbol was painted on the front. As they pulled away from the curb he saw Henderson coming out of the building with another agent. Henderson's jaw dropped as he recognized Matt speed by.

"Turn left here." Dismissing his career without a second thought, Matt held on to the door handle as Franklin peeled around the corner. "This old bus moves pretty well," he added, surprised.

The ex-hippie darted a sardonic glance at him and shifted into a higher gear. "I've had plenty of practice in quick getaways, D'Angelo. But I've got to admit, this is the first time I've gone looking for Carling, instead of the other way around. What's this about him being presumed dead?"

Matt gave him the essentials as they careened wildly through the traffic. "The one thing I never understood was why Carling attempted to have Jenna killed when she was on her way to phone the Bureau, but when that failed, he simply tried to discredit her," he ended, frowning. "The only explanation is that he must have decided her death would have lent credibility to whatever she'd told us over the phone. But that doesn't fit with his persona—he's a gambler, a risk taker. He must have had some other reason for letting her live.''

"He did.'' Franklin's capable hands tightened on the steering wheel as they turned onto Matt's street. "In fact, I'm inclined to believe that incident on the sidewalk was just what it appeared to be—an accidental nudge by a stranger, and nothing to do with Rupert Carling at all. Seeing Jenna in that basement corridor must have been like seeing the only person he'd ever cared for come back to him. He was in love with her mother—as much in love with her as he was capable of being,'' he amended. "He had to have realized who she was. He wouldn't have wanted to hurt her unless he felt he had no choice.''

"The next house on the—'' The blood drained from Matt's face. "What the hell—stop the van, Moon! Someone's *screaming*—and it's coming from my house!''

He was out of the vehicle before it had stopped, running up the walk and fumbling frantically in his pockets for his keys as he ran. They weren't necessary. Through his open front door Matt could hear the terrible screaming continue unabated, and as he burst into the house he drew his gun.

The screams were coming from the direction of his study, and as he sped down the hall he found himself voicelessly reiterating a desperate, inarticulate prayer.

Don't let anything happen to her, don't let anything happen to her, don't let—

He skidded to a stop just inside the threshold of the study. The room was empty, but the chilling screams filled the air, and looking up he saw a terror-stricken Ziggy, caught by her collar at the top of the curtain rod. He holstered his gun, feeling slightly foolish.

"It's the damn cat,'' he called over his shoulder to

Franklin as the other man ran into the room. "Hold on while I cut her down."

Pulling a pocketknife from his pants, he positioned a chair under the frantic animal. Standing on it and dodging her razorlike claws, he neatly slit the collar and Ziggy dropped to the floor. The deafening screams switched off like magic as she flew under a nearby chair, and in the sudden silence Franklin spoke.

"It looks like Jen left you a note."

Dropping Ziggy's now-destroyed collar on his desk, Matt picked up the envelope, frowning. He read the few lines scribbled there and felt his features gradually relax. Carefully refolding Jenna's letter, he slipped it into his jacket as his heartbeat finally returned to something approximating normal.

"I think we'll find her at the bus station. She must have torn out of here like a whirlwind—she's gone looking for you. Come on, we'd better find her before she hops a Greyhound."

"What's this?" Franklin was holding the slashed collar, staring at it curiously. "There's something sewn inside here. It feels flimsy, like onion-skin paper."

"It's probably just the lining." About to turn away, Matt hesitated, remembering the scene in Miss Terwilliger's kitchen. What had the woman told them?

"…I'd just finished sewing up a small—a small rip in the seam of her collar…"

"Let me have a look at that," he said sharply, but Franklin was already extracting the thin sheet of paper from the collar that had been its hiding place. Matt took it from him. It had been folded down to a long, thin strip, and he spread it out on the desk, smoothing out the accordion-like pleats, his eyes rapidly scanning its contents.

"E–Z Corp.," Franklin murmured over his shoulder.

"What's that—and why was this paper sewn inside your cat's collar?"

"The cat belongs to Miss Terwilliger—the woman who was injured in the hit-and-run I told you about. And I think she must have thought something in this fax could be used to expose the people who were threatening her. Jenna found a file on E–Z Corp. in Charles Parks's office the night she broke in." He paused, his eyes widening. "It's got to be the shell company that Parks set up for Carling's last scam! I think Ziggy just clinched the case against those two. Come on, we'll find Jenna and then I'll get this to Henderson…"

His voice trailed off. Across the room Zappa had come out from wherever he'd been, and one cream-and-brown paw was patting at an object half hidden beneath a chair. A single silvery note shivered delicately in the air.

In two strides Matt was beside the chair. He bent over and picked up the broken length of chain, the tiny bells attached to it ringing out like a warning.

"She never would have left this behind," he ground out. In Franklin's stunned gaze he read the same horrified comprehension he knew must be in his own. "Carling's got Jenna. Carling's got Jenna—and I wasn't here to stop him."

Chapter Fifteen

She'd been close—so *close*—to finding her heart's desire. Jenna drifted up from unconsciousness, fighting a wave of nausea. She'd dreamed that she had been exploring a cave, searching for a fabulous treasure trove that had been hidden deep in the dark rocky heart of a mountain. She'd had a map, but it had been lost; she'd had a light, but it had burned itself out. Still she'd gone on, blindly stumbling around in the blackness.

Until the mountain itself had fallen in on her, burying her under tons of stone and locking its treasure away from her forever.

She couldn't move. *Okay, the dream's over. Enough is enough,* she woozily commanded her limbs. *You're not buried under rocks, so snap out of it.*

As if they were weighted down themselves, with an effort she finally got her eyelids to open. For a moment she thought she was back in her dream but then her vision cleared and she realized she wasn't in a cavernous cave, she was in a cavernous warehouse. She wasn't pinned down, she was tied down—to a hard wooden chair, and so tightly that she really *couldn't* move.

Nylon cord in a cheery tone of canary yellow was bound several times around her waist like a particularly tight belt, and looking down she saw that the same nylon rope was lashed cruelly around her thighs and the seat of the chair. Her hands were bound behind her and although she couldn't see them, her legs and feet were also secured.

I must look like a big chicken, ready to pop into the oven, she thought in annoyed chagrin. *Is this supposed to be some kind of a joke?*

The last of the sickening fog cleared from her mind and all of a sudden she remembered everything—the cats yowling, the nauseatingly sweet smell of the chloroform, and Davis's face watching her as she feebly struggled in his grip and finally lost consciousness.

"We thought you were going to sleep forever."

It was Rupert Carling. His voice echoed through the vast, empty space, bouncing off the metal-clad walls at the other end of the building and then resonating back again. He was about fifty feet away and walking toward her, his stride leisurely, his hands in the pockets of his suit. Beside him was Davis, the thin man she'd first seen in Charles Parks's office a few nights ago.

Jenna stared at them as they approached, but she said nothing. She couldn't have spoken anyway, she thought, trying to take a deep breath and unable to because of the bonds across her chest. Her mouth was too dry with fear. About all she would be capable of producing right now would be a croak.

This time she really was going to die. It wasn't merely a possibility, it was a certainty. Hiding behind Charles Parks's couch, at risk of being discovered at any moment, she'd felt safe in the belief that nothing could truly harm her, that her future held a lifetime of happiness with the man she loved.

She'd been such a *fool.*

She swallowed the lump in her throat and fixed the well-dressed man in front of her with an unwavering gaze. He had the expensive good looks of a politician or a banker, she thought in cold appraisal, with a squash player's trim figure and attractively silvered hair. His even features were lightly tanned, as if he spent his weekends doing something robust and healthy, like sailing.

The little finger of his left hand was wrapped in white surgical gauze. Rupert Carling spent his weekends faking his own death, having people killed and going so far as to slice off the tip of his own finger to validate his deception.

"You've got her hair and her eyes," he said softly. "I wish it hadn't turned out this way, Jenna."

She felt as if she'd just been doused with ice water—first numb with shock, then galvanized into incredulous speech. "What—what do you mean? Whose hair? *Whose* eyes?"

Davis, standing off to one side, looked as confused as she felt, and with an impatient gesture Carling motioned him away. Coming closer to Jenna and giving her a searching look, he shook his head wonderingly.

"It's like seeing her ghost—Sara's ghost. When you ran into me that day at Parks, Parks at first I thought I *was* looking at a ghost. But since I don't believe in them, I knew you had to be her daughter."

"You knew my *mother*? You knew Sara? No—you're lying." Her lips thinned in denial. "This is another one of your manipulative games, Carling."

"It's a long story." He shrugged. "And let's face it—there's not enough time left in your life to hear it. But yes, I knew Sara and Franklin once, years ago. If things had worked out differently, I might have been your father, Jenna."

He reached out and laid a possessive hand on her hair.

She recoiled from his touch, unable to move completely out of range.

"You've lied to other people for so long that now you can't even tell when you're lying to yourself," she said, shuddering. "But even you can't believe that Sara ever would have chosen a man like you over my father. Franklin Moon is a decent, valuable human being. You're a killer."

He withdrew his hand from her hair abruptly, his features tightening with displeasure. "Franklin was a naive, idealistic patsy who was too damn stupid to know he was being set up until the noose was slipping around his neck. He was perfect for what I wanted—until he ran." Jerking his head at the waiting Davis, he started to turn away.

"Wait!" Carling paused, shooting her a disinterested glance over his shoulder. "Wait," she said urgently. "Are you telling me it was always *true?* Was it *you* we were running from all those years?"

His eyes widened, and then he grinned with real amusement. "He never told you? My God, the one thing I regretted was having to disappear without knowing that I'd finally destroyed him, but this is almost as good. You've always thought your father was crazy, haven't you?" Still chuckling, he glanced over at Davis. "Okay, get rid of her. I've got to be at the airport in a couple of hours."

His command was so casual that at first she didn't understand what he'd meant. A second later the realization hit her.

She'd just heard her own death sentence. No matter what she'd once told herself, what she'd once believed, *this* was what fate had in store for her—to be snuffed out in this abandoned warehouse, to die a futile, lonely death far from the man she loved. Matt would remember her as the woman who'd lied to him, who'd deceived him, and she would never have the opportunity to tell him the truth...

…but in this last second of her life she could finally see it for herself.

Because ultimately the truth was that even if her dream had been only a dream, Matt D'Angelo was the other half of her soul. He *had* been her destiny—and if she needed a mystical sign to convince her of that, all she had to do was remember the way his lips had felt on her skin, how his gaze had held hers across a crowded dinner table, and the incredible rightness of falling asleep in his arms, knowing that when she woke up he would still be holding her.

"The signs were all there. The signs were *always* there," she whispered as Davis raised his gun and took aim. "It *can't* end like this!"

She struggled frantically against the bonds that secured her, hearing the familiar sound of the bells on her ankle bracelet jingling madly. Even if she could buy a few moments of precious time by flinging herself sideways, she thought, her muscles straining as she tried to rock the chair off balance—someone might hear the shot and somehow she—

The chair was immovable. Davis's finger tightened on the trigger. She saw him squeeze off the shot.

An invisible *force* pushed her sideways, and the chair, with her tied to it, crashed to the concrete floor as an explosion of sound filled the air. It was like flying through a cloud during a thunderstorm, Jenna thought crazily. Was this death? Was it supposed to be so loud?

"You goddamn fool!"

Rupert Carling was on his knees only a few feet away from her. Craning her neck around uncomfortably, she saw that his face was contorted in pain and rage. The right leg of his expensively tailored suit was covered in blood.

My blood? she wondered, confused. *But I don't feel anything.*

"You shot me, for God's sake!" Carling's healthy tan had disappeared. His skin was a pasty white and his jaw was clenched as he glared up at his hired gun.

"I couldn't have! My God—Mr. Carling, I'm sorry!" Davis looked appalled. He reached down to help Carling to his feet, his outstretched hand unsteady. "There's no damn way I would have missed—not at that distance! All of a sudden the freakin' chair fell over, but I still don't get it. You know I wasn't aiming for you. You know that, right?"

"Hell, yes." Carling stood, wincing. "I trust you. There has to be something wrong with your piece. Let me look at it—and set the girl and the chair up again. I don't want you firing into concrete. The next time the damn ricochet might get me."

Davis handed his gun over and turned toward Jenna, still shaking his head. "Nothing like that ever happened to me before. I mean—I never miss—"

"Neither do I." His employer lifted his arm, the barrel of the gun coming up in an arc that stopped just to the left of Davis's spine, and fired.

The thin man was dead before he fell. He hit the floor heavily, his skull making brutal contact with the concrete, his hands still at his sides, his muddy brown eyes only inches away from Jenna's terrified stare, as if he had something vitally important to communicate to her.

"I trusted him. Live and learn," Carling said lightly. He walked over to Jenna and, grimacing as he put his weight on his wounded leg, hauled her upright with an effort. The bells on her bracelet chimed softly as the wooden chair rocked back into position. "I'd hoped I wouldn't have to be the one to actually do this—"

He stopped in midsentence. Looking up at him, for one crazy moment Jenna wondered if he was having second thoughts, but immediately she stifled the futile hope. Rupert Carling had just killed a man right in front of her eyes, with no more emotion than if he'd scraped something off the bottom of his shoe. He was completely detached from the rest of the human race. If she tried for a thousand years, she would never establish any kind of connection with the man, never find anything in him that she could appeal to. He didn't have a soul.

But maybe he'd had one once.

"You even wear the same perfume," he said, his eyes shadowed with something akin to regret. "Patchouli. I always knew when she'd been in a room."

"I'm not wearing perfume." Her voice was flat. "I don't—"

Suddenly the heady scent of spices and flowers and precious oils was almost tangibly overwhelming, swirling like a silken fog around her, wrapping her in a cloud of perfume so evocative that Jenna could almost feel the comforting arms around her, hear the soft voice calming her fears, see the blue eyes, so like her own, filled with a love so strong that time and space and eternity were barriers too flimsy to contain it. A silvery chiming note rang out, like a single ice crystal catching the light.

"I'm not wearing perfume," she said softly, meeting the uncertain gaze of the man who was about to kill her. "Sara is."

His mouth worked soundlessly and his eyes filled with fear and denial. Then he raised his gun and pointed it straight at her, his hand trembling. "No!" he hissed hoarsely, his finger tightening on the trigger. "I don't believe—I *won't* believe—"

He pulled the trigger, but at the same time his hand flew up in an awkward, jerky gesture, the gun spinning from his grasp and discharging in midair. On Rupert Carling's face was a stubbornly incredulous expression.

"I—I don't *believe,*" he gasped, clutching at his chest and looking down at the blood soaking the front of his shirt. He fell to the floor.

"Jenna! Jenna!" From the shadows at the far end of the warehouse Matt was racing toward her, his gun still in his hand. Then he was beside her, his hands cupping her face and those amazing golden eyes searching hers fearfully.

"Dear God—Jenna, are you hurt, *cara?* Are you all right?"

He was babbling, the frantic words spilling from him as if he'd been driven out of his mind with worry. She had to be still in shock, Jenna thought dazedly, because as he bent over her and sawed swiftly through the cruelly tight bonds of the nylon, she was sure she saw that he was wearing his St. Anthony medal. Then her arms were free and the ropes fell away from her legs and he was helping her to her feet and crushing her to him.

"*Cara,* I was so afraid we wouldn't be in time," he said, his words muffled against her hair. "And if we'd guessed wrong, I knew we wouldn't get a second chance."

"Who's we? And how did you know where I was?" Now *she* was the one who was babbling, she thought light-headedly, but somehow she couldn't seem to stop herself. "Matt—I left you a note and then I saw the photo, and Zappa and Ziggy must have tried to warn me but I didn't— I didn't…oh, Matt!" Her eyes filled with tears and she raised her head to look at him. "I thought I needed a sign, but the signs were right in front of me all the time!"

"Jen!" The voice was familiar, but until she saw Franklin hurrying toward them she couldn't believe what she was hearing, and then when he got closer she couldn't believe what she was seeing. Like Matt, he was carrying a gun. He held it stiffly away from his body, as if he was afraid it was about to explode in his hand. He saw her incredulous glance.

"I know. I always said violence didn't solve anything." He looked over at the lifeless bodies of Carling and Davis a few feet away, and grimaced. "They lived by the sword. Nothing less could have stopped them."

Feeling the shudder that rippled through her, Matt's grip around her tightened. "This is the address they gave as the head office of E–Z Corp.," he said, forcing a lightness into his tone. "And yes, I found your note—after Franklin found me. But the one you really should thank is Zappa." He attempted a smile, and fished in his pocket for something. "If it hadn't been for him we might not have realized you'd been kidnapped."

A tiny, joyful ringing filled the air as he held up the ankle bracelet that had once belonged to Sara Moon. Her hand trembling slightly, Jenna reached out for it and Matt dropped it into her palm.

She looked down at her ankle. It still bore the red marks from the nylon rope, but otherwise it was bare. A ghostly scent touched the air one last time, and then faded gently away.

Another, more pragmatic person might have had questions. But Jenna Moon believed in love, peace and understanding. All of her questions had been answered—except one.

"Matt, do you—do you believe in destiny?" she asked, those fabulous blue eyes worriedly searching his and those lush lips parted only inches away, awaiting his answer.

"*Destino?* I'm holding mine in my arms right now."

He smiled, watching the shadows disappear from those

eyes, and then…since he was a D'Angelo, and male, and holding the woman he loved more than life itself…well, he'd be crazy not to kiss her, Matt thought.

So he did.

Epilogue

"As soon as the kittens are weaned Edna's giving us one for our wedding present, Matt!"

Jenna had kicked off her shoes an hour earlier during an especially energetic rumba with one of Matt's uncles. Her feet peeked out from beneath yards of tulle and satin as she turned to her brand-new husband, her hand on the shoulder of Miss Terwilliger. The older lady still sported a cast from the knee down.

"I'll bring them over when they're bigger to meet their rapscallion of a father," Edna said in mock disapproval. Then she smiled. "I must admit, they certainly are adorable. The smallest male is such a scamp!"

"We're lucky we didn't get slapped with a paternity suit," Matt murmured as they made their way through the throng of guests. "I'll have to have a little talk with Zappa."

"That would be a prime example of the pot calling the kettle black," Jenna said airily, twiddling her fingers at Tiffany and Crystal. Sitting on the sofa, they were batting impossibly long lashes at a couple of Matt's handsome cousins who were hovering around them. "If you catch my drift," she added.

"Yeah, I catch your—" Matt stopped suddenly. Jenna

was popping a cream-filled cannoli from the nearby table into her mouth, and she stared at him innocently, licking her fingers.

"You mean you're—we're—" He grabbed her by the shoulders, searching her face incredulously.

"And you're supposed to be an FBI agent," she said, her eyes alight. "I'm almost positive, Matt. And I think Carmela and your mom suspect something—why do you think those two managed to organize a wedding in a matter of weeks?"

"*Cara*—I can't believe it!" He raked his hand through his hair, grinning, and then he gathered her in his arms and crushed her to him. His breath was warm by her ear. *"Ti amo, cara,"* he whispered softly. "I want a little girl. She'll look just like her mama, with big blue eyes and red-gold hair."

In the circle of his arms, Jenna gave a little laugh. The bells on her ankle bracelet chimed delicately, and then she went very still, staring over Matt's shoulder.

Her father was on the other side of the room, talking to Matt's mother. But that wasn't what had caught her attention. A few feet away from him stood a beautiful little girl, with huge dark eyes and long dark curls. Her gaze met Jenna's and the cherubic mouth curved into a smile. One tiny hand came up in a wave.

And then she faded away again.

"What is it, honey?" Love and pride glowed in those fabulous golden eyes. "See someone you know?"

"She won't have red hair, she'll have dark curls. And her eyes will be the most beautiful brown," Jenna breathed. She could still smell the faint scent of patchouli. "Keep good care of her for me until it's time for her to come into the world, Sara."

"What did you say?"

He was looking down at her quizzically. Jenna smiled up at him, blinking away tears of joy. "You know what, Matt? The universe is unfolding as it should—*exactly* as it should."

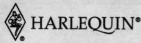

If you enjoyed what you just read,
then we've got an offer you can't resist!

Take 2 bestselling love stories FREE!

Plus get a FREE surprise gift!

Clip this page and mail it to Harlequin Reader Service®

IN U.S.A.	IN CANADA
3010 Walden Ave.	P.O. Box 609
P.O. Box 1867	Fort Erie, Ontario
Buffalo, N.Y. 14240-1867	L2A 5X3

YES! Please send me 2 free Harlequin Intrigue® novels and my free surprise gift. Then send me 4 brand-new novels every month, which I will receive before they're available in stores. In the U.S.A., bill me at the bargain price of $3.57 plus 25¢ delivery per book and applicable sales tax, if any*. In Canada, bill me at the bargain price of $3.96 plus 25¢ delivery per book and applicable taxes**. That's the complete price and a savings of at least 10% off the cover prices—what a great deal! I understand that accepting the 2 free books and gift places me under no obligation ever to buy any books. I can always return a shipment and cancel at any time. Even if I never buy another book from Harlequin, the 2 free books and gift are mine to keep forever. So why not take us up on our invitation. You'll be glad you did!

181 HEN C22Y
381 HEN C22Z

Name _____ (PLEASE PRINT) _____

Address _____ Apt.# _____

City _____ State/Prov. _____ Zip/Postal Code _____

* Terms and prices subject to change without notice. Sales tax applicable in N.Y.
** Canadian residents will be charged applicable provincial taxes and GST.
All orders subject to approval. Offer limited to one per household.
® are registered trademarks of Harlequin Enterprises Limited.

INT00

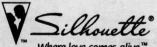

Spines will tingle...mysteries await...
and dangerous passion lurks in the night
as *Reader's Choice* presents

DREAM SCAPES!

Thrills and chills abound in these four romances
welcoming readers to the dark side of love.
Available January 2001 at your
favorite retail outlet:

THUNDER MOUNTAIN
by Rachel Lee

NIGHT MIST
by Helen R. Myers

DARK OBSESSION
by Amanda Stevens

HANGAR 13
by Lindsay McKenna

Harlequin invites you to walk down the aisle...

To honor our year long celebration of weddings, we are offering an exciting opportunity for you to own the Harlequin Bride Doll. Handcrafted in fine bisque porcelain, the wedding doll is dressed for her wedding day in a cream satin gown accented by lace trim. She carries an exquisite traditional bridal bouquet and wears a cathedral-length dotted Swiss veil. Embroidered flowers cascade down her lace overskirt to the scalloped hemline; underneath all is a multi-layered crinoline.

Join us in our celebration of weddings by sending away for your own Harlequin Bride Doll. This doll regularly retails for $74.95 U.S./approx. $108.68 CDN. One doll per household. Requests must be received no later than June 30, 2001. Offer good while quantities of gifts last. Please allow 6-8 weeks for delivery. Offer good in the U.S. and Canada only. Become part of this exciting offer!

Simply complete the order form and mail to:
"A Walk Down the Aisle"

IN U.S.A
P.O. Box 9057
3010 Walden Ave.
Buffalo, NY 14240-9057

IN CANADA
P.O. Box 622
Fort Erie, Ontario
L2A 5X3

Enclosed are eight (8) proofs of purchase found on the last page of every specially marked Harlequin series book and $3.75 check or money order (for postage and handling). Please send my Harlequin Bride Doll to:

Name (PLEASE PRINT)

Address   Apt. #

City   State/Prov.   Zip/Postal Code

Account # (if applicable)   **098 KIK DAEW**

HARLEQUIN®
Makes any time special®

A Walk Down the Aisle
Free Bride Doll Offer
One Proof-of-Purchase

Visit us at www.eHarlequin.com   PHWDAPOP

The romantic suspense at

HARLEQUIN®
INTRIGUE

just got more intense!

On the precipice between imminent danger and
smoldering desire, they are

When your back is against the wall
and nothing makes sense, only one man
is strong enough to pull you from the brink—
and into his loving arms!
Look for all the books in this riveting new
promotion:

WOMAN MOST WANTED (#599)
by **Harper Allen**
On sale January 2001

PRIVATE VOWS (#603)
by **Sally Steward**
On sale February 2001

NIGHTTIME GUARDIAN (#607)
by **Amanda Stevens**
On sale March 2001

Available at your favorite retail outlet.

HARLEQUIN®
Makes any time special ™

Visit us at www.eHarlequin.com

HIOTE